**PRAISE FOR**

# THE END
## IN ALL
# BEGINNINGS

"Accomplished, complex, heartfelt. The best novella collection in years!" —JACK KETCHUM, World Horror Grandmaster and Bram Stoker Award®-winning author of *Closing Time*, *Peaceable Kingdom*, and *The Box*

"Taff brings the pain in five damaged and disturbing tales of love gone horribly wrong. This collection is like a knife in the heart. Highly recommended!" —JONATHAN MABERRY, *New York Times* bestselling author of *Code Zero* and *Fall of Night*

"Literary affecting, chilling, and indicative of that old-school mentality meets new-school daring." —KEALAN PATRICK BURKE, Bram Stoker Award®-winning author of *The Turtle Boy*, *Kin*, and *Jack & Jill*

**PRAISE FOR**

# JOHN F.D. TAFF

"No one is doing what Taff does." —Josh Malerman, *New York Times* bestselling author of *Incidents Around the House*

"John F. D. Taff has rapidly become one of my favorite writers in the horror genre. His horror is grounded in our day-to-day lives, in our families, our work, our most private thoughts. His stories vibrate with emotion and life and his prose is cathartic, deeply satisfying, like popping the bubbles in bubble wrap." —RAY GARTON, Grand Master of Horror and author of *Live Girls* and *Ravenous*

**ALSO BY**

# JOHN F.D. TAFF

*All the Stars Die: Cosmic Horror Novellas*

*Dark Stars: New Tales of Darkest Horror*

# THE END IN ALL BEGINNINGS

## JOHN F.D. TAFF

*The End in All Beginnings*
Copyright © 2017-2025 by John FD Taff

Print ISBN: 979-8-9924837-6-5

Cover Art & Design by Sarah Sumeray
Interior Design & Formatting by Todd Keisling | Dullington Design Co.

Second Paperback Edition

No part of this work may be reproduced or transmitted in any form or by any means without permission, except for inclusion of brief quotations with attribution in a review or report. Requests for reproduction or related information should be addressed to the Contact page at www.badhandbooks.com.

Without in any way limiting the authors' and publisher's exclusive rights under copyright, any use of this publication to "train" generative artificial intelligence (AI) technologies to generate text is expressly prohibited. The author reserves all rights to license uses of their work for generative AI training and development of machine learning language models.

This is a work of fiction. All characters, products, corporations, institutions, and/or entities in this book are either products of the author's imagination or, if real, used fictitiously without intent to describe actual characteristics.

Bad Hand Books
www.badhandbooks.com

*To my grandparents,*

*Robert & Anita Taff and Floyd & Margaret Graham.*
*I knew you for too short a time—and one of you not at all!*

# TABLE OF CONTENTS

WHAT BECOMES GOD ............................................. 9

OBJECT PERMANENCE.............................................. 77

LOVE IN THE TIME OF ZOMBIES............................... 135

THE LONG, LONG BREAKDOWN.............................. 173

VISITATION............................................................. 219

AFTERWORD.......................................................... 265

AUTHOR'S NOTES.................................................. 269

ACKNOWLEDGMENTS ............................................. 273

# WHAT BECOMES GOD

*"God is a man-eater. For this reason, men are sacrificed to him."*

—The Gospel of Philip

# PROLOGUE

Was it two? Or three?

I'm just not sure anymore. I can't be sure of that.

I have dreams where there are just two, normal size, at the front, set up on biers.

I have dreams where there are three, two normal size, one to either side of the smaller one in the middle.

I'd like to believe there were actually three.

Believing that there were only two means…means…

There was a time when I believed…in a lot of things.

But no more.

Belief is a terrible thing. It demands sacrifice.

Once, I was a child, and I believed, and I sacrificed a thing of beauty for the thing I loved most, my best friend.

And it bought me nothing.

Nothing, that is, except disbelief.

Here it is, then, if you want it, if you can see it.

If you will take it.

PROLOGUE

**F**irst *I believed I could catch the moon.*

I hadn't been asleep long when the moon exploded.

I'd entered sleep roughly that evening, pounding my pillow into submission, thrashing the covers until they could fight me no longer.

When sleep finally came, though, it was indifferent, a familiar lover's torpid kiss.

And the dream came with it almost immediately.

I stood on the deck of my house. Only it was the house I'd grown up in, the house I'd been born into. That house never had a deck. Being back was enough to awaken in me some dim spark of loss—of childhood, home and family, whatever pain it might have caused me in my youth. Perhaps the fog of years or the acceptance of age dulled my mind to the sting of such memories.

Sighing heavily, I reached forward, grasping the rough-hewn railing of the deck I never knew and looked up at the silver-white light of the moon, impossibly big and full above me.

I had touched the moon one childhood evening.

Or, rather, I'd tried.

That early summer's evening, I had tried to catch the moon, trap it in a jar like the king of all fireflies. I had raced through the weed-choked empty lot behind my house for hours, leaving my father slumped in his easy chair, a pile of beer cans slouching at his feet, a half-lit cigarette slipping from his drooping hand.

My mother was gone on one of her countless errands—shopping or playing cards or having dinner at one of her friends' houses—all of which, I know now (and was dimly aware of in this dream) meant she was out with one of her lovers. One of the men who showed up frequently at the house during the morning or afternoon—always while dad was away—to "fix the sink" or "unstop the toilet" or "work on the furnace."

Together, they'd disappear for hours, and return sweaty and disheveled.

It would start when my dad returned home—the yelling, the throwing, the rage that echoed from the dingy walls of our small place until...

But that one evening, I'd felt larger than it all—as big as an eight-year-old boy can feel. While I rested in the field, munching on the crushed remains of a cheese sandwich I'd fixed for dinner, my breath rasping in my lungs, an empty jar sitting amiably beside me, I believed I could catch the moon.

*I believed.*

Or maybe I wanted the moon to catch me, to seal and take me away in its own glass jar, still smelling faintly of whatever condiment was used on the moon.

While I rested there, my older sister, Marcia, came crashing through the tall grass.

"What the fuck are you doing out here?" she asked. I saw the inexpertly rolled white cylinder in her hands disappear behind her bare back, where a single roll of baby fat still curved innocently from between the short hem of her t-shirt, the low waist of her torn, tight jeans.

All of fifteen, she was already smoking pot and getting laid and thinking about moving on to, perhaps, heroin or LSD and communal living and free love. Marcia had come out here alone to smoke, still fearing the anger of our parents, however fossilized and impotent it might appear.

And I could tell she feared what I thought, as well.

How strange, I realize now.

But with this also came the realization that she hated me with a loathing that reminded me of the secret looks my mother sometimes gave my father.

"I'm trying to catch the moon," I breathed, stale crumbs of bread flaking from my lips, one dirty hand stroking the smooth glass of the jar.

She stood with her mouth open for a moment, not able to laugh or speak. Finally, "You're a fucking retard. Just like the old man. Must run in the entire fucking family," she spat, hurtling each word forward like a striking snake.

With that, she turned away, strode farther off into the field, farther from me.

I never saw her again.

From what little my parents said about her afterward, I gleaned that she'd run away, hitched to San Francisco, joined some group of hippies. She died three years later, when I was eleven and she only eighteen, of a heroin overdose.

My parents didn't bring her home to bury her, didn't go there to attend the funeral. Later, when I was in high school, some acquaintance of hers told me that her friends had buried her with flowers in her hair.

He laughed as if this was some black joke, watched my uncomprehending face, shook his head.

My dream-self remembered all of this, but particularly how close the moon had been that heavy summer evening. It had seemed possible, *really* possible to touch it, to capture it.

I *believed* it.

How would it feel, I wondered, to run my hands along its grey ridges and dead dry scarps, to feel the impression of its craters beneath the tips of my fingers?

While I considered reaching out to touch it in this dream, it burst asunder like the husk of a dried, desiccated fruit.

There was a tremendous flash of light, painful even with closed eyes. I threw my hands up to ward it away, but it did no good. It penetrated flesh and bone and mind in one gigantic, formless pulse of light before it faded.

And it left a horror in its absence.

Where there was once one round face in the sky, there were now thousands, millions of jagged pieces, twirling and spinning in the darkness like fragments of a shattered mirror, each glittering the same argent as the former whole.

The space between these whirling shards was filled with jagged arms of purple lightning, and silvery faery dust, and the plumes of myriad explosions.

A moment earlier, and I felt I could reach out to stroke the face of the moon.

No more.

The vast space between the Earth and moon was magnified by the streamers and debris that filled the sky, seeming to come closer and closer, but never able to reach Earth.

And I realized through the mist of my dream, through the veil of years that separated the *me* of years and years ago from this me, realized how ridiculous this childhood dream was, this *belief.*

No one could touch the moon.

No one.

He was dying even then, I know now.

Dying not in teetering steps as old men die, but in great bounding leaps. As children gulp Kool-Aid on a summer day, he was taking death in, gulping it down, swallowing it whole. Not missing a drop.

*And the Kool-Aid Man says "Oh yeahhhhh!"*

Part of me feels anguish at the fact that it took so long for me to notice. The pale skin. The deep-set, bruised eyes. The thin arms and legs, as spindly as a monkey's. His lack of energy, of strength. He could never keep up with me. Couldn't run as fast or as long, climb as high, jump as far.

I never noticed. Well…that's not true. I did notice, but not until very, very late.

I think, though, that perhaps it was better that way. I never treated him any different, never looked to the days ahead—days very probably without him—and mourned his loss.

How that would change.

The frogs were Charlie's idea, not mine.

A few months before the sixties ended and the seventies began, we watched a man with the curiously Hollywood name of Armstrong walk on the moon in grainy, choppy black-and-white images on the hideous console TV in my mother's living room.

Charlie and I sat in enthralled silence, shoving handfuls of popcorn into our Kool-Aid-stained mouths, our hands greasy on the carpet.

"I want to be an astronaut when I grow up," Charlie said, his voice startling me. "I want to walk on the moon."

I laughed, imagining the other astronauts having to lean against boulders, pausing while Charlie caught his breath, or having to carry his backpack because he was too weak.

My mother, seated on the sofa behind us, stiffened.

"Brian!" she hissed.

She was alone, as she was often those days. My dad had walked out about a year before, and his absence—and the death of my sister just a few months earlier—left my mom deflated and listless. I could tell that she thought *she* was supposed to have been the one to leave, not him. When he left, though, either she lost interest in other men or they lost interest in her.

Though I didn't understand her reaction, I bit back my laughter, turned to Charlie.

I saw it in his eyes.

*Defiance.*

I shrugged, stuffed my mouth with popcorn and watched Armstrong bunny hop across the grey powder of the very moon that I had tried long ago to trap in a mayonnaise jar.

I wondered if I would be able to see his footprints from down here.

In my memory, the summers in my hometown of St. Louis were hotter and more humid than they are today. So much for global warming. The heat and the weighted air were oppressive, thick enough to take effort to draw into my lungs. My hair wilted, sweat

## WHAT BECOMES GOD

positively fountained from my pores. The air was so sodden that I became wet simply moving through it. Clothes adhered to my skin like hot towels in a sauna.

*And that's in the shade!* as the joke goes.

Water boiled from the air, yet was constantly replaced from some source I hadn't yet learned about in school.

Under my feet, the pavement became a griddle. Going barefoot was out of the question. The tar cementing sections of the road together wept onto the concrete, bubbled like black lava. Grass died in hours on lawns that weren't continuously watered.

The sun lasered layers of skin off my forehead, my exposed shoulders, the tips of my nose and ears.

No one wanted to be outside under that sun in those suburban, early seventies summers.

Except us kids.

Not that my friends and I had much choice. My mother, like most of the moms on the block, fed me breakfast early in the morning—as early, anyway, as she could drag me out of bed on a day with no school and no Saturday morning cartoons—packed my lunch, ushered me gently but firmly to the door, where I'd hear two things before being almost literally pushed out.

First was the warning not to bother her during the day, but be sure to be home for supper.

Second was the door locking behind me.

Getting back in the house—the coolly air-conditioned house—was possible only through visible blood, broken bones (again, visible) or imminent danger of an embarrassing *al fresco* bathroom incident (if you were a boy, only No. 2 would gain you access; either, if you were a girl, but only grudgingly).

There were other distractions, sure. Kickball, whiffle ball, hot box. Riding bikes to the local Quick Shop for candy or sodas or comics. The ice cream man's regular visits, announced by those tinkling bells that jangle something primal deep, deep within every child's DNA.

Following the mosquito fogger, running behind it or riding bikes, breathing in the dense, grey billows of smoke the contraption—usually perched in the bed of someone's truck—belched out. It smelled of gasoline and something lighter, headier and slightly botanical, but not in a good way. Like how some weeds smell when you crush them in your hands and they bleed out their thin, white sap. That I haven't died yet, after years of avidly inhaling that mosquito fog, still frankly surprises me. Who knows, though? Maybe it inoculated me against cancer. From what I can recall, the mosquitoes certainly never seemed to suffer from it.

We also had the woods.

We were in the woods that morning. Each in t-shirts and blue jeans cut down into shorts, clutching a brown paper bag with lunch inside. Canteens filled with Kool-Aid sweated at our hips.

My mother had been even more distant that morning, sitting at the kitchen table in her bathrobe, smoking a cigarette and drinking a cup of black coffee. She didn't say anything when I came into the room, made myself a bowl of cereal with the last of the milk in the refrigerator, didn't even look at me.

She seemed guarded, wary. There was a strong sense of fear that wafted from her; fear that I would say something to her, require her to do something for me.

*Feel* something for me.

I left without her saying a word to me. She didn't even tell me to be home for dinner.

Charlie, in contrast to my sullen, distracted mother, was very animated that morning. His hands moved as he talked, spots of color burned on his pale cheeks. His fish-white legs scissored back and forth, his head pivoting as if on a swivel.

It looked to be a good Charlie day, which, even then, was becoming rarer and rarer. I thought we might even make it to the creek before he needed to rest.

"So, did you read *Spider-Man* last night?" he asked, practically gasping out the words.

Unconsciously, I slowed my pace a little, literally gave him some room to breathe.

"Nah," I said, swinging my lunch bag before me.

"Nah? *Nah?* How can you not have read it? It's the final part of the story, Brian! I mean, jeez, the Green Goblin's high on drugs and you don't read it?"

I shrugged. Charlie gave me his comics when he was finished reading them and re-reading them. I had to hide them under my bed like dirty magazines. My mom didn't like me reading them. Said they rotted my mind.

I think she was really angry because she knew Charlie had *given* them to me. I think it made her mad to be confronted by the knowledge that my happiness could be had for something as simple as a 15-cent comic book.

She couldn't afford even that.

Charlie stopped walking, turned to me.

"Well, then how're we gonna talk about it today?" he said, exasperated. "I'll tell you *how*. We won't be able to, that's *how*."

"Sorry. I fell asleep. I'll read it tonight and we can talk about it tomorrow."

"But what about *today?*"

"I said I'm sorry, *Charles*. I'll have a full book report for ya tomorrow. *Jeez*."

"Screw you," he muttered, hesitantly making sure no adults were around to hear what his mother called "such language."

"And don't call me *Charles*," he pouted.

Also a mother thing.

"Don't get your undies in a bunch," I said, suddenly feeling the good-Charlieness of the day slipping away.

I punched him lightly on the shoulder. Not light enough, I saw later.

"Hey, I promise I'll read it tonight. *Promise*. Now, c'mon, let's get to the pond and grab a few frogs."

Charlie's frown clung to life for a few moments, then curled into a wry smile.

"Okay, then I'll give you the *Superman* comic my mom bought me yesterday and you can read that, instead. You'll *love* it."

"Supergay? No way. I hear he's *your* favorite, though."

"I don't think so," he said as we started walking again. "It's yours. That's why I'm giving it to you."

We were Marvel guys, not DC. You either get that or you don't.

*T*he woods.

They're gone now, lost, as the best chunks of America seem to be these days. Ground out, mowed down by the subdivisions and strip malls, gas stations and banks, McDonald's and Starbucks spit up in their places. At one time, the woods stretched from my little neighborhood to the Missouri River, miles and miles away. It was a terrific, dark, Germanic storybook of a forest, seemingly endless, though I suppose now that it wasn't nearly as big as my memory of it.

I will never know because I can't go back and walk its tree-canopied paths, jump across its narrow, high-banked streams or cross through wide, hilly fields where birds flew up from the ground like startled phantoms, or arm-thick black snakes sunned themselves atop abandoned wooden fence posts. There's only a narrow strip of my old woods left, encircling my old subdivision like a fringe of hair around an aging man's head.

The woods as I remember them exist now only in my memory, I suppose, and the memory of those who grew up near them. And the older I get, the more distant that memory becomes, almost illusory now, as if I've created it in the comfort of my middle years to give my sharp-edged childhood something soft, something to cushion it.

I believed it was, and even now want it to be, something that was *bigger* than me, yet didn't seem to be *against* me.

Too many things that were bigger than me seemed to be against me.

Isn't that the way of the world when we're young?

Does it ever really change?

The entrance to the woods was at the rear of our compact, ranch home subdivision. Here, the neighborhood ended in a broad arc. Two empty lots stood out, missing teeth in an otherwise blandly perfect smile. These lots formed a grassy bowl that sloped gradually down into a hollow.

From here, the dark, dense bulk of the woods rose, spread out before us. Entering here was dramatic, like slipping through the subdivision's gaping smile into the mouth of the forest, then down its dark, dangerous throat.

Inside, behind that moist, green curtain, were trees we had no names for, mysterious plants, the danger of snakes and snapping turtles, raccoons and possums, bees and wasps.

Inside, there was life that took almost no notice of us.

Inside, there was the *known* and the *unknown*.

Inside, we were the little gods of a little universe.

"Let's see if he's there," I said, trotting ahead, down the slope of the bowl. A creek twisted and gouged its way along the edges, where it flowed into a man-made storm drain, then disappeared into the side of the hill.

Across this creek, an ancient tree had collapsed, probably decades before we were born. It was huge, five or six feet in diameter, and it stretched from one crooked, slanting bank to the other.

Its wood was old and crumbly, like moist chalk, and many things made their lives under it, on it, inside it. Mushrooms sprouted from dark, damp holes. Clinging vines and nettles grew around it. Peel back a chunk of its flesh to reveal a dark scramble of beetles, pill bugs and spiders.

On most days, most sunny days that is, there would be at least one reptile sunning itself on the tree's wide back—maybe a black snake.

Or maybe the skink.

*My skink.*

I'd seen him for the first time a year earlier. At least, I thought he was the same one. Every time I passed this way, I stopped to see if he was there. Sometimes, he wasn't. More often, though, he was.

Today he was.

He was a broadhead skink, one of the larger varieties. We saw plenty of smaller skinks in our yards, blue racers we called them. These were small, sleek creatures, whip thin and just as fast. Their tails were a deep electric blue—the kind you usually don't see outside a science fiction movie. They'd snap off when you caught them, wriggling disturbingly for an hour or so afterward. Great for grossing girls out.

My skink was about seven or eight inches long and aerodynamically plump. His shiny, polished scales glittered a copper-brown in the morning sun. His head was a brilliant burst of orangey-red.

He watched me with his dark, tiny eyes as I approached the fallen trunk, gauging how close he would allow me to come before darting into the underbrush. We'd played this game before, many times, but today I was content to just stand and watch him.

To admire him.

I didn't move, didn't step onto the log. I just stood there and noted the funny way his rear legs splayed out and backward. The quizzical tilt of his head. The slow fade of red down his back, shining like a new penny.

He was the first thing in my world that I unabashedly acknowledged as beautiful.

I hadn't heard Charlie approach, but I heard him now, wheezing in my ear, could smell Cocoa Puffs on each breath blatted my way.

"It's just getting a tan, I guess."

"I guess."

"I don't know why you just don't grab it," he said. "Keep it in an aquarium in your room. That'd be *cool*."

As if hearing this, my skink flicked his head to the left, gave a dismissive, disappointed little twitch of his tail, and scampered away down the length of the log, then off below.

I turned to Charlie, frowning.

"No, that'd *suck*."

Truth was, though, I'd thought that very thing. I lay awake some nights when the air in my cramped little bedroom was still and heavy, not even stirring the model space ships hung from the ceiling with fishing line. I thought about catching him, bringing him here to live with me in my room, in some enclosure where I could watch him whenever I wanted.

But something struck me as awfully wrong about that plan, about that *desire*, and I never acted on it—at that point, at least.

It occurred to me that it wouldn't be the same in my room. My bedroom lamp wouldn't shine on his penny scales like the sun. His eyes might not look back at me with lively awareness through aquarium glass. His back legs might not splay out in such relaxation were he lying on a handful of grass wrenched from my yard.

No, it wouldn't be the same.

*We* wouldn't be the same.

Something told me that owning his beauty wouldn't be the same as appreciating it, would never match its benefits.

I knew that both the skink and I would lose something were I to capture him and bring him home. That something, as intangible as it seemed to me, I knew I would miss.

"I wish I was him…sometimes," Charlie said, his voice hushed, almost as if speaking to himself.

"Huh?"

"He's got the perfect life, you know," Charlie said, moving away, back up the hill. "No doctors, no hospitals, no being sick, no bossy moms."

I frowned behind his back. I didn't like it when he spoke like this.

I followed him, clapped him smartly on the back, collapsing his thin shoulder blades around my hand.

"Nope, not perfect."

"Ouch!" he yelped, turning toward me with a questioning look.

"He's got no comic books."

That said, we entered the woods.

Every story, all real stories, begin when you enter the deep, dark woods.

And so.

Once upon a time…

# WHAT BECOMES GOD

"Hey, wanna know what's funny? I watched *The Monkees* on TV yesterday afternoon and *Planet of the Apes* last night."

"Huh?" I asked, something I did a lot to Charlie's seemingly unconnected blurts of consciousness.

"The movie? *Planet of the Apes*. It was on TV last night."

"What about it?"

We'd made it to the creek by then, the main creek for which the one at the entrance to the woods was just a thin feeder. We sat on its banks while Charlie rested, caught his breath.

He let out a long, dramatic sigh.

"Hey, dillweed, are you even listening to me?"

"I'm listening." It was a lie. I was tying a knot in a long blade of grass, cooling my bare feet in the cold, flowing water of the creek.

And I was thinking, of all things, of my family, such as it was.

I dropped the knotted grass and picked the frail, white bloom of one of the innumerable trilliums that covered the hill and most of the ground under the trees. The plant, a trio of broad, limp, heart-shaped leaves atop a short, slender stalk, held onto the flower for a moment, then released it, snapped back. Its leaves seemed to droop a little lower at the theft of its flower.

"You're listening, huh?"

"Uh-huh."

I contemplated the torn bloom, twirled it between my fingers, smelled its no-scent.

"Good," Charlie said, as if from a distance. "I'm dying."

The flower fell from fingers that suddenly felt numb.

My heart stopped beating.

My blood refused to flow.

"What?" I asked, facing him.

"I said, dude, *you're lying*."

I heard it again, not what he said, but what I thought he said.

"What? What's up with you all of a sudden?"

"What did you say?" The rest of my body went as cold as my toes in the water.

"I said you were lying. Yeah, you're really listening."

"Oh," was the only word my throat would allow, and it was more a gulped syllable than a word.

"What'd you think I said?" he asked, his dark, bruised eyes narrowing, his pale, thin lips compressing into a slit, as if he were waiting for a specific response from me.

"Nothing." I pulled my feet from the creek, kicked the water from them before sliding into my battered Keds. "Ready to go?"

He nodded uncertainly, as if still waiting for something, surprised that it hadn't occurred.

"Yup," he said after a minute. "Let's go."

I got to my feet, offered him my hand. He let me pull him up, and I had to turn away once he was on his feet. I walked a few paces down the path ahead of him.

I couldn't risk even wiping the tears away without revealing them.

When I helped him to his feet, it was like lifting a twig, a feather.

When he came up beside me, he couldn't meet my eyes, either.

He knew I knew.

It was what he had been waiting for.

The pond was a flat, green glass, reflecting the sky and drifting clouds as if mirrored in an emerald. It was about an acre in size, shaped roughly like a comma or a comic book text balloon, a fat oval with a short, curved tail.

I crested the small rise that sloped up from the path, giving us a full view of the pond and the surrounding landscape. Its broadest curve spread directly beneath us, and the tail swooped out from the opposite shore and to the left. A farmer's field to the right was cordoned off from the pond by a rickety barb wire fence. Corn was just beginning to stand up in the field.

The path we were on hugged the right-hand shore of the pond, between it and the field. From here, this same path traveled deeper into the woods, to other sites. To an abandoned and derelict mill, with a small, crumbling concrete dam. To a deeply banked creek where a tree anchored a series of long vines that allowed you, if you were as crazy as we were, to swing out and over the creek, from one bank to the other, at least 20 feet in the air. To a strange junk pile made up of what looked like the complete, carefully arranged remains of a house—from an ancient television to a bathtub—minus the actual house.

Today, though, the pond was our destination. Charlie just didn't have the stamina to go farther into the woods.

He stood beside me, and we both surveyed the pond.

"Well, what're we waiting for? Those frogs aren't going to catch themselves."

He stumbled down the path, and I followed.

Where the trail came to the edge of the pond, curved right, there was what, on a map or a much larger body of water, would be a bay. This small, protected harbor held some unidentified animal that, when it heard us approach, would emit an aggrieved squeal and splash into the water. We thought it might have been something cool, like a beaver or an otter. It was, in all probability, just a pissed-off muskrat.

Today, though, no splash. It must have been sleeping or off on an errand. There was only the multiple, smaller splashes of the frogs and toads.

Charlie wasted no time, not even to take off his shoes. He waded ankle deep into the pond, bowed at the waist like one of those toy glass birds filled with red water.

"Dude, your mom's gonna kill you," I said with some surprise. Charlie usually followed each of his mom's very many rules scrupulously, no matter how silly they seemed.

He got that faraway look again, as if seeing mountains on the distant horizon. "Sometimes, you know, I wish she were dead. Both my parents, really. I wish I could kill them, so that they wouldn't look at me like I'm already…"

My eyebrows shot up and my mouth dropped. "Charlie…"

"Just sometimes, you know…so they wouldn't have to see me… wouldn't have to…well, you know."

He shot his hand into the water, hauled out our first catch of the day, a good-sized leopard frog.

"I'll hose my shoes off at your house."

His face, usually so set and hollow, filled, shone like the sun.

I stood up, left my own shoes on, and joined him.

We ate lunch shirtless and shoeless on a rise overlooking the pond. The former hung from a nearby tree branch, dripping brown water; the latter scattered across the top of the hill where they'd landed after we'd kicked them off.

Charlie lay stretched flat, feeding pretzel sticks into his mouth like lumber into a sawmill. He stared unblinking into the sky. I took the last mouthful of warm grape Kool-Aid from my Boy Scout canteen. It was weak—my mom never used enough sugar—and metallic tasting, but I gulped it greedily.

Then, I lay back, too, feeling the solid hill beneath me, the downy grass under my sweaty, grimy head.

"It's kind of weird when it's out during the day."

Halfway up the sky was the pale sketch of the moon.

"Yeah. That is weird."

Charlie turned to me quizzically, expecting, I guess, my usual "What?" He eyed me with some surprise, then resettled his head, looking straight up.

"The next Apollo mission is going up soon. Apollo 17. They say it might be the last one."

I grunted noncommittally.

"Remember what I told you when we watched Apollo 11 land on the moon?"

"You still want to be an astronaut?"

He nodded.

I didn't laugh this time. He smiled, I think in gratitude, turned back to the sky.

"I hope it's not the last one. I want to walk on the moon."

I saw the shadow of a bruise on his upper forearm, where I'd lightly punched him earlier.

"I need to train, I guess," he said, interrupting my solemnity. "Train. *Practice.* You know, like the astronauts."

"Hmm," I replied, nodding yet having no clear idea what he meant.

Then, he sat bolt upright, back rigid, eyes wide.

"What's the matter?" I yelped, sitting up, too.

"Experiments," he said. "We need to experiment. To see what kind of stresses my body will have to take."

He didn't even wait for my "Huh?"

"Frogs. We'll experiment with frogs." He rubbed the side of his head absently. His breathing was rapid, shallow and sharp, and I really did begin to worry.

"Okay," I said, still not completely following him. "Let's go get some frogs, then."

"We don't have anything to put them in. How'll we get them home?"

"No problem. We'll come back tomorrow and..."

Like a delicate bubble, his excitement popped. His narrow, ashen chest caved in, his shoulders, red and indented from the ground beneath them, slumped.

He looked at me with a face full of disappointment. It was weary and defeated beyond his years, knowing failure and pain and some bigger loss, vague and undefined, hanging somewhere in the distance.

"I can't. I have a doctor's appointment tomorrow."

He spoke it in a whisper, like a terrible, guarded secret or a magic phrase that, once uttered, can never be called back.

I stood, with no reply on my lips, in my mind, in my heart, and helped him up. We put on our damp shirts and shoes, squelchy and reeking of the pond, and returned down the path and out the maw of the woods.

"What's wrong with Charlie?" I asked my mom, later that night, as she passed by the open door of my room.

I was already in bed. She hadn't tucked me in or read to me or even told me to go to bed. She didn't make me dinner or speak to me much that evening, for that matter. Since dad left, we no longer had that type of relationship. It was very close to no relationship at all. As if we, too, had left each other, even though we were still here.

I saw her shadow hesitate outside my door. It struck me that she must have been dreading this question, or another like it, for a while.

She turned to my door, eased it open. She didn't come in.

"Why?"

I shrugged beneath my covers.

"I dunno. He's tired and sick all the time."

My mother mulled this over, probably weighing what little I knew against the danger of imparting even a little more knowledge.

"Charlie's...well, got some problems," she said, her words slow and slurred. She'd been drinking beer alone that night, and I could smell her breath from where I lay.

"But, hey, who doesn't?" she said, trying to sound brighter, but barking out a harsh and bitter laugh. "It's not like we don't have our own problems, right?"

By we, I knew she meant herself.

And by problems, I knew she meant me.

"Is he gonna be all right?"

She snorted, but it sounded weak and defeated, and again, I thought her response was as much meant for her as for Charlie.

"Shit, kid, I dunno."

Moving to leave, she stopped when I asked her a final question.

"Can I help him?"

She paused, half-turned from me, then flicked the light in the hall off, plunging us both into darkness.

"Pray."

I fell asleep thinking of my mother's single word response.

*Pray?*

At that time, I'd last been in a church when my grandmother, my mom's mother, died. She'd been a dour old Baptist, full of verse and venom, which she administered liberally to anyone within striking range.

That my mother had married a Catholic—*a Catholic!*—became the reason for years of animosity directed at her. But it hardly mattered in reality. My mother's two sisters and two brothers hadn't married Catholics, yet received their full measure of my grandmother's ire.

I'd only ever been to church in the company of grandparents. My mother, soaked to the bone in Jesus' blood three days a week while growing up, used my father's Catholicism as an excuse to extricate herself from attending church altogether. My father, whose grasp on Catholicism could fairly be called tenuous at best, attended church only on Christmas and Easter.

On occasion, each of my grandmothers would arrange to take my sister and me to church with them, at least until Marcia became old enough to say "No" and make it stick. When my father's mom, Grandma Jean, took us, we were always freshly bathed, wearing our best clothes, teeth brushed, shoes shined, hair combed. These outings were, it seemed to me, more social than anything else. They were chances for her to show us off to friends, to take us to breakfast afterward, to show someone, whoever that might be, that she, at least, was not neglecting her grandchildren's eternal souls.

When my mom's mom, Grandma Rebekah, took us, there was no breakfast or socializing. Going to church with her was like being escorted to the doctor for an inoculation against something dreadful and most likely life-threatening, like incipient Catholicism. I think if Grandma Jean had left us to our own devices, so would have Grandma Rebekah.

## WHAT BECOMES GOD

These instances, while completely different in tone and scope from each other, never gave me any glimpses into the meaning of religion. I had no framework on which to build an idea of God beyond some great, bearded, toga-wearing, cloud-dwelling old man who, evidently, somehow, for some unknown reason, made everything and then became pretty pissed about the whole deal.

It wasn't so much whether I believed or disbelieved in God.

I didn't know enough about him one way or the other.

So, *pray* to him?

I barely even knew him, and I suspected that he felt similarly about me.

And I'm supposed to ask him for a favor?

I believed there must be a better way.

Entering the woods by myself was a little scary.

It sometimes felt as if the woods were alive; a huge, sentient thing that would simply swallow me, lose me in its vastness.

There were paths leading everywhere inside it, and we hadn't—couldn't—explore them all. Sometimes it felt as if it moved those paths, deliberately altered landmarks to confuse us, to keep us within it, wandering its shifting trails, lost forever.

I'd gotten out of bed early that morning, dressed and eaten a quick, quiet breakfast alone, in a house that felt as aggrieved as my mother. In the garage, the heart of my dad's abandoned kingdom—just as his recliner, which neither my mom nor I sat in, was his abandoned throne—I dumped the loose nuts and bolts from a five-pound can of Eight O'Clock coffee. I left the garage, still smelling of my dad's absent car, my dad's absence, and set off.

I passed Charlie's house on the way to the woods, noticed that his parents' car was already gone. My heart gave a little twinge.

With a peanut butter sandwich, a canteen filled with lime Kool-Aid, an apple and my empty coffee can, I parted the dark green curtains, stepped backstage.

A few hours later, and I had a coffee can literally packed with frogs and toads of all kinds. I even managed to snag a huge, slimy bullfrog weighing at least a pound. I immediately named him Armstrong. Holding him was like trying to grasp a slick, naked muscle, but he went into the can with the rest.

I used a sharp stick to punch several air holes through the plastic lid, careful not to press too hard and injure the frogs. The entire can jumped and jostled, filled as it was with indignant amphibians.

I washed my sticky hands in a clear part of the pond. Atop the rise, the bouncing can at my side, I gobbled my peanut butter sandwich and my apple, drained my canteen.

My eyes closed and my head was filled with the drowsy red light of the sun shining through my lids. I thought of staying there for a while, resting my head, sleeping there. And I almost let it happen. Already, I could feel myself see-sawing down into sleep, like a leaf dropped from a tree.

But the coffee can thumping against my thigh brought me back.

I had to get home and find more comfortable—and more spacious—accommodations for the frogs.

I had to get them ready to meet Charlie.

Because I believed they would save him.

"Acute lymphocytic leukemia, if you're interested."

We were in Charlie's room later that day, sprawled on

## WHAT BECOMES GOD

the floor, reading comics. He had them all—*The Fantastic Four, The Incredible Hulk, The Invincible Iron Man, Captain America, Daredevil: The Man Without Fear, The Avengers, The Mighty Thor, Dr. Strange, The Uncanny X-Men.* And, of course, *The Amazing Spider-Man.*

I was several pages into a *Marvel Team-Up* pairing The Thing with Spidey when he spoke those words.

"What?"

He smiled at the comfortable familiarity of my response.

"That's why I can't go outside just yet. I got my first drugs today, and my mother wants me to stay inside."

I swallowed, looked away from a panel where The Thing was telling the villain, in his gravelly, Brooklyn voice, that it was clobberin' time.

"Oh," I replied. "What's…um…what's that?"

"My body's making too many little blood cells," he said, matter-of-factly paging through an issue of *Luke Cage: Hero for Hire.* "It's a cancer."

My tongue seemed stuck to the roof of my mouth. My throat felt clogged with shards of glass. I didn't know what to say, how to react, what to do.

So, I tried to follow his lead, flipped the page of the comic I was no longer reading. A New York building was collapsing onto the villain, who'd been knocked into it by a great orange, rocky fist.

But I couldn't focus, couldn't make the comic book words come together in any way that made sense any more than I could Charlie's words.

"I got the frogs," I croaked through my sharp throat and numb tongue.

He forgot the comics, snapped his head to me.

"You did? Really?"

His eyes, which had looked flat and dull, pushed into their sockets, now actually seemed to protrude, to shine with life. His cheeks flushed, and his mouth moved for a moment around syllables that were unspoken.

"Yeah," I continued. I wanted to bury his earlier words, what he'd said, what he'd meant, with words of my own. To cover them with talk of frogs and astronauts and comics and whatever until both of us forgot what it was he had said.

Forgot that he was dying.

"About fourteen of 'em. They're in coffee cans right now on my front porch. My mom wouldn't let me bring them inside."

"Didja poke holes in the lids, because…"

"I'm not stupid, dillweed. I know frogs need to breathe."

He closed his mouth, pursed his lips. His mind was racing, I knew. His breathing came heavy through his nostrils.

"Okay, okay. We've got to plan. To make a plan. Get everything ready. We need to get started right away, because they won't…"

His voice trailed off as his eyes met mine

*Live long…*

He didn't say it, but it hung there over his head, like a comic book hero's words.

This was probably the only time I appreciated Charlie's mom interrupting us.

His bedroom door, already cracked, flew open wide, and Mrs. Greenwell strode in, eyes narrowed and scanning the bedroom. She did this quite often, looking shocked and vaguely surprised, as if she hadn't been altogether sure that this door actually led here. Then, her look faded quickly to one of mild disappointment tinged with whatever passed for embarrassment with her.

Years later, I realized that she expected—no, *wanted*—to catch us

## WHAT BECOMES GOD

at something, smoking pot or lying around naked paging through *Playboy* or selling nuclear secrets to the Soviets. That she never found us doing anything more interesting than reading comics or playing Mouse Trap was, I think, a great disappointment to her.

"Oh, well, Brian," she stammered, lurching to a halt halfway into the room. "You're still here."

I smiled vacantly up at her from the floor.

"Well, ahh, yes, Charles has had a tiring day today, and he needs to get some rest, you understand. Some quiet time."

She looked down at the slick of comic books spread across the carpet of Charlie's room, and the upturned corners of her thin, severe mouth drooped down to, what was in all probability, their normal position.

She didn't like comic books any better than my mother. The difference, though, other than the money to buy them, was that she was unable to deny them to Charlie because he was—

"He knows."

Her eyes—hell, my eyes—snapped wide, drilled into him.

"He knows *what*, Charles?" she asked, blinking, hands playing with the neckline of her sundress.

"About me. About the doctors."

Some of the tension in her body sloughed away at that, thinking I knew this and no more.

"Oh, Charles, now is that really the kind of thing two young boys need to be—"

"About the acute lymphocytic leukemia."

I saw, I know I saw, the whites of Mrs. Greenwell's eyes as they rolled back in her head. What she'd been saying died in her throat, faded softly like a radio slowly being turned off.

"Charles!" she breathed, though it was weak and more a force of habit. "Such language."

"It's okay," he smiled up at her. "I just thought he should know. And I just thought you should know that he knows."

Her face, usually so fixed, so set, fell into what I was sure, had this occurred before a mirror, she would see as a distressing network of lines, creases and odd, pulsing veins.

"Well," she creaked. "I think it's time for Brian to go. Perhaps if you're feeling well tomorrow, he can visit."

"Sure," Charlie said. Then, he scooped up a pile of comics, straightened them, handed them to me as I got to my feet. The top one showed the Sub-Mariner erupting from the sea in a spray of foam.

I took them, told Charlie I'd see him tomorrow, edged around his passive, unmoving mother and out the door.

And I felt something for her. Sympathy, I guess, or perhaps pity or as close to either of those as an 11-year-old can get.

With me, Charlie seemed to be using the knowledge of his illness like bird crumbs; hints dropped at appropriate moments to lead me somewhere without overwhelming me.

But with his mother, Charlie used it as a weapon.

He wanted her to know that I knew.

He wanted it to hurt her.

I left his house clutching the slippery stack of comics. I wondered where I'd hide them from my mother, who was in the living room when I came in. She was wearing a wig, taken from a supposedly "secret" box at the back of her closet, a tight blouse, a mini-skirt and thigh-high go-go boots.

I stopped, frozen in the doorway, as much by the sight of her as by the need to hide the comics.

But she hardly even turned to see me. She looked at herself in the small mirror above the davenport, daubed at her face.

"Oh, good, you're back. I'm going out tonight. Gotta date, Brian-baby."

I nodded in silence. This was not the mother I'd grown accustomed to over the last few months.

"There's hot dogs and beans in the fridge for dinner, but don't eat them all. They've got to last all week."

She pursed her lips, applied lipstick, blotted it with a piece of tissue.

Her eyes found mine in the mirror.

"Oh, yeah, your father called and said he was coming by to see you. Maybe he'll even take you out for a hamburger or something. The hot dogs are just in case he's still an asshole."

I dragged a limp french fry through a puddle of ketchup pooled on the paper wrapper of my hamburger and tried to decide whether my father was an asshole. I wasn't sure. It seemed my mother had given me a fairly weighty responsibility in deciding if an adult—my father, no less—was an asshole.

Still.

Which implied, of course, that he had been one before.

I couldn't decide. My dad, when he was around, was more a problematic equation, one that I'd never devoted any real effort in solving. The few functions I'd previously assigned to him—paying bills, putting food on the table and clothes on our backs—seemed to be working just as well with him gone as they did when he was here. If this were an actual equation, then, he'd be a zero.

"So, what've you been up to?" he asked, watching me eat. He hadn't taken more than a bite or two of his own meal. "How's school?"

I know my brow must have knitted in confused annoyance at this question.

"School's been out for a month."

He nodded, his eyes closing slowly. I watched his face, lined with unspoken stress, fractured with failures both real and perceived, break into a sort of brave, crooked smile.

"Sure, I know that. Just forgot, I guess."

Another long, awkward pause in a meal that was mostly an extended, awkward pause. He poked at his fries, took a long, gurgling sip from his own soda, sighed.

"How's your mom?"

I knew then, knew in a flash of thought, knew in a way no child should know, that this visit, this meal had nothing to do with me, his missing me or loving me.

I was simply a line, a road that led to my mother and whatever emotions still lingered in the ghost of their dead relationship—jealousy, pity (self or otherwise), the longing for what was and is no longer.

In that regard, this meal was no different than a drunk phone call or a late night drive by the house, slowing to see what lights were still burning.

I was the picture he couldn't bear to throw away, the phone number he couldn't cross out.

The face, fogged by memory, he just couldn't forget.

I was just a way for him to conjure her.

And I hated him for that with a bright, flaring hatred that seemed so naked to me that I blushed, feeling the heat in my cheeks.

"She never believed in me, you know."

I brought my eyes to his, saw the sadness there, going deep, deep, as if the backs of his eyes were miles distant. That look, at once so pitiable yet also so inexplicably loathsome, struck a chord in me.

As much as he'd hurt my mother, damaged her pride in some way I was too young to discern, she'd hurt him, too.

And her hurt cut deeper, affected him at a much more basic level. It seemed to drain a vital essence from him, deprived him, in some way, of himself.

"If only she'd believed in me. That's all it would have taken. Just an ounce of belief that I was good enough, that I amounted to something."

He took a small bite of his hamburger, chewed it mechanically, swallowed it.

"You believe in me, don't you, Brian?"

That was not a question.

Seemingly everyone, everything, wanted or needed my belief these days.

But I didn't stop to think about my answer. If I had, I think I'd still be sitting there today.

"Sure, Dad. I believe in you."

A little groan escaped his lips, and he managed to jam the soda straw in his mouth to block it.

"Don't ever stop believing in me, son. That's all I need. All I ask."

It was more than I could give him, though.

More than I could give anyone for a long time.

"Jeez, that stinks," Charlie yelped, yanking his head back and waving his hands a little prissily in front of his face.

I had to agree. The smell that wafted from the coffee can was dense and wet and rotten. It was equal parts decaying grass clippings, oozy mud and concentrated frog slime. Even for a young boy schooled in all things gross, it was repellant. So we leaned in, sniffed it again.

"Ughh," I groaned. "Smells like your underwear drawer."

He half turned to me, his eyes narrowing. "Been sniffing my underwear? How else would you know?"

"Give me a break!" I said, opening the next coffee can. "I smell 'em from here."

Soon, we had all six cans open, and a veritable mini-plague of frogs was let loose on my front lawn. Charlie and I attempted to corral them as I explained my sorting system.

"The toads went into their own cans. Three to a can. Two cans. Then, the leopard frogs, two to a can since they're bigger. That's four cans. Then, Armstrong gets his own."

"Armstrong?"

I pointed at the green mound squatting motionlessly amidst the hopping clamor.

"You named the bullfrog 'Armstrong?' Cool."

I helped him hose out their living quarters, pulling fresh grass and recapturing the frogs. Lids went back on, and we placed the coffee cans in the shade.

This was several days after the dinner with my father. In that period, I hadn't heard a peep from Charlie. I tried to visit many times since that day we'd read comics sprawled out on his floor, showed up dutifully on his front porch.

Every day, I was sent away by his mom, not ungently, but with perhaps too fine a sense of control. It was as if she were the gatekeeper of Oz, denying access to the Wizard. Or a priest guarding entrance to the inner temple of a secret god.

That morning, though, Charlie had shown up at my door. He looked smaller than usual, thinner, paler, as if someone had spent the last few days first erasing, then lightly re-sketching him.

He was breathless from his short walk to my house, and the hectic red spots normally brought to his cheeks were a disturbing yellow-gray. The only color at all on his face came from his two blazing blue eyes, which shone out from their bruised sockets like baleful stars in a dark winter sky.

Tucked in the crook of his arm was a thick, wire-bound composition notebook, an assortment of pens clipped to its cover.

"Ready?" was the only word he was able to rasp out.

I was still in the t-shirt and shorts I wore to bed. Sleep encrusted my eyes, and my King Vitamin cereal—my mom's cheaper replacement for Cap'n Crunch—usually indestructible, was now, I knew, turning to mush in my bowl.

"For what?"

Charlie smiled, and that smile is the one that I remember every time I think of him now. The day I snapped open the paper and scanned his name in the obituaries, that smile floated in my mind, smeared through my tears though it was.

That smile was all it took to get me moving.

"For the experiments! The astronaut training program begins today!"

The composition book was filled with empty charts. As he paged through the notebook, explaining what he'd done, I imagined him in his Spider-Man pajamas, propped up in his bed, pencil flying as he mapped out the course of his idea, which had been in his head for the last few years.

He'd divided the testing of our candidates into six main categories: Isolation, Stress, Acceleration, High-G, Altitude, and Recovery

Each main section occupied several pages, with descriptions of each test and spaces for notes about the candidates, identified only as "Subject 1," "Subject 2," and so on.

**JOHN F.D. TAFF**

Charlie unclipped one of the pens, then, on the page of the first test, "Isolation," he wrote "Armstrong" under "Subject 1."

"I figure since you already named the big guy, we should go ahead and name 'em all."

So, this is how we ended up:

Subject 1:Armstrong
Subject 2:Buzz
Subject 3:Collins
Subject 4:Bean
Subject 5:Conrad
Subject 6:Shepard
Subject 7:Mitchell
Subject 8:Scott
Subject 9:Irwin
Subject 10:Duke
Subject 11:Young
Subject 12:Glenn
Subject 13:Kirk
Subject 14:Spock

Those last two, I admit, were my idea, and Charlie met them with cool silence. But having no alternatives himself, he noted the names in the book, shaking his head.

Once this was accomplished, we sat on my front porch for a little while, so Charlie could rest, regain his strength. He was breathing harder than usual, even though we hadn't really been doing anything strenuous. As I looked at him, I saw his thin arms and legs, pale as frogs' bellies themselves, were covered in a constellation of yellow, green and purple bruises.

## WHAT BECOMES GOD

"Are you okay?" I asked, both realizing and not realizing what I was asking. The obvious little question of right now and the vague, bigger question that seemed to go on and on.

"I'm fine," he snapped, not looking at me. He'd answered the little question, but I knew he wanted me to think it was the bigger question.

Right there, sitting on the porch and feeling the emptiness of that answer, the angry, phony defiance, right there is when I first became afraid.

"Isolation will be the first test, 'cuz it's the easiest." He solemnly opened the notebook, inscribed the date under "Isolation."

"What do we do now?" I asked.

"Got a shovel?"

That afternoon, in the cool shade of the side of my house, near where the metal box of the air conditioner shuddered, I dug holes for seven coffee cans. As Charlie crouched beside me, I buried each of them up to the rims, leaving about an inch of the metal above ground. Then, I fitted the plastic lids, secured them snuggly, and enlarged the air holes to ensure the frogs had plenty of air.

"What's the point of this again?"

"When you're in space," he began, in the huffy, professorial tone he sometimes adopted, "you have to spend a lot of time alone."

"They're not alone, though."

He shot me a veiled look.

"But they're pretty isolated, aren't they?"

I had to give him that.

"So...ummm...what are we looking for?"

Charlie stood, wobbled uncertainly, bent to wipe dead grass from his ghostly knees.

"Well, we leave 'em here for a day or two...and see if...well... if they're okay."

I considered this for a moment.

"You mean…if they're *alive*?"

Charlie seemed uncomfortable, then color, the color that had been missing from his face this morning, flooded his features.

"This is the easiest test of all. If they can't even live through this, what's the point?"

I hauled myself up to ask him what the heck was wrong with him, but found myself looking at his painfully thin back, his shoulders hitching as he stalked back home.

That night, death was very much on my mind.

My experience with death, at that point, was limited to distant relatives who meant little or nothing to me; matronly great aunts or senile third cousins left to dawdle toward death in yellowed, antiseptic nursing homes. I remembered funerals, the powdery smell of flowers, the vibrato of organ music, the dark clothes, the shuffling of feet.

And the tears.

It always made me feel a little scared to see my mother cry. It unnerved me to some extent, not knowing from where that depth of emotion rose. As with any child, it never occurred to me that my parents had a life before me or outside mine. If I barely knew, or as was more often the case, never knew at all, great-aunt Alma or cousin Henry, my parents couldn't have known them all that well, either.

And if those emotions—those raw emotions shed between the viewing and the somber meal of ham and cheesy potato casserole and macaroni salad—were so strong, so deep, how much stronger, how much deeper would they be for someone known, someone loved?

## WHAT BECOMES GOD

I thought about Charlie, about his doctors, his unspoken illness, his pale skin, his hurt eyes.

I thought of his death, what it might be like without him. Playing hot box or reading comics. Or walking through the woods without him, without stopping to rest or leaving early. Going where I wanted at my own pace.

I felt the tears start, hot and unwanted, and I threw the covers off.

I crept outside in pajamas and bare feet, went to the garage.

Quietly, I emptied the largest box I could find, took it outside.

I dug up the seven coffee cans and let the frogs come out and hop around for a while, until I could not keep my eyes open any longer.

I placed them all inside the box, curled up beside it.

I fell asleep, the clear sky flickering above me, the damp grass soaking through my t-shirt.

I thought of death no more that night.

"Can you believe it?" Charlie crowed after we'd opened all seven cans and released our trainees. "All alive!"

He practically shouted that last word as we watched them hop all over the thin slice of yard between the two houses.

I didn't tell him, never told him how I'd awoken at dawn, soaked with the cool dew that slicked the grass. How I'd decanted all of the frogs back into their isolation chambers. Took the huge box to the garage. How I'd silently washed my hands and feet, toweled off in the bathroom, slipped back into my own bed without waking my mother.

He snapped the composition book open and happily scrawled something in the first box for each subject.

One word. *Alive.*

I saw that word, and knew it had a bigger meaning for Charlie. Charlie had his own construct of beliefs he was building. The survival of these frogs meant more to him than what it meant to me. I knew that even then.

We let the frogs stay outside for a while, filling a depression in the yard with water from the hose and letting them soak in it. We ate our lunch there, keeping them corralled, eating with fingers that smelled of fishy mud.

"One more night," he said as he crumbled his garbage into a ball, stuffed it into the empty brown paper sack.

"What?" I asked, less because I didn't understand him than I'd hoped that I hadn't heard him correctly.

"One more night," he repeated. "They've got to show me they can do it. I've got to believe they can live for one more night."

I knew I was in for another mostly sleepless night in the side yard.

Over the next two weeks, everything accelerated, moved toward an end that seemed increasingly to have been there from the very beginning, burning at its secret heart.

The frogs survived their second night, spent mostly out of their coffee cans with me sleeping beside them on the side yard. The next morning, Charlie seemed satisfied with that part of the testing, uplifted almost, and began excitedly checking both the "Isolation" and "Stress" boxes beside each frog's name.

"Why are you checking both boxes?" I asked, not wanting to disturb the mood.

"What's more stressful than spending two days in a coffee can jammed in with other frogs?" he said.

## WHAT BECOMES GOD

I couldn't disagree, so I left it at that.

"Now, next on the list is Acceleration," he said, tapping the tip of the pencil against the page. "How do we manage that?"

"We've got to get them moving fast," I offered, peering over his shoulder.

"Yes, that's exactly what 'acceleration' means, Einstein."

I shrugged and waited for him to find the answer.

"Your mom…"

"What about her?"

"You mom…her truck…we need to go for a ride," he said excitedly, racing around to the front of the house.

His idea, revealed in breathless spurts of information, was ridiculous but workable.

It involved half a dozen large, plastic Formula One cars we'd bought from the dime store years ago. Each was about a foot long, with fat plastic tires and a molded plastic driver glued to the seat.

We removed each plastic driver, replacing it with two frogs to a car, jammed into the seat in a sitting position and bread-tied into place. Armstrong was exempted, on account of his not being able to fit into a car even by himself. Spock was exempted, too, for no good reason.

A length of rope was knotted to each car, looped around the front end.

Next, we had to ask my mother to go for a ride in her truck. When she was in a good mood, which was getting more and more rare those days, she'd take us out in the truck, just a little Chevy, letting us climb into the open bed once we were out of eyeshot of Charlie's house. If Charlie's mom had ever seen him standing in the bed of that truck, speeding through the subdivision, getting onto the highway, standing there with his hair blowing in the wind, his eyes as big as dinner plates, his thin hands clutching the roof of the cab, she might very well have preceded her son in, well, you know.

We secreted the frog-filled racecars in the bed of the truck, went into my house and cajoled my mother into taking us for a drive. After several minutes of begging, she finally gave Charlie a long, hard look, grabbed her keys without a word and stood.

"I suppose you could come with me to the liquor store," she said, crushed her cigarette out in an already full ashtray and motioned us out to the driveway.

We lost six of them that afternoon. Two shot out of their cars when he heaved them off the back of the truck and onto the road, their ropes uncoiling like umbilici. One other popped out when his car struck the pavement, ejecting him like a villain in a James Bond movie.

Those three were lucky, well, not as lucky as the out-and-out survivors, but luckier than the other three we lost. They ejected and hit the pavement rolling and seemed, at least from our vantage speeding away, to be okay. If, that is, they weren't hit by cars once we lost sight of them.

The remaining three suffered fates that were, well, *horrible*. We didn't torture them or butcher them or anything. I mean, we weren't serial killers in training, but we were boys, with all that *Lord of the Flies* shit and everything.

We comforted ourselves with the thought that those who'd died had sacrificed themselves so that the others might live.

That's what Charlie said, anyway.

*Sacrifice.*

As if that ever helps.

Well, suffice it to say, then, that the other three were lost in more horrifying ways. Two involving the bottom of their car literally scraping away when it lost three of its wheels. Concrete is not kind to soft plastic, or to even softer frog flesh. The sixth fatality involved the breaking of the rope and the small plastic car and its single amphibian driver disappearing under the wheels of a larger truck, a semi, bearing down on us and honking and honking for a reason my mother never knew.

Three tests down, and our crew of astronauts was reduced to just eight. After the High-G test, which involved tying them by their legs and swinging them around at rapid velocity, there were only five left. Unfortunately, three subjects—Armstrong among them—upchucked all of their guts during the test, literally. And then there were five:

Subject 5: Conrad
Subject 8: Scott
Subject 9: Irwin
Subject 10: Duke
Subject 11: Young

And just one test left. Altitude.

Unfortunately, I failed to notice that Charlie's health continued to worsen during the three days it took us to get through these tests. I'd been fooled by the energy, the passion that was burning through him, choosing to see it as such when it was really only one thing. His disease.

Passion is a fuel that doesn't consume what it burns. Disease, though, burns the whole fucking house down, torching anything within, taking everything with it.

He had grown noticeably thinner over those three days, when I hadn't thought that was possible. His skin had taken on a thin, insubstantial quality, like vapor. It was the color of smoke, too, grey and ashy. His eyes were receding into his face, and veins began to show in his arms, his legs; pale blue lines like the routes on a map leading someplace you didn't want to go.

But his energy remained high, and his mother continued to let him come out with me when I showed up on their front porch each morning. She held the door open for him as he sidled past her, carefully negotiating the single step that led from inside the house to the concrete pad of the porch. On more than one occasion, I caught her eyes as he eased himself out of the house. She wasn't watching him. She was watching me, and her eyes held a complex mixture of deep, deep sadness, gratitude and bitterness, anger, I think, at my having this time with him, time she would never have. And all if it counted against her own.

But she let him go, until that day.

I showed up that morning as usual, a box of Ziploc bags tucked under one arm, a kite under the other.

She came to the door, looked momentarily confused at the items I carried with me, then cracked the door an inch or two. She didn't move her face or body into that crack to talk to me. It was done merely to let out her voice, which she kept low and whispery.

"Not today, Brian," she said, wincing at my name. Maybe it was because she was afraid that he might hear her talking with me. Maybe she loathed saying it because it was the name of a boy who would live. Her son, his name, would die. Mine would go on, and she was on the verge of never being able to forgive me for that.

"Not today," she said, shaking her head as if she were sorrier than I was. "He's...tired...very tired. We're getting ready to take him to the hospital."

"Okay," I said, not really knowing exactly how to respond. "Is he...I mean...okay? Will he be around later?"

Her eyes narrowed to slits and her mouth chewed words it seemed unable to spit out. Bitter words. She shook her head, let the door close its few, begrudged inches slowly.

I stood there for a minute or two, not sure where to go, what to do.

I went home, stomped to my room, slammed the door.

Hours later, my mom opened the door, stood in the doorway.
"No dinner tonight, kiddo?"

"No thanks."

She waited a moment. I think she belched. I could smell beer on the air.

"Charlie?"

I nodded in the darkness, said nothing.

There was silence between us, and I knew that her drunken mind was reeling from thought to thought, trying to figure out what to say to fill it.

I finally did. "I mean, nothing's working. The doctors, the medicines, all the stuff his mom won't let him do. It's not helping. He's still...still...gonna..."

"Have you prayed for him, kiddo?"

"Yeah, sure, but..."

"Sometimes prayers work better when you sacrifice something."

I blinked, frowned.

"Sacrifice something?"

"Yeah," she snorted. "I don't mean a goat or lamb or anything like that. I mean give up something, something you love."

I thought about that for a while.

"I gotta make a *trade* with God?"

"Look it up, it's in the Bible," she slurred. "Okay, well, get some sleep. If you get hungry in the night, there's peanut butter if you want a sandwich. G'night, kiddo."

"Night, mom."

She closed the door.

*A sacrifice.*

*Something I love.*

I fell asleep with coldness riming my heart.

The next morning I rose early, shrugged into clean clothing, grabbed five Ziploc bags from the kitchen pantry. I tiptoed through the living room, my mom slumped on the couch, snoring heavily.

Outside, I went to the coffee can, retrieved the frogs, sealed each in a clear plastic bag. Leaving these on the side yard, I went into the garage and found my kite, a big, black, bat-shaped thing, complete with a reel loaded with 500 feet of string.

Working quickly, I wrestled the kite from the garage, grabbed yet another spool of kite string. I collected the wriggling bags of frogs, then walked a block or two down to the entrance to the woods.

I placed the kite and reel onto the dewy grass, sat with the baggies filled with frogs between my legs. I used the spare spool of string to tie the bags together, then tied this bundle to the underside of the kite using a special knot my dad had taught me before he left.

Ironically, it was a knot that untied itself when pulled on.

I rose, lifted the kite. It was heavy, but I thought it was still able to get off the ground. So I set it down, nose in the air, unspooled about fifteen feet of string, and walked away. When I'd pulled the string taut, I took a deep breath, raced away from the kite, sending it jerkily into the air.

It waivered, did a few dipping loops, then grabbed the wind. It lofted itself into the sky on a shallow angle, burdened by its increasingly agitated payload.

I stood below it, grimly playing out the line.

*Altitude.* That was the last test.

No.

*Sacrifice.* That was the last test.

That another might live.

After about a hundred feet of line played out, the kite soared, as if the weight of the frogs beneath it, squirming and jostling in the confines of their plastic bags, meant nothing.

Two hundred feet.

I held the other string in the hand that wasn't keeping the kite tethered to the Earth.

I wanted to think that they were just frogs.

That it was all for my friend, Charlie.

That I wasn't mean or horrible or cold-hearted.

I convinced myself that all of these things were true.

I pulled the string.

Somewhere, more than 200 feet over the canopy of the woods, the plain little knot my father had taught me how to tie unraveled, pulled through itself.

Free now from this string, the five little plastic parcels it had held tightly as babies to the breast of their mother came away from the kite, tumbled through the air, fell, fell, and then were lost in the dark treetops.

And I felt nothing as I let the other string play out completely, detach from the reel, pull from my hand.

I felt nothing as I watched the kite ascend into the clouds, growing smaller and smaller until it was just a black pinprick against the silent blue of the sky, gone, disappearing utterly.

I went home with just the spare reel, which I carried to my bedroom, past my still snoring mother.

I climbed into bed, fell asleep clasping the reel in both hands across my chest like a corpse clutching a lily.

The next morning Charlie was gone.

To the hospital, my mother told me at breakfast. She'd spoken to his mother over the phone before I got up. She related this to me slowly, quietly, all the more so because she was hung over.

*Charlie was...well, it was bad.*

*He might not make it through this, might...well, you know...*

I sat at the kitchen table, bleary-eyed, having trouble processing this.

A cereal bowl was set before me, an unopened box of Cap'n Crunch standing over it. My favorite, but too expensive my mom always told me. Who knew how long she'd had that box, hidden away, ready to set before me for just this occasion.

I focused on the wrong things as she spoke.

The plastic milk jug sweating.

The spoon that rested in the bowl, nicked and marred by what looked to be several trips around the garbage disposal.

A stray length of my mother's hair that curled around her ear, grey and colorless in the morning light.

*Die? Was that it, mom? Charlie might die? How was that possible? I prayed for him. I sacrificed for him. Wasn't it good enough? Wasn't I good enough?*

But I didn't say any of that.

## WHAT BECOMES GOD

What I did say was, "Just what the hell does he want?"

It's a testament to how poorly my mother felt that she didn't launch a hand across the table to smack my face.

"What does *who* want?"

"God. What does he want from me anyway?"

My mother thought about this for a moment.

"My ma always used to tell us that God only wants two things from us: faith and sacrifice. But grandma's a whack-job."

She ducked her head, sipped at her coffee slowly.

I wanted to rail at her, to shake her, to sweep all the stuff from the kitchen table and roar at her, and *through* her, at God.

*I gave all that to you, and still you do this?*

*What else do you want?*

And it came to me, a thought so pure, so dazzling in its stark obviousness that it vibrated through my body like an electric shock.

The frogs. They'd been Charlie's thing, his belief.

*I'd sacrificed the wrong thing.*

Numb, I rose slowly, shaking, left the kitchen, left the house.

And just walked.

I don't know that there was a coherent thought in my head, just rage, resentment at what I was being forced to do.

Pure anger that vibrated down to my bones, set my teeth on edge, made my scalp crawl.

I slowed when I realized that I'd reached the top of the bowl in the woods, where the fallen tree stretched across the ravine, touched a hill on the other side.

I didn't consciously walk there, though I knew exactly why I was there.

I wanted to be quiet, so quiet.

The sun was out in the empty, blue sea of the sky, shimmering in the heat.

And he was there, my skink, there as always sunning atop the log, his eyes closed in sleep or whatever pleasure a lizard experiences.

But he wasn't *my* skink, not really, not ever.

I stood there, reached out and touched the rotten wood of the tree trunk to steady myself.

I thought of Charlie.

I realized, standing under that broiling sun, that Charlie wasn't mine either.

I'd been hanging onto Charlie as if I could have prevented his death, as if I had the right to. It was as selfish a thought as catching this skink and imprisoning him in a glass aquarium in my room.

Trapping him for my pleasure, regardless of what it meant for him, how it felt for him.

In my own way, I wanted to do the same thing to Charlie. I wanted to keep him, protect him, sure, but keep him mostly. So we could hike into the woods and catch frogs and eat sandwiches and drink Kool-Aid that tasted of metal canteens. So we could argue and read comic books and call each other names and do stupid things like test frogs for an astronaut program.

*Forever.*

Standing there, I knew it could never last forever anyway, even if Charlie weren't dying—didn't die.

That thought went deep enough to hurt, and I found myself crying, tears dripping from my cheeks, wetting my already sweat-soaked t-shirt. The pang of that thought—it was the first time I'd ever experienced it.

It was the pang of something slipping away, something you

thought never would, never could. And you were powerless to prevent it. It was the sliding away of love, something, someone so deeply loved that their absence seemed impossible, irrecoverable.

It was so raw and new that it tore my heart out.

The tears cooled my cheeks but did nothing to prevent this emotion from growing, and then turning, as emotions so often do, into anger.

I couldn't cope with that feeling of loss. It was like staring into an abyss, teetering on the edge of something so dark, so profoundly empty that invisible tendrils coming up from within its bottomless depths threatened to pull you in.

To prevent that, my mind simply flipped the feeling over into anger, rage. So much easier for a child to process.

Shaking, and now—not from the tears—I narrowed my eyes at the skink.

Why should it have the perfect life it had?

Why not Charlie?

Surely, Charlie was more deserving of it than a lizard?

What if I could give that to him?

*Belief.*

What if I could give him this perfect life, trade it for his own sickly, terminal one?

*Sacrifice.*

I gritted my teeth, felt every muscle in my body tighten.

The skin of my forehead crawled across my skull, and I stepped forward slowly, quietly.

The skink continued to sun itself on the log, oblivious.

My hand fumbled absently across the ground until it closed on a branch, short and thick as a club.

I lifted it quietly above my head, stepped forward again.

The skink glittered in the sun, its coppery scales so achingly beautiful that my breath caught in my constricted throat.

*But no.*

Tears streaming down my face, I brought the stick down, whickering through the hot summer air. I saw the arc of it descend toward the skink.

Right before it impacted, I think I saw its eyes open, sensing something amiss but not quite realizing what it was.

The branch struck its hindquarters, flattened them against the log.

A great gout of blood vomited from its mouth, followed by the pink wedge of its tongue. Its black eyes seemed to roll in their orbits, and it turned sharply to see what it was that had struck it.

I swear, swear that there was some recognition in those dark, glistening eyes, some disappointment.

*Sadness.*

That was like a match touched to the tinder of my heart.

Roaring, weeping for what I'd done, what I was about to do, I jerked the branch up again, brought it down with all my might.

Shining copper was blotted out by a shocking burst of red that spattered the log, rained down onto the leaves and grass. Beneath the *whack!* of the branch against the fallen trunk, there was the crackling of tiny bones, the awful flat sound of something like meat slapping against a hard surface.

My pulse raced and my vision waivered. Heat seemed not just to pound down on me, but also to radiate from me in great, pulsing waves. Sweat literally poured from my skin, and the tears…the tears fell unabated.

I wasn't just weeping anymore, I was bawling, crying like a newborn wanting something, needing it but unable to express or even know what it was. Streamers of snot ran from my nostrils.

My great, braying cries echoed from the hills.

My rubbery legs gave way, and I fell onto the log, half kneeling, half slumped over it.

The branch fell from my shaking hands, tumbled into the brush on the other side of the log.

I kept my eyes closed for many, many minutes, not wanting to see it…what I'd done.

When I finally did open them, hot and sticky and filled with tears, I saw.

The skink, *my skink*, was a smear now, a bloody, misshapen mess. Its guts had erupted from the ruin of its head, coils of purple and pink, smeared with red. Its beautiful coppery scales were slicked with blood, the way water beaded on my father's freshly waxed car. Its spine was crushed, legs smashed, skin pounded into the decaying bark of the tree.

I had taken its beauty as surely as I'd taken its life.

At least its head was smashed, too. I don't think I could have confronted those eyes again.

I looked at it for a long, long time.

When I finally pulled myself up, when I made my way home, I was crying.

When I fell into my bed, I was still crying.

For me? For the skink? For Charlie?

I had no idea.

I slept a kind of sleep, filled with nightmares that seared through me unremembered but leaving a horrible, harrowing smear across my mind.

Feeling woozy and disconnected, I sat up in my bed. The house was quiet, and the sunlight filtering through the curtains in my room was the golden, diffuse light of early morning or later afternoon.

I'd either slept all day or all day and all night.

I got out of bed, went into the kitchen. It was definitely the morning of the day after.

My stomach growled and twisted almost to the point of nausea. The box of Cap'n Crunch still sat unopened on the table, my bowl and spoon where my mom had set them yesterday morning.

Quietly, I got the milk out of the refrigerator, opened the box of cereal and had two giant bowls. It fell into the pit of my stomach, somehow without seeming to fill it; as open and empty as the rest of me felt.

Putting the milk back into the fridge, the dishes into the sink, I went into the living room, peered out the window.

Charlie's parents' car was in their driveway.

That meant, well, it meant either, or—

I shot out the front door, let it slam behind me. I didn't worry about what time it was or waking my mother.

Filled with a twisting sense of dread and anticipation, I raced across the street, bounded onto the front porch of Charlie's house, lifted my hand to knock on the front door.

*Which was open.*

Not all the way, mind you, just a crack.

It seemed all the worse that it was open just a bit.

I pushed at it timidly, waited for it to swing open all the way.

"Charlie?" I called into the empty doorway. "Anyone?"

I stood there in the open doorway for a moment. The air that floated out of the house seemed wrong, violated. And there was a smell, something I couldn't place…and another just underneath it that played at the edges of my senses.

Knowing it was a mistake, sensing that it was something that I would regret, I stepped inside. Instantly, the house's atmosphere washed over me, vibrating with echoes of violence, promises of more to come.

"Charlie?" I whispered again, stepping through the foyer and stopping.

Right there, all alone on the white wall of the hallway leading to the family room, was a smeary red handprint. It looked too red against the unforgiving white of the wall, still tacky.

I moved to the other side of the hall to avoid coming close to it. Watching it as if it might leap at me, I stepped into the family room. The living room, dining room and kitchen made one great, open space at the back of the house. Everywhere I looked, it was a shambles.

The dining room chairs and table were upturned, scattered, broken. The light fixture hanging over the table was shattered. There were huge scars on the vinyl floor of the kitchen, slashes across the wood of the cabinets. The door to the refrigerator was open, and a spill of food and liquid disgorged from inside.

On the other side of the room, though, it was worse. The furniture had been thrown over. Lamps lay on the torn carpet, which was absolutely shredded in some areas. The television was smashed, leaned against the fireplace. Pictures on the wall were askew, their glass shattered. Books were tossed from their shelves, lay everywhere like stricken birds.

But that wasn't what kept me from taking another step into the room.

*It was the blood.*

It was sloshed over the carpet, splattered against the walls. It dripped from a lampshade, stained the curtains, dotted the faces in the crooked family portraits like some strange, contagious pox. Extravagant red sprays even stained the ceiling.

It trickled down the windows, soaked into the drywall, dripped down the masonry of the fireplace.

And everywhere, everything bore slashes, broad swipes that cut through the wallpaper, leaving it in tatters. The curtains were shredded, the carpet looked like someone had ice-skated over it, cleaving it, raising huge slashes across its tasteful, tan surface.

My lip was quivering now, my body shaking. I could feel a cold wave that rolled down my spine, spun like a frozen cyclone in my stomach. Suddenly, the weight of all the milk I'd consumed with the Cap'n Crunch pressed unmercifully on my bladder.

I took a nervous faltering step farther into the carnage, then another.

Pushing aside a broken kitchen chair, I stepped from the slick vinyl kitchen floor onto the carpet of the family room. I moved through the riot of furniture, stepping carefully to avoid as much red as possible.

That's when I saw them.

Charlie's parents.

At least that's who I thought they must be.

Their peaceful appearance amidst the carnage—laid stretched out side-by-side, holding bloodied hands—belied the intensity of the violence done to them.

I could make out which was Charlie's mom only by a lock or two of her hair that wasn't matted with blood and gore. Otherwise, there wasn't enough left of her or her clothes to be sure. Her face wasn't just covered in blood, it was gone, removed.

Across the very top of her scalp, I could see deep rents, three parallel lines that cut down to her skull, and had peeled back to expose the shocking white of bone beneath.

Her eyes were gone…just…*gone*. Her throat had also been slit, and the wound was ragged and gaping.

I looked over to what I assumed was Charlie's father. He was never around much, which made it hard for me to recognize him. He was mutilated, too, but his wounds didn't look as *angry*.

After a minute, I realized two things.

First, I had wet myself. I felt a large, growing area of warmth that spilled across my crotch, down the legs of my jeans.

Second, they had not died there like that.

Someone had laid them out there, together.

*Someone.*

Perhaps still in the house.

My heart lurched, and a low, quivering moan escaped my lips.

I stepped backward, keeping my eyes on the pair of dead bodies.

"Brian," came a voice from behind me.

It was Charlie's voice, that I knew.

I also knew, before I turned, that he wasn't Charlie, not anymore. Something in the voice. There was a flat, thin tone, a coldness.

And—the thing that really frightened me—a *hissing* quality to it.

I turned slowly to face him.

If there had been anything left in my bladder, I'm sure it would have gushed out at that moment.

"What happened to me?" he asked, pleaded.

He was Charlie.

And he was a monster.

Somehow, I could tell it was Charlie, though what stood before me was more lizard now than boy. He was still about Charlie's size, standing upright, his clothing hanging in shreds and tatters. His clothes, like the room around us, were stained with blood.

But his skin was no longer pale, pallid. It was now brown and tan and a coppery orange that deepened into a dark red around his head and face. His skin was rough, scaly, covered with bumps and furrows.

His bare chest was thicker, more muscled, longer even. His legs had shortened and thickened, too, and his arms were powerful looking. The hands that he held out to me were spatulate, ended in fingers that were long, tapered and wickedly clawed.

A tail, plump and sinuous, fell from his backside, curled at his feet.

Only his eyes looked the same, those same grey, determined eyes now peering from a face that was pushed out into a kind of blunt snout.

"Charlie?"

"Brian...what...what happened to me?"

I could see his tongue when he talked, peeking through the flat slit of his wide mouth. It was a moist, pink wedge.

*Oh my God, what have I done?*

"Charlie...your parents..."

He flicked his head first left, then right, his eyes darting quickly around the room.

"Had to...had to kill them. They screamed...oh, God, Brian, they screamed so much. I couldn't take it...couldn't. But now they don't have to know, don't have to see me."

My heart, already chilled at this point, froze over like a pond in winter.

"Charlie...you killed them? Your parents? You..."

His eyes flicked back to me at an astonishing speed, his head cocking like a confused dog. "Had to, didn't I just say that? Had to."

He regarded me coolly, looked me up and down, stopping at the stain on my jeans.

"Milk, milk, lemonade," he said, and he uttered a series of short, raspy barks that I realized was laughter. "You smell like piss, man."

He leaned forward, and it took every ounce of effort on my part not to flinch.

"And *fear*."

His flattened nostrils, shaded a deep, deep indigo, flared, and he snorted.

"I'm sorry," I said. "Charlie, I'm sorry, so sorry."

His eyes, which were even then starting to darken, as if black ink were rolling into them, stopped their crazy flitting and focused on mine.

"For what, Brian?"

It was in the tone of his voice.

*He knew.*

I swallowed, trying to get my mouth wet enough to make words.

"It was me...I did this to you. I just wanted to give you the perfect life."

He chittered his strange laugh at me, leaned in again.

I smelled it on him, that smell I sensed upon entering the house.

It was a musk, something oily and densely reptilian. Unpleasant.

"I know," he hissed, and now it was a hiss. His pink tongue darted out, seemed to be smelling me as I was smelling him. "Killed it. Gave its life to me."

"I'm sorry, Charlie," I moaned. "I just wanted to help you. I didn't want you to..."

"Die?"

I nodded.

"I guess I should thank you then," he said, slurring the words, mostly whispering them now.

His eyes had gone fully dark.

"It's not perfect, Brian," he murmured. "But it's gotta be better than dead."

He turned quickly, took a step toward the staircase in the foyer.

Before I could react, he spun around, crouched low, came at me. "Remember me, Brian."

With that, he slashed at me, then dropped to all fours and scurried out of the room and up the staircase.

I stood there for a moment, then felt a line of fire across my chest. Looking down, I saw that my shirt was torn open in three lines. Blood pulsed from the wounds, soaked the shirt.

I took two or three lurching steps into the hallway, feeling the house close in around me. My chest burned, my head swirled and I felt nauseated enough to vomit.

Slumping against the bloody handprint I had tried so hard to avoid earlier, I saw Charlie's bright, coppery form slither down the stairs, stand silhouetted in the open doorway.

He clutched a big canvas pack in his clawed hands. The pack was heavy, stuffed with whatever he'd gone upstairs to retrieve.

"Almost. Perfect. Now," he said with great difficulty.

And with that, he crouched down, darted through the front door.

I tried to get up then, to follow him at least to the door, to see which direction he went.

But I knew. I knew.

My eyes fell to the foyer floor, where several items had spilled from the pack as he left.

*Comic books.*

One was an issue of *The Amazing Spider-Man.*

On its cover, the webslinger fought with the white-lab-coat-wearing Lizard.

I fainted with a trembling smile on my face.

# WHAT BECOMES GOD

And that's where my mother found me.

Amazingly, she was sober.

More amazingly, she was sober for the rest of her life.

There were police, lots of police, lots of questions, but I couldn't answer many of them. I'd come over to see Charlie, found the door open, saw the carnage, was attacked.

No, I didn't know who it was.

No, I didn't know why I'd been attacked, left.

No, I had no idea what happened to Charlie.

But I knew. I knew.

Things got fuzzier, though, the farther away I got. Within a few hours, I was doubting what I'd seen, what I'd done.

Maybe the police were right. Maybe there had been a psychopath that had broken into the house, killed Charlie's parents, kidnapped him. Maybe I had stumbled onto the scene as the killer was leaving, and he'd attacked me, too.

There was a funeral several days later. My mom and even my dad attended with me. They held hands and paid a great deal of attention to me. But it was temporary. My dad drifted away again afterward. But my mom never went back to drinking.

I think about that ceremony now, and, like I said, it's *fuzzy*.

Were there two caskets at the front of the church?

Or were there three?

My mind, I think to protect itself from the impossibility of what had really happened, tells me there were three…had to be three.

But I think there were two.

Only two.

I look down often at the claw marks raked across my chest, my heart...at the scars they've become. I touch them lightly, the raised, gnarled skin there, and I remember.

As if I could forget.

# EPILOGUE

For years, there were psychiatrists, medications, nightmares.

Eventually, I rose above them all.

*Hah, sure!*

Now I'm a day trader in New York City, and I believe in nothing.

Well, that's not precisely true. I believe in two things. Money and numbers.

Money's all that matters.

And numbers don't demand sacrifices in order to work.

About five years ago—twelve years after all this happened—I went back to my hometown, back to the subdivision. I hadn't been there since I'd left for college. My mother had moved away long ago.

I parked my car in front of my old house—how small it looked now, peaceful. A new family lived in Charlie's old house. Children played on the lawn, their mother waved to me absently from a chair on the front porch.

I wondered if she knew. But she had to, it was in all the newspapers, the television reports.

I was appalled that a few coats of paint and some new carpeting could erase what had happened there.

I waved back, hefted the heavy bag I carried, and walked away down the street.

The path was as familiar to me as if I were still eleven years old. Back to the woods.

I stood in the clearing at its entrance, still so much like theater curtains. I lingered there for uncounted minutes, nervous as an actor with stage fright. Eventually, sighing heavily, I pushed through these curtains, took the stage.

It was a cool, late spring day. There was a threat of rain, and clouds bunched together, pushed atop each other in the sky. The air smelled of ozone and dark, green leafy things.

I walked the path, still worn, down to the little hill where the fallen tree had been, relieved that it was still there.

Where else would I look?

I clambered down the hill, caught myself on the tree trunk, still somehow solid after all these years. To either side, the undergrowth was thick, lush. A few trillium here and there, their white flowers like polka dots against the verdant green.

They made me think of that day so long ago now, in these woods with Charlie.

I wasn't sure he'd actually still be here, but where else would he go?

"Charlie," I said, my voice cracking. "It's me, Brian. Sorry it's taken so long. But I brought you something."

I lifted the heavy bag, set it down onto the log.

I waited a few minutes, my ears straining to hear something, anything.

But there was just the chirping of the birds, a distant lawnmower, the gentle whisper of the wind.

I brushed a few tears from my eyes, absently touched the scar on my chest through my shirt.

Turning away, I set off up the hill.

When I heard it.

A slither of plastic. A patter of things falling, hitting the ground.

I spun, took a step back toward the log.

The bag I'd brought, filled with an entire year's worth of Marvel comics—and a few DCs thrown in just to piss him off—had drooped over the far edge of the trunk, spilling some of the comics into the deep weeds.

I peered into that darkness, past the spray of fallen comics.

I thought I saw two eyes there, glittering from the darkness.

The curl of a boy-sized body, glittering like pennies in the afternoon sun, the sinuous sweep of a tail curled silently in the brush.

I thought I saw something in those eyes.

*Recognition*, perhaps.

Thanks. Perhaps.

I left the bag of comics, backed away up the hill, returned to my car.

I've been back every year since with another bag.

My dreams these days are mostly of numbers, spreadsheets, margins, calls. Dollar signs.

*Mostly.*

But every so often, perhaps three or four times a year, I dream of him, of Charlie. He is no longer the boy I knew, and that's okay. Even in my memories, my dreams, I have no right to hold him there, like he was.

I dream of Charlie as he is now, curled beneath a fallen tree in the woods of our youth. He is beautiful, vibrant with color and life.

In these dreams, he sometimes suns himself on the top of the log, sparkling reds and oranges and shiny coppers. His eyes are closed, drowsy.

I see him curled beneath the log, atop a pile of soggy, faded comic books, *Spider-Man, Iron Man, Captain America, The Fantastic Four.* Maybe even a *Superman* or two.

It is the perfect life.

And these are the good dreams.

# OBJECT PERMANENCE

# PART I

He was there again today, standing in the corner, arms limp. He wore nothing, but didn't conceal his nudity. I got so little company those days that his presence could actually be comforting if it weren't for the total lack of features on his face.

I don't just mean that his features were indistinct or forgettable. I mean he had none. No eyes, ears, nose, mouth. His head was a smooth, shining white ball atop a lanky body. He gave me the impression of a living bedpost.

In fact, the only recognizable thing on his entire body was his erect penis, jutting into space.

Like its owner, it had very little detail. No veins, no pores, no dark band to mark where he'd been circumcised. Only the small hole at its tip was visible. I half suspected that, were I to stand and examine the top of his head, I'd find a similar dark hole.

But, of course, I couldn't. Violent ones like me were strapped into a jacket and leashed to the padded wall. No sudden movements to alarm the staff. I mean, Christ! I'd already killed three or four people.

I forgot.

God help me. That's the problem.

I had a mantra of names that I recited hour after hour, day after blurry, drug-fogged, endless, run-together day. Everyone I knew or had known, being very careful to leave out the ones I knew were dead.

I shuddered to think what might happen if I were to remember them.

The ones I forgot were the problem. I tried so hard to remember, but sometimes the drugs and the electroshock therapy—Yes, Virginia, there is a Sears DieHard!—made me forget.

And that scared me.

What happens if I forgot myself?

It's like the light bulb in the icebox. Is it really off when you close the door? Or is it on all the time?

An interesting question.

And I couldn't tell if I was the icebox or just another light bulb.

"And how are you today, Mr. Stadler?" Dr. Benton asked keeping his distance.

"Fine," I answered in a noncommittal tone. He'd already forgotten about me and moved straight to the words and numbers on the chart he held tightly.

"Any side effects from the electro-convulsive therapy?" he asked, almost not expecting or wanting an answer.

"No more than usual," I answered, moving slightly, enough to cause the metal clasp on the leash to jingle against the jacket straps.

He looked up, trying not to appear to have done so too quickly.

"You don't like talking to me, do you?"

"Don't like you, Mr. Stadler?" he asked. "Why would you say that?"

"No, you don't know me enough to dislike me. You just don't like to talk with me."

He considered this, plainly uncomfortable. "Well, it could be the fact that you've assaulted six staff members in two years. Maybe I don't want to be the seventh." He smiled, tight and grim. "If you have any trouble, I'll be back again in three hours. We can discuss it then. And we can move you into your own room tomorrow…if you'll cooperate."

He turned and rapped sharply on the little Plexiglas window high up in the padded door.

"Wait!" I pleaded as the door drew open and light from the corridor—outdoor light, sunlight—crept into my room.

"I didn't mean to. I try so hard…to remember. But, they're falling away like leaves. I'm afraid of the shock treatments. Afraid they'll make…afraid I'll forget *me*."

This held him in the doorway for a second. But he turned and left, the door closing behind him, and I heard the sound of the bolt slide into place.

I began the mantra immediately.

After the first run through, I thought for a moment, then added my own name.

"Where do you go when you're not with me?" I raised my head as much as possible from the thinly padded table. "I mean where do you go? What do you do?"

"I go home. I see other patients. What kind of question is that, anyway?" He laughed, flicking the tip of a needle that seemed to appear from nowhere.

Alarms went off in my head, but the two burliest interns the institution could dig up were nearby in the small room. Not much more that a strapped-down person could do other than comply.

"You need to lie still for a moment," Dr. Benton said, swabbing my forearm.

"So, where do you go?" I repeated. I saw one of the interns roll his eyes. They wanted the main event, enough of this talky stuff already.

"I told you," he paused, the tip of the needle poised to pierce the skin. "I have no idea what you're asking. Or why, for that matter."

"It's an icebox question," I laughed, lowering myself back onto the bed.

"A what?"

I felt the needle slip into my arm as easily as if it had found a hole made for it. There was that disturbing feeling of something foreign jetting into my body as he plunged down on the syringe, and the drug rolled into me like fog. Almost immediately, I felt warm and heavy, a dribble of sticky pancake syrup.

"You know, like does the light in the icebox really go out when you close the door? Didn't you ever think about that when you were a kid?"

"Well, yes," he hesitated, wondering about the connection.

"What do you do when I'm not there to see you do it? Do you even exist when I don't think of you?"

"Just relax, Mr. Stadler," he motioned, and the interns came toward me, towering walls of crisp white.

On went the electrodes with their jelly, the mouth protector, the close-fitting cap, the chinstrap.

"Doctor," I mumbled. "Will I remember you?"

"Yes, Mr. Stadler. You will. You've been through this procedure before."

As I slipped into unconsciousness, I thought I smelled ozone, sharp and acrid.

Then, blessed light.

Oh God, not her.

She stayed the longest of all.

And I could barely stand to look at her.

She's built like a cheerleader, with curves that caused neck injuries just looking at them. Nice ass, perky, high-school tits.

Then there was her skin.

The entire surface of her body was a scab, a thick, crusty wound, constantly healing, but never quite.

Unlike the nude man, she moved about, though never getting close to me. And she didn't speak. But when she moved, the sound! The sound set my teeth on edge, because it was rough and grinding and sandpapery.

Fissures and faults cracked opened on her body when she moved, exposing something underneath as deep and glistening as her skin was thick and dry. The angry red of that raw flesh gave way almost immediately to cloudy yellow tears that trickled down her body.

She was a monstrosity.

She didn't seem to notice me as she paced across the confines of my cell, her feet rasping the floor.

I'd tried talking to her, but the most I got was a slight glance, an inclination of the head, a flick of the eyes.

I had no idea how long I'd been there or—

Oh, yes. The shock treatment. I'd—

*Forgotten.*

Shaken, I launched into my mantra of names, reciting aloud,

enunciating each slowly so that both mind and tongue wouldn't forget how to pronounce them.

The scab woman stopped her pacing, turned to face me, startling me so that I broke off mid-name.

Her face moved, her cheeks stretching and bulging, her mouth contorting as if in pain.

Her eyes blazed at me.

There was a tearing sound, horribly loud and strangely intimate.

A rush of fluid spilled from her lips, streamed down her chin and neck.

Her lips stretched across her face slowly, with a sound like someone pulling a hunk of bread from a crusty french loaf. Teeth, shiny and moist and gummy pink, flashed between them.

*A smile.*

Suddenly, my head spun. The electric smell of the treatment room buzzed inside my nostrils, and my stomach tightened.

I think I screamed before I threw up, before I fainted.

She stood over me and smiled that wound of a smile down at me, fierce and triumphant.

I awoke in the infirmary—sort of a strange place to have inside a facility that's basically a big infirmary itself—and the nurses were not happy. A violent one in here usually spelled trouble. I had injured two staff members on one of my first visits years ago.

This time I was the one who'd been hurt. Didn't remember how. I must have fainted, gouged my head on one of the jacket's buckles. Pretty nasty, especially considering that I hadn't been found until the next morning. And head wounds bleed a lot.

At least I thought it was my blood. I hadn't been able to get a good look at the cut. They had me strapped down pretty tight

No one to talk to here, even though it was the first time I'd seen real people in days. They were real, I guess, even though they all looked so nondescript, so plain, so—

*Forgettable.*

Dinner was fed to me—couldn't be trusted with my hands free for a moment, much less possess a spoon—by a bored bull of an orderly. Large kid, maybe twenty-three or twenty-four. Looked like a college ball player who had learned the hard way that those professors really *were* just passing him so that he could catch the winning pass in the Rose Bowl.

Quick, efficient and neat, he slid the soft, grey starchy food into me in just ten minutes.

After, it was lights out. I saw the shadow of the guard outside the infirmary as the orderly left. Then, the loud click of the lock engaged.

I wasn't sleepy, but I no longer fought the drugs they snuck into me.

The bed spun, threatening to throw me against the walls, and my stomach lurched uncertainly.

It passed, and I slept.

But not a long or particularly restful sleep.

I awoke and there he was, standing in the corner.

The third of my nightmare visitors.

With disgust, I noticed the smell. It was pervasive, overwhelming. I was at its mercy since I couldn't even reach up to cover my nose and mouth.

It was like someone had emptied every bedpan in every bathroom in the hospital there in that room. I tried to breathe through my mouth, but it did little good. I drew the odor in with every breath, shed it with every exhalation.

The air in the small room seemed to ripple with its foul load. Unable to bear it any longer, I leaned my head as far over the side of the bed as I could without breaking my neck, vomited my dinner.

I lolled there groggily for some time, my head inches from the puddle I'd just let loose. Still the odor of excrement filled my nostrils. As I pulled myself back onto the bed, I caught sight of his silhouette in the corner.

His outline was rough and lumpy; misshapen. Not the smooth, true lines of a real person.

He moved.

A cold chill swept through me when I realized that he was coming toward me.

I rustled the covers, clinked the buckles and clasps on my jacket in an attempt to gain the attention of the—probably sleeping— attendant outside my door.

My voice, however, seemed locked in my throat.

My movements neither brought the orderly nor stopped the figure, which was now at my bedside. The overwhelming odor flowed from it in waves. Its proximity made my sensitive stomach spasm in anticipation of another bout of vomiting.

It took a moment for me to see its form distinctly, but when I did, I would have rubbed my eyes in disbelief had I been able.

Its body was a bulging, twisted mass of dark material, glistening in the thin light that leaked in under the door.

*Shit.*

Without warning, a hand emerged from the blackness, grasped me.

I screamed at its slick, warm touch, thankful then for the heavy leather of the straitjacket. Its flesh squished and slurped as it squeezed my arm, and I realized, sickeningly, that it was attempting to get its arm under me, to lift me.

*To embrace me.*

I didn't struggle as it lifted me to my feet, drew me close. The jacket dropped jingling to the floor, and I felt the creature's warm putrescence press through my paper-thin gown.

A part of me seemed resigned to this, calm and accepting, even grateful.

Its embrace tightened, and instead of being uncomfortable, I found myself actually sinking into the form. The sensation was both repelling and strangely soothing; as pleasant as stepping into a hot bath.

As I oozed into it, I began to feel slightly dizzy, light-headed. Drunk almost. Then, even the sensation of him being there—the thickness, the warmth, the overpowering smell—disappeared as I sank deeper.

I felt as if there were nothing now, and I was hovering over a deep chasm.

A part of my brain screamed at me from a distance, which seemed farther and farther away.

It had nearly consumed all of me at that point, but my hands clutched at its chest as if hanging onto a doorframe. This purchase, however, was slippery, gave way.

I found myself, somewhat against my will, pulling back, retreating from that warm embrace. The more I pulled, however, the harder it became. Like quicksand, its body held me as I struggled.

It tried to squeeze me into its form, enveloping me in its arms. But I caught them, slick and muscular as two snakes, and we wrestled.

With the strength that only the truly desperate can muster,

I wrapped my ankles around the foot of the infirmary bed and leveraged my weight against its body. With a terrific squelching, I wrenched myself from it, flung it from me. It spun across the room, splattered against the wall, lost all form and slid to the floor.

I stood there for a moment, stunned, dripping with shit, covering my eyes, in my nose, down my throat.

But I remembered.

*I am Chris Stadler.*

I remembered *everything*.

Wobbly, I fell to my knees, and my head smacked the floor wetly. Barely conscious, I retched what little there was left in my stomach into the mess that was the room. When there was nothing left, I continued to vomit, until I was sure the only thing coming out of me was blood.

You'd better believe that the doctors, nurses, orderlies and the poor people that had to clean up that mess wondered how a person could be so full of shit.

I was accused of deliberately "retaining stool," as they put it, and placed on a modified, high-fiber diet along with plenty of monitored potty breaks.

I didn't fully understand what happened that night, but I was changed. I felt different somehow, more aware of myself, who I was, where I was.

I remembered for the first time in years what had happened.

I was put there two years prior by my only living relative, my great-aunt Olivia Hardison, because of a supposed advanced degeneration of my memory, similar to Alzheimer's disease. I had been under the impression that whenever I forgot someone, they ceased to exist.

## OBJECT PERMANENCE

Doctors call this object permanence, and it's something that babies experience, then grow out of.

I was put there because I forgot.

But now, I remembered.

I knew that I needed to see my great-aunt.

And something told me that she wouldn't be very thrilled to see me.

Night again. Whatever they were giving me had made me so regular that I was exhausted.

I replayed in my mind what had happened and why. One thing was apparent. The reason for placing me here—that people and things I forgot disappeared—was not a delusion. I knew that. It really happened.

And, I could control it, had controlled it, used it like a power.

But why did my aunt have me committed?

Why were they so hell-bent on keeping me pumped up on drugs?

What could I do to get out of here?

At about 2:00 a.m., she returned.

The straitjacket dropped from my body, fell to the floor.

So did my institution-grey pajamas, and I was nude.

She moved toward me, chilling in her aspect and intensity.

Crackling like dry toast, she knelt, and a thrill of perverse exhilaration raced through me. She hunkered on the floor, then stretched out. In a parody of enticement, she ran her hands roughly over her scabrous form, flakes falling from her curves, a sound like sandpaper over wood.

Then, she slowly opened her legs, spread them with all the abandon of a centerfold.

I could scarcely see in the dim light, but as her legs parted, that horrible tearing sound came from between them. A vertical gash opened where her sex should be, deep and red and wet.

I nearly jumped when she reached out, grabbed my naked leg with her rough hand, pulled me down. Initially, I resisted, but I succumbed.

I sank slowly to my knees. Her legs encompassed me in their strong, craggy embrace.

I nearly passed out with revulsion and pleasure as I entered her.

It seemed to last forever, the thrusting, the grunting, the tearing and rasping.

As we neared climax, she put her mouth to my ear, and in a partially recognizable voice, gasped, "Remember!"

There was an explosion within me, and I passed it into her.

As I watched, she became a new woman, complete, healed and whole.

And as shockingly beautiful as she had been hideous.

She smiled at me, but I couldn't see the color of her eyes in the darkness.

I rolled off her, and a wave of exhaustion swept through me, more profound than anything I had felt in the last several days.

I was swept away.

When I awoke, I was covered with rust-brown dried blood. She was gone.

I stood, very wobbly, and looked out the tiny window of my cell.

Although the lights were as bright as ever in the corridors, there was no one about.

*No one.*

I frowned at this, and pressed my face against the glass for a better look.

As I did so, the door, to my astonishment, moved, swung open without a sound.

For a moment, I stood there—naked, cold, covered in flakes of dried blood—and did nothing. Then, I took two tentative steps into the bright hall.

I half expected a team of orderlies, doctors and police officers to round the corner and club me back into the room. Then, it'd be a return to the drugs and high-fiber diet for me.

But no one came.

Confused, I walked farther down the corridor, out of the secure wing, past the nurses station, past the administration offices.

No one was here. Not even the other patients.

I was somewhere near the lobby of the infirmary when I realized what was going on.

*I'd forgotten them. All of them.*

They were gone, as gone as if they'd never existed.

This didn't make me feel as great as I might have hoped. Although a big part of me was glad to be rid of them, another big part was dazed and lost.

I had to see Aunt Olivia.

I smiled at my reflection in the infirmary's glass door; a demonic figure, nude and red and leering.

With a purpose, I padded slowly down to the staff lounge for my first unattended hot shower in more than two years.

A canvas laundry sack was the closest thing to a suitcase I could find, and I filled it with everything I could. Toiletries and aspirin, canned foods, office supplies. The employee locker rooms turned out to be a treasure trove of money and clothing. I left with more than $4,000 in cash, an assortment of credit cards, and a pair of jeans and a t-shirt that seemed made for me.

Slinging the heavy sack over my shoulder, I went outside into the parking lot and looked back at the facility. It was, in my estimation, the most unassuming building I had ever seen. Low slung, one story, with minimal glass, and bricks that blended with the wooded surroundings. It seemed architecturally designed to fade into the background and be forgotten, along with its inhabitants.

I had also found the keys to a '12 Dodge Dakota, which took me some time to identify among the parked cars. I hoisted the laundry bag into its bed and climbed into the cab.

I started the truck, pulled out of the parking lot.

*I remember you, Aunt Olivia,*

*I'm coming to see you.*

*I think you'll remember me.*

# PART II

The road wandered into town, seeming as surprised at the town's existence as was Chris. He slowed down immediately, the truck's tires fishtailing on the newly paved road.

MISSION SPRINGS, the crooked, brown road sign read. POPULATION 234.

Chris sat there for a moment staring at the sign, the truck idling amidst the dust raised by its abrupt stop.

Mission Springs. The memories came rushing back.

*"It's the family curse, my dear boy,"* Aunt Olivia had laughed. *"Or the family blessing. It all depends whether or not you're on the receiving end."*

Anger flashed within him, as bright as it had the day she'd spoken those words.

*"Memory is your protection. Remember those dearest to you, and they'll live forever unchanged. Forget your enemies, and they will disappear as certainly and as permanently as if they had never existed."*

In the end, Chris had broken ranks with his domineering great-aunt, for a reason or reasons still unclear to him. Something had happened, something the old woman didn't like or couldn't tolerate. So, she'd committed him in the institution.

Coldness stirred in his stomach at the return of these memories. If the old lady was capable of kicking his ass once, she could do it again.

But he had to know...to remember.

Lifting his foot off the brake, he rolled into town with the road.

He had no clear idea of exactly where he was going, but the house and its surroundings leapt out at him, dragged more memories from the clogged recesses of his mind.

He'd played ball there, on the side yard, as a kid. The big oak in the front still supported the tire chain his uncle Frank—an unexpected chill as that name surfaced—had hung long ago. In the dormer, high atop one of the Victorian house's many gables, was his old room. There was the mailbox he ran to every afternoon to wait for the rare and precious letters from his father.

The house was still and picturesque. Autumn had come with its palette of reds and browns. Morning sunlight flooded the expanse of the property—some fifty or sixty wooded acres—giving it a golden, lush aspect.

His heels clumped up the half dozen steps that led to the huge, wraparound porch. A hammock swung sullenly in the early morning breeze. Children's toys were scattered here and there, a fine coat of dew sparkling on their surfaces. Stepping over them, he hesitated, wanting desperately to turn back, to run away and truly forget this place and the other memories it held.

He heard his knock on the heavy wooden door echo through the cavernous house. It didn't take long for someone to answer it. A hand pushed aside a corner of the sheer curtain covering the door's glass, and Chris heard a startled intake of breath.

## OBJECT PERMANENCE

After some fumbling with the locks, a man drew the door open slowly. He was perhaps sixty or so, dressed casually but warmly for a Midwestern autumn morning. He looked on Chris as if he wasn't sure whether he should let him in.

"Good lord," the man whispered, his breath puffing out in clouds of fog. "How did you get out?"

Although the only memory of this man that came to Chris immediately was his name, Uncle Joe, there was something cold and off-putting about him.

"Well, come in, I suppose," Joe said. "Any man who could manage that deserves at least a cup of coffee and some breakfast."

They wound their way through hallways lined with family pictures, faces barely glimpsed, barely remembered. In the large, airy kitchen, Joe poured him a cup, handed it to him. He drained it quickly, hoping that its warmth would steel his muscles, stop them from shaking. But it didn't. Nonetheless, he held out his cup for more.

"How much do you remember?" Joe asked.

"A little more all the time, especially after seeing this place."

Best to play it safe with everyone and pretend to know a lot less than you do.

Which shouldn't be hard.

"Are you planning on staying?" Joe asked, looking over the rim of his thick, porcelain cup to see what kind of reaction this elicited.

*He's as scared of me as he is of her.*

"I don't know," Chris answered, setting his cup down. "Where is she?"

"In the breakfast room. If you want, I could…"

"No thanks," he smiled. "I've managed quite well for the last couple of years without any help from the family. I suppose I can deal with this, too."

As he turned, Joe caught hold of his shoulder. "She's not as patient as she used to be."

But Chris's smile only tightened. "Neither am I."

He took a shortcut he wasn't aware he knew. Through the butler's pantry, across the hallway, through the parlor, his path unfolded before him with each step.

The breakfast room was at the rear of the house, looking out to the woods. It wasn't part of the original structure, but had been added by Uncle Frank when Chris was still a kid. Another chill at that name, and Chris remembered that he was Aunt Olivia's husband.

He paused outside the pocket doors that opened onto the breakfast room. The slight clinking of metal on china drifted through the partially closed door.

Self-consciously, he smoothed his shirt, ran his hands through his hair. He caught himself, smiled. Old habits—and fears—die hard.

He swallowed, wet his lips, and drew the doors open.

She sat with her back to the doorway, and even seated, it was obvious she was tall and carried herself proudly. Her long, grey hair fell over her shoulders, spread across the royal blue silk robe she wore. A tea service sat on a small table to her side, and she held a newspaper outstretched before her.

"Well, you're finally up. Good, I need a little company," the woman said without turning around.

"Good morning, Aunt Olivia," he said in a loud voice.

She dropped the newspaper to the floor, all but leapt from her seat.

"You!" was the first thing she said, and Chris could see she was truly startled. A second later, her face looked as if she were angry with herself for letting him know she was surprised.

**OBJECT PERMANENCE**

"Well, dear boy," she said when she'd collected herself, "you're back. I hope it's because the doctors have been able to do something for you."

Her face—lined, but not seriously so for a woman who claimed to be eighty-three years old—was now cool and even, displaying no more thought of the matter than she probably showed when she ordered breakfast this morning.

To Chris, she looked older, though, more worn than before she sent him away.

And more afraid.

He could feel her fear. It flowed from her in waves, just as it had earlier from Uncle Joe.

She motioned him to a seat next to hers, poured him a cup of tea.

"The doctors did a lot for me," Chris answered, trying to be as matter-of-fact as she was.

"Not the least of which was to disappear quietly. I've already forgotten the entire incident."

He sat, took the cup of tea from her as she looked uncomfortably at him. Her eyes, so brown they were black, fixed on him.

She reached for her tea.

"You didn't." she said, slightly hesitant. "*All* the doctors?"

He smiled as he took a loud, long slurp from the little china cup of tea she'd handed him.

"And to think you were so dead set against doing the very same thing for me. That's why you were there in the first place. You do remember *that*, don't you, dear boy?"

She returned his smile with one so cold, so full of loathing and menace that he actually shivered as he gulped the last dregs of tea.

"I don't remember a lot. I know you're the reason that I was held there, pumped full of drugs and wired to a car battery. If nothing else, you've got that to answer for. The rest will come back to me in time, especially the more I'm in this house."

He drained his cup of tea and stood, feeling her angry gaze boring into him. "I've got to unpack, but we'll have plenty of time later to talk about what went on before. I'll take my old bedroom. That should jog some memories."

He bent to kiss her cheek, but she didn't stir. As he drew the pocket doors open to leave, Aunt Olivia turned to him and said, "I've been more patient with you than anyone, because you were my favorite. But you haven't learned anything. Some things are best left forgotten, dear boy.

"When I forget you this time, it will be permanent," she said.

He paused in the open doorway, turned back to her.

"Like Uncle Frank?" he said, and smiled as the color drained from her face.

He reclaimed his boyhood room, unpacking quietly so as not to disturb a small child asleep in what used to be his bed. Dumping the empty laundry sack in a corner, he carefully bent to see the boy's face. Peaceful and innocent as only a sleeping child can be. He looked exactly like a cousin he'd known from his childhood, Ben.

*Must be one of his kids. The old lady had such a hold on the family that they all tended to hang around.*

But as Chris stood, surveyed the room and its furniture, the toys, the comic books, the dirty clothes and sneakers, it suddenly felt strange, too familiar.

He left the room quickly, before the creeping realization had a chance to gel in his awakening mind.

## OBJECT PERMANENCE

The house was still quiet when he left a little later. He needed to take a walk, clear his head. Uncle Joe was in the backyard, chopping firewood. When he waved, Joe pretended not to notice him and went on chopping.

The tree-lined street stretched quite a distance before another house appeared. Continuing past this, the street met another road—Main Street, of course—that wandered through the heart of Mission Springs. He turned right there, knowing the way toward the few shops and businesses that made up downtown.

Little had changed that he could see from the last time he was here. Although this was a small town, and they tend to age more slowly than big cities, it made him feel slightly uneasy.

Few people were out, which seemed odd for a farming community where everyone is up early. Those he passed seemed to know him and appeared shocked to see him. They flashed wary, benign smiles, or threw a quick, "Good morning," then turned away.

A big, black '52 Chevy pulled up alongside him, and Uncle Joe leapt out, scampered around to the passenger side. There, he opened the door and offered his arm. Accepting it was a gloved hand that Chris immediately recognized.

Aunt Olivia unfolded gracefully as a butterfly from the cocoon of the car, stretching to her full, regal height. She looked around, took note of everyone near her, dismissed Joe with a motion.

"You probably don't even remember that you used to accompany me on my morning walks, do you?" she asked as the car pulled away.

He shook his head, and she reached out toward him, took his arm, cozied close. As she did so, he suddenly remembered walking with her on many occasions, her holding his arm like this.

"I have a house that I want to stop by this morning. Do you mind? I'm sure they'd love to see that you're back safe."

She smiled at him, feral and uncompromising, but he assented without a word.

They walked for some blocks, Chris listening as the old woman prattled on about this house or that, this family or that. He said little, grunting or nodding when he remembered something or someone to whom she referred.

As they rounded a corner onto Third Street, a nervous tingle started in his belly. Aunt Olivia paused long enough to notice his discomfort. She smiled, reinforcing his belief that she was taking him somewhere for a purpose.

"Cold, dear boy?"

He looked down the street at the row of widely spaced older homes and wondered why this scene should make him nervous. "No, no. Just a feeling, really. Déjà vu."

"Well, I should hope so. You've certainly visited them enough. They'll be upset if you don't remember them," Aunt Olivia clucked. "Quite upset, I should say."

They continued on, but Chris noticed that the old woman was no longer subtly leading him. She wanted to see exactly how much of his memory was coming back, if he could find his way to their destination on his own.

He slowed his pace, carefully scanned each house as they passed. But they looked only remotely familiar, like landmarks passed day after day on the way to another destination.

The street ended in a cul-de-sac, and another great, old Victorian mansion sat there. But while his aunt's house seemed to shine and invite, this house glowered and grimaced. Drapes were closed tight in its many windows.

He paused before the house, his stomach churning, and he knew this was the place Aunt Olivia wanted him to find.

"I haven't seen the Archibalds in so long, well, I've almost forgotten them," Aunt Olivia leered at him.

He snapped his attention to her, anger, fierce and bright and violent, coursing through him. But, of course, he didn't know why.

She noted his reaction, expected it. "Not to worry, dear boy. How could I forget them? You'll thank me when you see I've kept them exactly as you left them. Exactly." She took the lead again, almost pulling him up the walkway that led to the front porch.

Paper Thanksgiving decorations, the kind found on the cinderblock walls of school lunchrooms and tacked to bulletin boards in public libraries, were taped haphazardly to the windows. A large paper turkey, faded and tattered, was stuck to the front door, haggardly resplendent in its pop-up tail of reds, golds and browns.

His first knock brought no response, nor did his second or third. On the fourth, he heard someone fumbling with the lock, and after a moment, the door opened a tiny crack.

"Hello," he said. The girl behind the door hissed in a breath, then fainted to the floor, the door swinging open into the house.

Chris immediately bent to her aid, grabbing her wrist, slipping an arm under her neck. From somewhere in the house, he heard the confusion of feet on hardwood floors and voices calling, "Emma! Emma, who's there?"

"Ma'am," Chris said, lifting her head, "Are you all right?"

As he brought her head up, a spray of brown hair covering her face slipped away.

The scabrous woman from the institution. The one he'd made love to and healed.

The one he'd thought was a delusion.

Shock, confusion and nervousness raced through him as the voices and the footsteps came closer, but he ignored all that, focused on her face. He reached out, stroked it absently, feeling how cool and soft her skin was.

"Emma, what's the matter? I thought I heard the d—,"came a woman's voice, which ended in a gasp when she saw who was cradling her.

"You! Why did you come back?" the woman said, wrenching Emma's still comatose body away from him. "After what's been done to my daughter…your wife! To us!" She lifted Emma onto her plump lap, rocking and stroking the girl, who was beginning to come around.

"And you, you witch! Get out of my house. I'll not have you here."

"Well, good morning, Mae," cooed Aunt Olivia. "You're looking well today. Pray tell, where are the grandchildren? I trust they're all in good health."

At the mention of the children, Mae blanched, fell silent.

Emma had begun to come around, and then her eyes snapped open.

"Chris," she whispered. "It *is* you." She took his hand, brought it to her face and kissed his palm.

"Wife? I…I don't remember you."

"I know, but it'll come back. It'll all come back. I promise," she said, stroking his hand and kissing it.

Without realizing it, he'd begun to cry, and his tears plopped to the polished floor, beaded there. Angry and ashamed, he stood, dragged his hand across the well of his eyes.

"I'm sorry," he choked.

**OBJECT PERMANENCE**

He knew he was sorry, believed it to the core of his being. Even though he was not sure why.

Reaching out, Chris offered a hand to both women. Emma took it eagerly, but Mae hesitated. Finally, she relented, and he hauled her to her feet as well.

"Well, enough of the heartfelt family reunion. I'm here to visit," Aunt Olivia said, removing her gloves. "Bring everyone out to see me. Hurry, it's been so long I've nearly forgotten them."

This time, color rose red and hot in Mae's cheeks, but Aunt Olivia disregarded her, sat slowly and regally on a sofa in the parlor as if she were the Dowager Empress preparing to receive guests of state.

Mae returned a moment later, a throng of older people shuffling behind her with eyes downcast, faces sullen. They filed into the room, stopping in turn before his aged aunt, who reached out and clasped their limp hands in hers. She spoke a few words to each, in a bright, high voice, and then they left.

Chris wondered at this odd ritual and the reactions of each of his wife's family members. This was not the delight, boredom or downright antipathy most people exhibited when greeting guests. Rather, it was dejection, an uncaring acceptance of some fact that had been fought against and lost to long ago.

Mae ushered them all out, and when Aunt Olivia had greeted the last, Mae prepared to leave the room as well.

"Mae?" Aunt Olivia sang. "I do believe you've left somebody out. Where's Thomas? Wouldn't want to forget him, would you? "

Mae stood in the hallway near Chris and Emma, silent and wide-eyed.

"Mae?"

"Please. Just this once. Please. Let him be. He's so close, so close," Mae cried, burying her face in her hands.

Aunt Olivia rose from the sofa in a shot, strode into the hallway with frightening speed and determination. She grabbed Mae by the front of her dress and shook her, the veins on her bony hands practically popping.

"Where is he, Mae? You damned old fool, you'll never learn!" she screamed. Emma curled up to Chris, who was snapped out of his reverie by this outburst.

Mae's head rolled loosely on her neck, and she looked plaintively upstairs.

Aunt Olivia unclenched her fists, pushed Mae from her, and dashed up the stairs at a pace that astounded Chris.

"Do something," Emma cried, looking at her husband.

He disengaged himself from her embrace, ran up the stairs after the old woman.

When he reached the top of the steps and followed the shouts and shrieks, he saw several people in various states of distress outside the bedroom door. They quickly parted as he passed. Inside the room, light from a stained glass window colored the swirl of people. Their faces, their gestures struck him with the intensity of a medieval tableau.

All of the activity seemed to center around a massive bed that occupied much of the room. At the center of its four, thick wooden posts, a tiny figure huddled, clutched the covers. Pale and drawn, the man seemed only fitfully aware of what transpired around him. And when he did show any awareness, it was the same resignation that Chris had witnessed from the other family members downstairs.

Aunt Olivia stood at the side of the bed, her eyes closed, clutching one of his hands tightly in both of hers.

The old man was dying.

Aunt Olivia was preventing it, not helping, Chris realized.

Preventing.

As she held his hand, a remarkable thing happened. Color returned to the old man's cheeks. Focus and a sparkle of awareness swam into his eyes, and the trembling of his limbs stopped. His free hand lost its convulsive grip on the sheets, and his breathing returned to normal.

"Fool!" Aunt Olivia hissed at him, throwing his hand to the bed. "You're lucky that you didn't die, Thomas. I would have made your family pay dearly."

The old man, who now didn't look so old, hung his head upon his breast, dejected and utterly beaten. The twinkle Chris had seen in his eyes just a moment ago was gone.

Aunt Olivia turned and saw Chris standing in the doorway, the others skirting him gingerly in their attempt to leave the room.

"I have a surprise for you, Thomas," she said, turning her death's head grin on him. "I have someone who's come back to see you and your family."

The man raised his head, looked in Chris's direction.

Tears welled in his eyes and spilled down his cheeks.

"Please, let me die. Just let me die," he whispered.

"I'll be back next week to see how you're doing, Thomas," Aunt Olivia said, as if nothing had happened. "Well, Chris, are you coming?"

Chris shook his head. He needed to remember, and this was the place, these were the people to help him. If for no other reason than they seemed to be afraid of Aunt Olivia.

Of course, they were afraid of him, too, but he needed to get to the bottom of that.

"I thought you might stay," the old woman answered, chuckling a bit. "Do you think you can remember the way home on your own, dear boy?"

"How could I forget?" he answered, and she accepted his response with another chuckle.

"I'll see you tonight at dinner, then." She walked slowly past, touching his shoulder lightly on the way out. He heard her steps fade down the hallway, down the stairs. The front door opened, closed, and the entire house seemed to expel a long-held breath.

Suddenly, Mae dashed into the room, pushed past Emma and Chris, rushed to the side of her husband. His head lay on the pillow, eyes staring into space, silent tears spilling down his cheeks. Mae held him tight, and they both cried.

"Chris," Emma whispered, taking his hand and pulling him from the room. "Come on, we've got a lot to discuss."

"I know."

# PART III

She led him from the house into the backyard garden, brown and wilted from the autumn. Bare stakes, turned earth and the detritus of dead plants were scattered here and there, giving the landscape a peculiar, ravaged look. Only the trees farther back in the yard lent any color to the surroundings.

A picnic table squatted amidst this, its boards grey and warped, its top uneven. They sat side-by-side. She held his hand tightly in hers, studied him for a minute.

"I didn't know if you would come back," she said. "I mean, I didn't know if you'd be able to.

"I guess what I'm trying to say is…I didn't know if you'd remember."

And she hugged him, buried her face in his neck and cried. He felt her tears, warm against his flesh on this cold morning, trickle underneath his shirt and down his shoulder. He returned her embrace.

And remembered.

The almost prophetic curve of the small of her back. The smell of her hair. The sound of her breathing. The softness of her skin.

His wife. A bit older than he remembered, but it was she who had appeared to him at the institution. Was that a delusion?

"Shh," he said, his love for her returning in a blast of memory that shivered through him more powerfully than the damp, cold air. "I'm beginning to remember everything. And some of it I wish I could forget."

She pulled up, wiped her eyes. "That's in the past. We settled it before she sent you away. I know you never meant to hurt us. You loved us so much that you wanted to keep us the way we were. You know it can't be that way."

"You're going to have to help me," he said, taking her face gently in his hands. "I don't remember everything yet. That's dangerous. Aunt Olivia is playing a game with me, trying to see how much I remember. When she finds out, she'll try to get rid of me again. I need to know some things. Can you tell me?"

"Of course."

"From what I can piece together from my memory and what happened this morning, Aunt Olivia has some sort of power that holds this town just the way she remembers it, the people, the things, the landscape. They all stay the same forever. Is that right?"

"Yes," she said, her face trying hard not to express surprise that he didn't remember even this.

"Okay, bear with me," he sighed. "That's the strangest part, and I wasn't sure whether I really was crazy for thinking that. But I have that same power. Is that right?"

"Yes. In fact, you're the only other person in the family who does. You were sort of her second-in-command. She was grooming you for something."

"Right," he said, standing suddenly and pacing. "I remember that. She knew I had the power—object permanence, she called it— and she wanted me to do something. To help her with something. But what was it? Did I ever say anything to you about it?"

## OBJECT PERMANENCE

She shook her head.

"Shit. All right, we'll leave that at present. Walking with her today, I felt that it was something we'd done before, often," he said.

"Every day. Olivia split the town into sections, and the two of you would take a walk every morning. That way she could see everyone and everything in town once a week—"

"Because she needed to," he interrupted. "That's it. To maintain the control, she has to remember. And to remember, she had to see everyone regularly, to keep them in mind."

"Before she sent you away, you told me something that you thought was important. You said that she didn't always do this every week. She began by seeing everyone once or twice every couple of months, then it became once a month. Only recently did it become once a week. You said that it meant something," Emma said.

Chris stopped pacing, stunned. His mind, racing as it was, locked its brakes and squealed to a stop.

Aunt Olivia was getting older.

She was *forgetting*.

He was sure of it. That's what he'd known before she had him institutionalized.

And then it all came back, like a dam crumbling, washing over him, threatening to sweep him along with the flow.

She wasn't just grooming him to take over.

She was growing old and losing her memory, and she wanted to make sure that he was around to remember *her*.

That way, she could arrest the downward spiral of her life, because her powers were becoming ineffectual on herself. When he was around, he could prop up her failing memory, make sure she never aged, never changed.

And she could continue her grip on the town.

For some reason, he had broken with her, refused to participate. And she had used her power on him, but his own power had kept him from being forgotten altogether, just as hers protected her. Instead, she drove him to the brink of insanity, and the results were two years on drugs and electricity.

That's why she was keeping him around, to see if he remembered all this. To see if it was possible to try to convince him to help her again.

Ruefully, in the jumble of memories that returned, Chris knew that he'd done the same thing to Emma and her family. Held them by the force of his memory, whether they wanted to or not. It was plain from this morning's scene that they did not want it.

But he did know that as part of realizing what Aunt Olivia was up to, he'd let his wife and her family go. It was both the hardest and the easiest decision he'd ever made, and the pain it had brought settled on him now as if he'd only come to this conclusion a moment ago.

He turned to look at his wife, seeing the affection in her face, and realized how much he owed her.

"I remember now, almost all of it," he whispered to her. "I know she was using me. That she's forgetting things, and wants me to do the same thing to her that she's doing to this town. If you have any doubts about it, I still won't do it. It's wrong.

"No, more than that," he reconsidered. "It's evil. And, I've got to stop it."

"Chris, she can hurt you. She's done that already," Emma said, standing and hugging him again.

"I know what she's capable of." He returned her hug, this time with the full force of his memories. "There's just one thing that bothers me now. And it's something I think I knew before she sent me away.

"If I was helping her while I was here, who was doing it before me?"

## OBJECT PERMANENCE

The sky was dark when he left the Archibald house, its face frowning on him as he walked down the tree-lined street. It was hard having to part from Emma again. But he had to confront his aunt, had to find out what she was up to. And that meant having to stay away from Emma and her family. They were bargaining chips now, something his aunt could use against him. He would bring no more harm to this family than he already had.

The sunset had come in a heartbeat, the temperature dropping precipitously. He wore only a denim jacket he'd taken from one of the employee lockers at the institution.

Halfway to Olivia's house, the moon rose, three-quarters full, and bathed his path in silver-white light. Leaves blown in the wind became shards of delicate glass drifting in its pearly light.

In the distance, he saw blue smoke curl above the trees, floating up from the thick chimney that perched atop the roof of his aunt's house. He quickened his pace, and was clumping up the porch steps and letting himself in seconds later.

The house was warm and smelled of fireplaces. He stripped off his denim jacket and hung it on one of the staircase finials, then headed up to his room.

The second floor was dark and quiet, and he saw no one. His door was ajar, and a thin wedge of light pushed into the hallway from the room. Slowly, he opened the door, poked his head inside.

As he did so, a shape launched from the partially lit room. It caught him in his midsection, tumbled him back into the corridor, knocked his breath away.

His hands worked blindly to catch whatever it was, a shock of thick hair, a smooth expanse of squirming skin.

## JOHN F.D. TAFF

"Gotcha!" it yelled, wrestling free from him and climbing to its feet. Chris gulped in a breath, looked up.

It was the small boy Chris had seen in bed this morning. No more than eight or ten years old.

"You're getting old," the boy laughed.

Chris pulled himself up to a sitting position against a door on the other side of the hall, returning the smile as good-naturedly as possible.

"Yeah, too old for that game. I had a cousin who used to do that to me all the time when I was…"

He stopped in mid-sentence as his eyes became accustomed to the low light and he got a good look at the boy.

"Who are you?" he whispered, his mouth suddenly dry.

"Aunt Olivia said you might not remember," the boy said, kicking out roughly at one of Chris's feet. "You really don't know, huh?"

"Oh my God…*Ben?*"

"See, how could you forget me?" he said, slightly petulant.

Dumbfounded at the implications of this, Chris stumbled to his knees, crawled over to where the boy stood, his head hung low.

"Ben?"

He reached out, lifted the boy's face. It was wet, and he realized Ben was trying to contain his sobs. They caught in his chest, hitched in his lungs.

Without warning, he grabbed hold of Chris, and bear-hugged him.

For the second time today, Chris was bathed in tears. Ben clung to him, twitching and gasping at the force of his sobs.

Chris patted him on the back, returned his embrace.

*This boy was ten years old when I was five,* he thought. *That would make him a 34-year-old man today.*

But right here, right now, Ben was only ten years old.

## OBJECT PERMANENCE

Because that's the way Aunt Olivia chose to remember him.

Chris found himself tearing up at that thought, at all that had been denied Ben by his aunt's cruel, hateful memory. He was locked in a life of toy cars and bicycles and playing army. It might have been fine for a while, but he hadn't known adolescence and all of its joys and heartaches. Hadn't known girls or women, and their strange and frustrating thrills.

"You said you'd come back if anything happened," Ben sniffed, pulling away and roughly wiping his eyes. "Said you'd come back to get me. Is that why you're back?"

Chris, too, wiped his eyes, pulled himself up. Ben's words brought back a vow he'd made just before Olivia had him committed.

*If she does anything to me, if she sends me away somewhere, you've got to promise to be good and do whatever she says. Wherever I am, I'll come back to get you, and we'll move away from here. Far away. I'll take you somewhere you can grow up.*

"Yeah," he said. "We're gonna get out of here. But, you have to wait until everything's ready."

Ben looked at him, his face flushed and doubtful.

"You don't remember everything, do you?"

"I think if one more person asks me that, I'll scream," Chris laughed. "But, no, I don't. Aunt Olivia doesn't know that yet, and I don't want her to, either. Understand?"

"Sure. I was just getting ready to head down for dinner. It's only Uncle Joe, Aunt Olivia, you and me tonight," Ben sniffed, still containing his hitching breath.

"Well, then, let's go."

"Okay. I have something to show you, but after dinner. Last one there's a butt head," he yelled, stomping on Chris's foot and taking off down the stairs.

Collecting his wits, Chris hobbled after him, tripping him in the library and getting to the dining room first.

Dinner was a restrained, uncomfortable affair, with Uncle Joe trying gamely to start conversations that evaporated after a minute or two. Eventually, he gave in to the silence, too. Aunt Olivia said little throughout the meal, and Chris followed her lead, fearful of revealing too much of what he didn't know.

Before coffee and dessert, Chris excused himself from the table, followed closely by Ben. When they reached the landing at the bottom of the back staircase, Chris stopped and whispered to Ben, "What is it you have to show me?"

"A note."

"From who?"

"From you, dork," he answered, dashing up the steps with more energy than Chris could muster after such a big dinner. He followed slowly, hearing wisps of quietly animated conversation between Aunt Olivia and Uncle Joe drift to his ears. Nothing was intelligible, but he got the distinct impression it was about him, and that his aunt was admonishing his uncle about something.

Cresting the stairs, he heard another sound down the hall, from his bedroom. It was the sound of things being thrown around, of something big being moved. As he came through the doorway, Ben was crouched behind a huge, old oak dresser, prying up one of the floorboards.

It popped from its place with a hollow, wooden knock. He reached in and fished around for a second, pulling out a small envelope.

Ben stood, sweaty and covered with dust. He took two steps forward and held the envelope out to Chris with a shaking hand.

## OBJECT PERMANENCE

Chris touched it, and immediately remembered what it contained, and it chilled him to his marrow. He ripped it open anyway.

Confronted by the cold reality of his own handwriting, echoing his memories, he fell back onto the small bed.

He finally remembered everything.

And he knew what he had to do.

"We need to find a photo of Uncle Frank."

Although the big house was relatively empty, Chris was still nervous about creeping around in it with Ben like two thieves. Aunt Olivia was, no doubt, reading in the library. Uncle Joe would be playing a solitary game in the basement billiards room.

And everyone else? Chris was not really sure just where everyone else was, and this tugged nervously at the back of his mind. Some four or five whole families lived in this house or on the adjacent property, but he'd seen no one except Aunt Olivia, Uncle Joe and Ben.

He didn't have a good feeling about the fate of the others.

Despite their best efforts, floorboards creaked and furniture shifted as they prowled through the house. Aunt Olivia's room was on the first floor, unfortunately very near the library. Ben and Chris skulked down the narrow hallway that led past that room.

They were close enough for Chris to hear the crackling fire, the turning pages of the book she was reading. The library's pocket doors were pulled almost shut, and Chris and Ben crept past the slim opening, crouched and holding their breaths, pausing to look into the room. Fortunately, much of their stealth was unnecessary. The old woman sat in a wingback chair facing the fire. All that was visible was the crown of her grey head.

Each taking a quiet breath, they proceeded down the hall, coming to a door that Ben indicated, with a tug on Chris's sleeve, led to Aunt Olivia's room. It swung open easily, without a squeak. The room inside was bathed in dim pools of golden light, cast from two enormous hurricane lamps that sat on nightstands on either side of a great canopy bed, turned down in preparation of Aunt Olivia's imminent slumber.

The furniture was not just old, but ancient by American standards. The pieces had to be at least as old as Aunt Olivia. Dark wood paneling, mahogany or cherry, Chris could not be sure in the light, dominated the large room; an imposing dresser, a dressing table and a mirror, a tall wardrobe. All of it with the dull burnish of old, well-cared-for wood.

Chris moved inside, looking around, quickly trying to take it all in and decide where she might keep a photo of her dead husband.

The wardrobe had been one of Uncle Frank's pieces of furniture, Chris remembered, so he opened it first. Dozens of outfits hung there, all men's clothing. She hadn't gotten rid of these in more than twenty years.

He dug through these frantically, the room beginning to make him uncomfortable. It was as if her bedroom were a microcosm of the town. It felt as if nothing had changed in here since the 1800s.

But that was ludicrous. Aunt Olivia was old, but she couldn't be that old.

Could she?

Finding nothing in the wardrobe, he pushed everything back inside, closed the doors carefully. He spun around, momentarily concerned by the look of fear on Ben's face, and caught sight of a desk tucked away in a dark corner.

As he approached it, he could see that it was a closed roll-top

## OBJECT PERMANENCE

desk with a vaguely unused air about it. With a nervous glance back toward the door, he quietly unrolled the cover.

Everything inside was neat and tidy and dust-free, leading Chris to believe that someone used the desk regularly. Drawer after drawer held papers or files or stacks of meaningless magazine covers dating all the way back to 1867.

When he drew open the bottom file drawer, though, something nearly popped out at him. It was a small silver picture frame, heavily tarnished. But, the photo behind the glass was turned backward, its yellowed side showing.

His hands trembling, he pulled the backing off, slid the glass and photo out, turned the picture around.

Uncle Frank.

Although the memory was dim and blurry—and the man in the photo was dressed in the clothes of someone far older—it was him.

Chris removed the photo, slid the glass back into the frame, and placed it gently in the drawer.

When the sound of a door opening into the room startled him.

He spun around and saw Uncle Joe emerging into the room through what appeared to be a hidden passage.

"Liv?" he said. "I thought I heard you…"

Ben gasped, and Chris quickly stuffed the photo of Uncle Frank down his shirt.

"What the hell are you two doing in here?" Uncle Joe demanded, surprised and confused and very frightened. "Your aunt is not going to be happy when I tell her this.

"Didn't take you long, did it?" he snapped at Chris. "She got rid of you once, you little shit. And she can do it again. You, too, you ungrateful little bastard!"

As Chris straightened, prepared an explanation, he saw Ben close his eyes tightly.

117

Then, an amazing thing happened.

Uncle Joe disappeared.

Without a sound, a flash. He neither faded nor flickered.

He simply ceased to exist.

"What?" Chris asked, his mouth open to its limit. He turned to Ben, who looked at him like a child who knew he had done something wrong. "Did you do that?"

Ben nodded his head.

Taking a deep breath, Chris closed the desk drawer.

"Come on," he motioned for Ben to follow him through the secret door Uncle Joe had used. Chris could not remember ever having seen such a door, and suspected that no one else knew about it either.

In fact, if what he was thinking turned out to be correct, the existence of the passage was knowledge shared only by Aunt Olivia and Uncle Joe.

And, quite possibly, Uncle Frank.

The door led to a set of narrow stairs. At the top, another opened into a small, rumpled bedroom.

Uncle Joe's.

Somehow, this did not surprise Chris.

Without pausing, he led Ben by the hand down the dark hallway back to their room. Once inside, Chris pulled the photo out of his shirt, set it on the table.

And he and Ben talked.

# PART IV

"**Y**ou have it, don't you Ben?" Chris whispered, sitting on the bed next to the young boy. "You know what I'm talking about. The gift Aunt Olivia and I have."

Ben looked scared. He may have been thirty-four years old chronologically, but he was still only a 10-year-old boy, and a frightened one at that.

"Mom..." and here his voice caught. "Mom told me not to tell anyone. Ever. She said I'd get into a lot of trouble. That Aunt Olivia would take me away from her and Dad. Just like she did..."

"Yeah?"

"Just like she did to you," he stammered.

And another memory, long buried, dropped onto his head with the emotional weight of an anvil. Aunt Olivia *had* taken Chris himself away from his mother when he was very young. Probably when she found out he had the power. And she'd scared away his father. That's why he'd written only occasional letters, which became ever more occasional before ending completely.

"So, Aunt Olivia doesn't know?"

"No, no."

"What did you do to Uncle Joe?" Chris asked, his mouth going dry.

"I…umm…remembered him."

Chris frowned. That was not the way the power worked. When you remembered people they remained, they continued to exist just as they had in your memory. It was when you forgot people that they disappeared.

"I don't understand," Chris said. "You mean you *forgot* him."

"I remembered a fishing trip he took me on about eight years ago to the Northwest Territories in Canada. In the middle of nowhere. I remembered him as far away as I could."

In an instant, Chris realized what he meant. That was not the way his power worked, but

Ben's power obviously manifested itself differently.

"You mean, now he's in…"

"Canada," whispered Ben.

"Holy shit," Chris muttered.

"I'm sorry, Chris," the boy said. "I didn't mean to. I was scared. He was going to hurt you again, and me, too."

Chris hugged him close.

"That's okay. I think Uncle Joe had it coming for a long time. Besides, I don't think you hurt him."

"Are…are you still going to take me with you when you leave?"

"You bet. But first, I'm going to need your help. How early can you get up in the morning?"

The sun rose on a clear morning that belied the frigid November temperatures outside. From Chris's window, the grass, burdened under the weight of the frost, looked like the lank, grey hair of a corpse.

He glanced at his watch. 6:45 a.m. The old lady would be having her breakfast about now. Time to take a shower and get down there.

"Hey, kiddo," Chris shook Ben. "It's show time."

The photo of Uncle Frank was tucked inside the front of his shirt, rubbing uncomfortably against his belly as Chris clumped down the staircase. She was waiting there, impatient, looking at her watch.

"Did you forget the time?"

"I'm sorry, Aunt Olivia," he said. "Two years of sleeping late, sleeping practically all day at the institution, is a hard habit to break."

"Well, no matter. We'll just be a little late, that's all," she said as if not hearing him. She pulled on her long, rabbit fur-lined gloves with a small flourish. "Do you know where we're going today?"

"Yes," he answered, and she looked up at him, surprised.

"You do?"

"Yes. My choice," he said, offering his arm. She took it slowly, looking askance.

"Well, what is your choice, dear boy?" she asked, smiling. And this nearly ruined Chris's whole plan, for it was the first genuine smile he'd seen from her since he'd returned to Mission Springs. It lit up her face, smoothed away the years and the bitterness and the anger. In an instant, she looked younger than she had when he saw her only yesterday morning.

He knew that it was because of him.

He was beginning to remember her.

She placed a gloved hand on his cheek, planted a tiny, musty kiss there. He could smell her sachet, violets and powder, and his heart ached in his chest. He remembered her caring for him when he was a child. How she had looked on most everything he had done with delight and pride. How she had been father to him when there was only his mother, and both when even she had gone.

Then he realized why Aunt Olivia was smiling. Because she thought she had her old boy back, before he learned the secrets, before he became difficult.

Before he challenged her.

"Well," he said. "If memory serves, my surprise."

He drew away from her, opened the front door of the house, and closed the door to his heart.

They spoke as they walked, and Chris noticed a slight pause, a hesitation on her part as he chose his path. There were very few houses along this stretch of the county road, so she came this way seldom.

"You simply mustn't keep an old lady in suspense," she said. "Where are you taking us?"

"Well, you remember the Hunters, don't you?"

"Why yes," she said, clapping her hands like a delighted child, her smile returning. "You never did like Mike Hunter, did you? Well, I'm afraid that I've let things slip since you've been gone. I wasn't able to hold Mike all by myself."

Cold mist rose off the sparkling grass of the pastures they walked by as the sun struggled over the low hills. The freshly asphalted road nearly shone, looking as if no car had ever touched it.

"I've been meaning to ask you about something," Chris said, and her hold tightened. "You weren't able to keep Mike Hunter. Is that what happened to the townspeople?"

Silence for the span of several footsteps.

"I'd hoped that you would help, that you would stay here," she breathed. "But, you wanted something else. It's so hard to do it all alone. And, other than you, no one in the family inherited the power."

She looked away, down the road, at nothing in particular.

"Without someone to help me, I'm beginning to age, and everything that entails. Including the loss of my memory," she said. "I've always thought how ironic it is that our power works on everyone but ourselves. If we want to be remembered, we need another. You can't remember yourself."

Chris thought back on his experience in the institution, to his struggle with the strange shit man and his encounter with the scab woman. And he knew that what she said was not so.

It *was* possible to remember yourself.

"Without you around, dear boy," she said, patting his hand, "I've no one to remember me.

So, everyone in the town suffers."

"It seems that there's a lot fewer people than I remember," he said after a minute.

"Forgotten."

A simpler word never held more damning meaning. She was losing her grip on the town because she was losing her memory. And the one thing the townsfolk probably most desired was coming true, and hurting them as badly in the long run.

He thought of his father-in-law, how badly he wanted to die. How close he came. He remembered that, just a few years ago, he wouldn't have even gotten that close.

They walked a while further in silence, passing several white clapboard farmhouses. No smoke rose from the chimneys of one or two, and Chris wondered if their owners were still there. Or if they'd simply disappeared one day when Olivia Hardison had forgotten them.

"And the rest of the family?"

She shook her head. "I could only hold on to so many. And the fights. Ahh, after you left, more of them felt braver, freer to argue with me. It was all I could do to keep Uncle Joe.

"And, Ben!" she chuckled. "Now there's a puzzle. He stayed no matter what. He's never manifested object permanence, but he must have some low-grade version of it protecting him."

*If only you knew.*

"Surely you've come back to help me, even after our fight. You see the good in it. So many people gone. So many," and her voice caught, tears welled in her eyes.

"I can see this much," he said. "It's wrong to hold people in our memories like this, no matter how good you think it is. It's wrong. Who appointed you to decide when and if a person should die or live forever?"

Her grip on his hand loosened, and she looked away.

"You didn't feel that way about Mike Hunter," she snapped. "Not about Emma or her family."

That stung him.

"I was wrong, I know that now. Emma knows it. She's forgiven me."

In the distance, the landscape changed, a small dip in the road masked the little glade that was his goal. He needed to keep talking, to keep her off balance so she wouldn't realize where he was headed.

"So," she said, her voice flat and dull. "You do remember. I'd thought we might be able to start over. I can see that I was wrong. Again."

"Again," he reiterated, increasing his pace as much as she would allow. "I can see *you* still haven't learned. Didn't you see the pain that you caused yesterday morning at my in-laws' house? Didn't you see how badly Mr. Archibald wanted release? To die?"

## OBJECT PERMANENCE

She spun on him, her face a twisted mixture of contempt, spite and hatred. "How can you say death is best? How can you argue that wanting to die is good? It's not. That's what's really evil. To want to be forgotten, to desire death.

"What I have is a great gift, and I share it with everyone that I know and love. What do I get in return? Fear. Hatred. Betrayal. Has that stopped me? No. Because, it's for their own good!"

Almost there. The photo still chafed reassuringly.

"No," he said, beginning to walk again. "It may have been good at one time, for a while maybe. But not for as long as you've done it. Not for centuries. That's selfish."

Her demeanor changed, and she looked at him through narrow eyes. "How long have you known that?"

"That you're older than you claim? Not very long."

"How?"

He held his answer in check. He stopped, and she turned to face him, not realizing or even caring where they were.

The elaborately scrolled cast-iron gate simply read, HOLY MOUNT CEMETERY.

"It was Uncle Frank at first, wasn't it?" he said, giving this bombshell plenty of time to hit the target before going on.

It had the desired effect. She gasped, shocked beyond measure. It had always been family taboo to even mention his name.

"What?"

"I mean you two had the power at first, right? He used it on you, you on him," Chris said, the words beginning to spill from his mouth. "But that wasn't good enough for you, was it? Next, it was your children. Uncle Frank went along with that. Then, it was the rest of the family. Your sisters, your grandchildren, nearly everyone related to you.

"I suspect that's when Uncle Frank began to have a problem. But when it really started was when you wanted to remember the town; to hold it—and everyone in it—this way forever. So that nothing would change, nothing would grow old. And no one would die."

She stood before him as if physically stunned. Her jaw hung open, and her hands went limp at her sides.

"There were arguments, I remember that from when I was little. Uncle Frank was a quiet man, but not as weak-willed as you came to think. And when that failed, he used his power to counteract yours. Because, in the end, he was more powerful than you, wasn't he?"

She said nothing, stared at him unbelievingly.

"So, you killed him. I don't mean forgetting him. I mean you really murdered him. Or was it Uncle Joe, his own brother?"

"I don't think Frank even knew we were having an affair," she whispered. "Frank didn't see the good in what I wanted for this town or our family either, just like you. He was a fool. But, Joe... He didn't have the power, but he had the will."

"How did he do it?" Chris asked, shivering at the flood of cold memories that she was dredging up.

"With a hammer to the back of the skull. Quick, relatively neat. The police, of course, knew. But what could they do? I threatened them and their families.

"He never had the gift his brother had, though his brother used it on him. I don't know how old they were. I do know that Frank had been alive during the Revolutionary War. The tales he told of it..."

She drifted off at that, and Chris took the opportunity to fish the photo out of his shirt.

"You know that I'm not here to help you," he said. "I'm here to stop you, to put everything right again. Just like Uncle Frank tried to do."

"Of course I know that, dear boy," she said. "But you can't stop me. I killed Frank. I sent you away once." She spat the last word at him, a sarcastic taunt.

"I always have Joe to take care of you in more mundane ways, should that prove necessary," she smiled again, tinged with the malice he was accustomed to.

"That's where you're wrong. Joe's far, far away. I made sure of that. I did remember to bring some help with me," he said, whipping the photo out and taking a long look at it before he held it out to her.

"Where did you get that?" she screamed, tearing it from his hand and recoiling.

Chris ignored her. He concentrated on the face in the photograph, formed an image in his mind, closed his eyes.

"What are you doing?" she yelled, grabbing his arm and shaking him.

"Dear lord," she breathed. "Dear lord, you can't mean to— Oh my God! You can't remember him. He's *dead*!"

The image formed, held.

There was a sound nearby, from within the tiny cemetery. It was a gentle, scraping sound, as if something were pushing through the earth.

A groan vibrated low on the air, rattling the ribs in Chris's chest.

Movement, an eruption of soil.

A headstone fell.

The clink of stone against stone.

Something rose from within the shadows of the little glade, pushed its way from the ground.

Aunt Olivia fell to her knees.

The shape stood to its full height, then ambled stiffly toward them.

The gate creaked open, and the figure walked into the early morning light.

Chris felt like falling to his knees, too.

Uncle Frank.

He was nothing more than an articulated skeleton, his skin drawn taut and shiny and a peculiar color of dried brown across his bones. His hair was long and disheveled, and stood out in waves from his head. The smooth outline of his skull was interrupted by two distinct holes; one near the crown, the other toward the side. They were ragged and quite large, and they glared darkly like two dead eyes. The remnant of a black suit clung to him, tattered and worm-eaten.

He took another step toward them, the bones of his shoeless feet scraping the asphalt as he shambled forward.

Aunt Olivia uttered a tiny, barely audible squeak.

"Who?" he asked, in a booming, strangely distance voice.

"Me," Chris answered, bracing for whatever came next.

The dead man looked upon Aunt Olivia, and his face twisted in confusion.

"I remember you," he said more softly, reaching out to stroke her grey hair with his gnarled, leathery hand.

She screamed, scrambled from his touch.

"No, no. I'm sorry. I've apologized to you every night since then. If I could have brought you back, I would have."

"It is good that you didn't," the dead man rumbled. "Perhaps you've learned."

"No," Chris said, his voice breaking. Uncle Frank snapped his dead eyes back to Chris. "She hasn't learned. She's held the town in her memory ever since you died. I have the power, as well, and she's trying to get me to help her. But I won't."

Uncle Frank remained still for a moment.

## OBJECT PERMANENCE

"Why do you remember me?"

"You've got to help me so that everyone here can go on the way they were meant to be. You knew this in life. That's why she had you killed."

The dead man began nodding his head slowly and awkwardly. "Yes, I remember."

They both turned toward Aunt Olivia, who was still on the ground.

She had closed her eyes tightly.

Chris knew what she was doing. He had seen her do it many times before.

He had done it many times before.

She was forgetting him.

A weird feeling of disassociation rippled through his body, and he felt himself grow insubstantial.

"Help me, Uncle Frank!" he yelled, doubling over in pain.

"Noooo!" yelled another voice.

*Ben.*

The young boy rose from behind one of the tombstones in the cemetery. His face was ashen, and Chris could see, even through his disorientation, that he was shaking and petrified.

"Ben!" he gasped. "Remember what I told you."

Then, all was searing agony. He felt as if his head was being ripped in half. Dozens of memories spun around inside his brain, half-remembered, departing.

She was sucking them out of him, leaving him nothing more than a hollow husk.

Suddenly, he remembered his experiences at the institution.

And he fought back.

Climbing to his knees, dizzy from pain, he clenched his teeth against the assault and closed his eyes.

He was rewarded by an unbelieving scream from Aunt Olivia and an instant lessening of her attack.

Opening his eyes, he saw she lay sprawled on the ground, her eyes wide and glassy. She was fumbling with her purse, struggling to open it.

"She's got a gun!" Ben yelled, and Chris saw him snap his eyes shut forcefully.

Aunt Olivia screamed under Ben's power, and the gun fired.

A spray of material, grayish and powdery, exploded from the dead man's back, ripping through his suit and carrying a patch of it in its wake.

Uncle Frank stumbled backward a step, but made no sound. As if awaiting a signal, he slowly, gently closed his eyes.

*The dead remember,* Chris thought. *And the dead can forget.*

Aunt Olivia wailed in wide-eyed agony, and dropped the gun. She brought her gloved hands to her head as if to hold it together.

Chris felt her trying to fight, but her attack was split between the three of them, and it was weak and flagging.

Sadness descending over him, he closed his eyes, too.

There was a keening, upward spiraling shriek, which flooded his senses.

Then, silence.

Panting, his heart beating wildly, he opened his eyes.

Ben was to his left, trembling, his eyes still tightly shut.

Uncle Frank stood in front of him, near where Aunt Olivia had been.

She was gone, forgotten.

The dead man turned to Chris, his dark eyes staring.

"All is forgotten," he said. "Now, I implore you to release me from your memory, so that I may join her."

"Of course," Chris whispered, his throat dry. Ben stood beside him, his small hand seeking the comfort of Chris's.

"Release those you love," the corpse intoned. "Memory is too cruel."

With great solemnity, Uncle Frank closed his tattered eyelids. And so did Ben and Chris.

A moment later, they were the only two on the road.

On the way home, the effects of Aunt Olivia's passing became noticeable.

"You're bigger," Chris said, stopping in the road behind Ben.

"Huh?" the boy said, and was startled by the deepness of his own voice. "Oh my gosh, what's happening?"

Chris smiled. "You're growing up. Without Aunt Olivia around to keep you down, you're progressing to your true age. That'd be around thirty-four or so, right?"

"I guess so," Ben answered, beginning to feel nauseated. "I don't feel like I'm thirty-four. I feel like I'm ten."

"Well," Chris said, putting his arm around the boy's shoulders. "I'd bet that you're about twelve right now. Which means that we better get out of town quick and move where there are a lot of girls. Something tells me that you're going to need them."

The house, too, had begun to show its real age. The porch was warped, the paint peeling, and pieces of its siding were cracked and hanging. Inside, furniture had collapsed under its own weight.

The house groaned and creaked disturbingly as they quickly packed their bags, adding clothes grabbed from other rooms. Ben had already begun growing out of the clothes he was wearing. A fine sheen of peach fuzz covered his face, and he was getting taller, lanky.

Once back outside, they climbed into the Dodge pickup, and Chris started the engine.

"Where are we going?" Ben asked.

"To get Emma. To get my wife," he said, throwing the truck into reverse just as the roof collapsed into the house, shattering the upstairs windows and raising a large cloud of cement and plaster dust that rolled across the yard.

Emma sat in front of the remains of her own house, her head in her hands. As the truck approached, she looked up, wiped her eyes.

"Emma?" Chris yelled, leaping from the cab. "Are you okay?"

She collapsed as he approached, sobbing hysterically.

"I thought she'd killed you. I thought she was punishing us again," she said, gesturing toward the pile of rubble that used to be her home. "I didn't think you'd come back again. Ever. I…"

"Shh," he whispered, pulling her to her feet, crushing her in his embrace. "For better or worse, it's done. She's gone and forgotten. And the town's going back to the way it would have been without her. Everything's been released.

"Your parents?"

"Gone," she sniffed. "I'm sad, but happy. Just the opposite of how it used to be when she held us all in her memory. I'm glad my mother and father finally got to rest after so long. Glad that they got to finally see the real you. The *you* I knew and fell in love with. And never forgot."

He hugged her again, kissed her lightly.

## OBJECT PERMANENCE

"I don't want to talk about memory or forgetting again. Ever. It's a hateful art," he said, opening the truck door and helping her in.

Their luggage tumbled in the bed as the truck squealed through the curve that led out of town.

As they passed, the road sign that once read MISSION SPRINGS, POPULATION 234," rusted from its post and fell into a dense stand of weeds by the side of what was now a crumbling, poorly maintained back road.

And faded, faded.

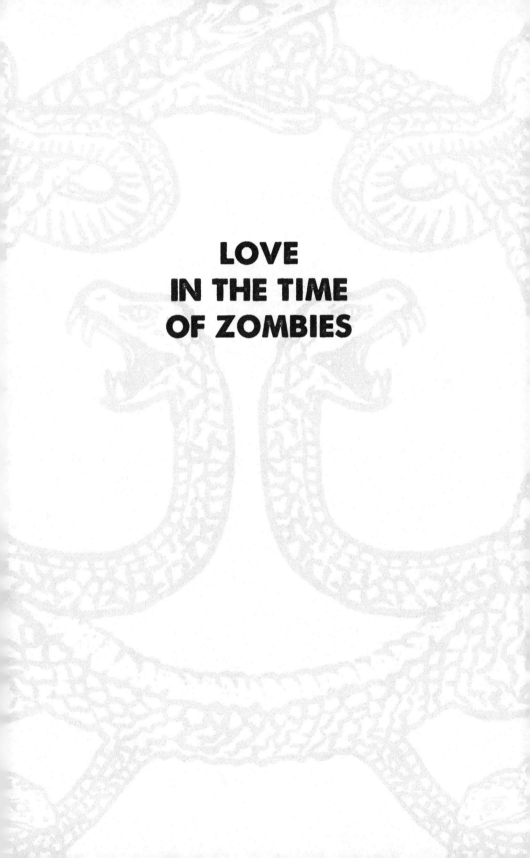

# LOVE IN THE TIME OF ZOMBIES

It was inevitable: the scent of bitter almonds always reminded him of the fate of unrequited love. It was their smell—*her* smell—a cloud of aroma that hung in the air because of them, followed them, emanating from them so powerfully that it was almost visible, like wavy lines of cartoon odor.

Durand told himself that he'd still love her even if she smelled of, well, what she looked like she'd smell of: rotting meat, clotted blood, the fish-stink of pus, the sweltering, bus-stop smell of urine or even the hazy, brown smell of feces.

But now, just almonds, burned, bitter almonds. And the Linda Ronstadt disc on the CD player in the store, playing "Long, Long Time" over and over again. That's all he had left of her, of it all.

Millstadt was a small, isolated Midwestern town in the middle of hundreds of miles of flat farmland, stretching from horizon to horizon, like a horizon unto itself. When it came, whatever *it* was, the world—if the world had any thought of Millstadt whatsoever—quickly forgot the rural community.

Durand had awoken that morning, like any other, to go to work at the cement plant. He'd showered, dressed, ate a bowl of Count Chocula over the cluttered sink in his trailer. He didn't listen to the TV or radio or read a newspaper, not that they'd have been much help that morning. The papers were too late to cover it. By the time it happened, there was no one left to write the news, edit the news, read the news. And the radio and TV were filled with, well, static mostly, and screaming.

He drove streets that didn't seem unusually quiet or empty to him. On Main Street, though, he began to sense that something was amiss. A few cars were parked diagonally in front of Millstadt Hardware, the Busy Bee Cafe and Dover Pharmacy, as on most mornings. But more than a few cars were simply stopped mid-street, doors open, some running.

More disturbing were the bodies, sprawled still and dark. Durand recognized Ina Thorpe from the DMV office—she was the only nice one there—Mr. Tucker from the Feed Store, and was that little Bobby Chavez sprawled on the curb, one sneaker tumbled across the sidewalk and a pool of dark liquid growing beneath him?

In a daze, Durand had stopped his car, reached beneath his seat to get his gun. It was a .45, registered, loaded and ready for business. He carried the gun cocked and pointed at the ground as he crept up on the body of Mr. Tucker. Bending, he saw a dark smear on the asphalt beneath Mr. Tucker, and he snatched his hand back.

*Terrorists!*

Still crouched, he scanned the stores that lined Main Street, their roofs, their windows, the likely hiding places for any Jihadists or Iranians looking to off a few Americans in Millstadt. When he returned his attention to the street, he saw stout Ina Thorpe roll over, saw blood running from a ragged wound that had opened the side of her face enough to reveal her small, peg teeth grinding a wad of something that looked awfully like part of her own cheek.

# LOVE IN THE TIME OF ZOMBIES

He saw Bobby Chavez's shoeless foot twitch violently, as if electricity had passed through it, then suddenly stop. Saw him crawl to his feet, fix Durand with one good eye; the other cloudy pink and turned impossibly in its socket toward the sky.

And he heard the low, gassy moan that escaped Marty Fretwell, a guy he had gone to high school with, as he shambled slowly in his direction. It was the deep, satisfied belch of a person who had just pushed himself from the dinner table. The only things that Marty Fretwell wore were a stained pair of white Fruit of the Loom briefs and an open-mouthed expression of absolute blankness.

His near nakedness aside, though, the worst of it took Durand a moment to absorb.

Marty Fretwell was missing his right arm.

It hadn't gone quietly, either. It had been ripped off, or *gnawed* off. What remained was a mangled red mess that dangled from his shoulder like wet fringe. Blood still pumped sluggishly from the wound, spattering the street and the side of Marty's naked body with each lurching step.

"You've got a gun, for Chrissakes!" Durand could tell that it came from behind the cafe's glass door, held open just a crack. "Shoot them!"

*Shoot them?* Shoot a couple of neighbors who'd been hurt in a goddamn terrorist attack?

Then, Marty Fretwell was trying to wrap his one good arm around him. Durand, disgusted but confused, wriggled in the man's slick grip, pulled away and stepped directly into Ina. With her two good arms, she clamped onto him with a strength that belied her age; as if she'd won him as a prize at the county fair and was unwilling to give him up.

"Jesus, Ina! What the f—"

139

Her teeth clacked together an inch from his denim work shirt, with a sound like a pair of garden shears snapping shut.

"Shoot her, you idiot! Do you wanna end up like one of them?"

Durand saw that they were closing in on him. All of them bloodied, all of them moving slowly and haltingly.

"Like them?" he yelled, stepping away from the weird, advancing group.

"Zombies!"

*Zombies?* The voice might as well have said werewolves or vampires or honest politicians, as far as Durand was concerned.

Then, Bobby Chavez darted forward with astonishing speed, coming in below his gun, clamping onto Durand's jean-clad left calf with his dirty, blood-grimed mouth.

A moment of astonishment was followed by one of pain. The kid had bitten him, not hard enough to get through the denim, but enough to hurt.

"Fuck this shit!" Durand yelled, and kicked like he'd done when he punted the ball for the winning field goal at the high school football championship years ago. Bobby Chavez flopped through the air about three feet, landed hard on the pavement.

"Fucking shoot them you fucking fucktard. Shoot them!"

He'd never shot at another living human before, and even when the clip was empty, that record would stand.

The first shot went wild, striking Tucker's car in the radiator, which hissed in exasperation.

Durand took a deep breath, aimed more carefully, shot again.

This time, it struck Ina in the chest, raising a little red bloom that soaked through her sweater and the tasteful, lace-topped white blouse it covered, knocking her ass over tea-kettle backward.

There was a long, raspy sigh of frustration from the cafe, as annoyed as Tucker's radiator.

"Have you ever seen a movie? In the head, in the fucking head!"

Durand swallowed, raised the gun again.

A flash and a kick, and the top of Marty's head, surmounted by a halo of wild bed hair, disappeared in a red haze. The rest of his body stood there for a moment, spun in on itself, fell to the road.

There was an excited, high-pitched whoop of encouragement from the cafe.

Quickly, before he could lose his nerve, Durand dropped Tucker as definitively as he had Marty.

Already, both Ina and Bobby were moving again, climbing to their feet.

Ina's head exploded. The little pair of silver glasses she wore on a chain around her neck went spinning off into the air, nothing left to keep them draped over her bosom.

The boy came on, limping a bit, his one eye still dead, still pointed upward.

"What are you waiting for? Do it!"

Durand grimaced in anger at the goading voice, closed his eyes and pulled the trigger.

When he opened them again, Bobby Chavez was minus both his sneakers and both his eyes.

Durand stood there for a moment, turning his head, surveying what he'd done.

*Four people I know, four neighbors, and one of them a kid for Chrissake. Dead. Sprawled on the street, leaking blood, headless.*

And he'd done it. He, Durand Evars.

"Unless you're planning on giving them mouth to mouth, get in here, dammit!"

Durand stumbled into the cafe, collapsed into a chair at an empty table. His heart was racing and his entire body was shaking. He ran both hands over his head, through his hair and took a long, trembling breath. Through his interlaced fingers, he heard the click of the cafe door being locked.

He came back to reality at the sound of a glass thumping onto the table before him. Orange juice sloshed, pooled near his hand.

"Sorry. You need something to drink, and that's the strongest stuff this place's got." It was the voice that had been shouting at him before.

Durand nodded his thanks, took the glass, drained it.

"Coffee?"

"Uhh…sure…hold on a sec." He heard the guy dash behind the counter. "Milk or sugar or anything?"

Durand shook his head vaguely, looked up. The voice belonged to a man he guessed to be in his early twenties , scruffy in the way that generation thinks is attractive, with uncombed hair and an unshaven face. He wore a torn, hooded sweatshirt that zipped up the front, splitting the one word, AUBURN, that arched across it.

He watched the guy grab a china coffee cup, fill it with black liquid. The coffee was hot, strong, bitter; he took several long sips, let the steaming liquid trickle down his tight throat.

"Scott Gibbons," the man said, offering his hand.

Reaching out absently, Durand shook it. "Durand Evars."

Gibbons took a seat at the table.

"For a minute there, I thought you were gonna end up as one of them," he said.

"What the fuck happened?"

Gibbons looked at his half-empty cup of coffee.

"Well, that's probably gonna require a whole pot. I'll make a fresh one."

# LOVE IN THE TIME OF ZOMBIES

Scott told him that the news had started on CNN at about one o'clock in the morning. Strange, multiple reports of people being killed in what looked like random attacks all across the globe. The automatic assumption was a large-scale, coordinated terrorist attack. But when the same reports started coming in from Pakistan, Iran and Saudi Arabia, this theory went by the wayside.

Right before the news went off the air, there were the first hesitant, disbelieving reports of the dead rising and attacking the living.

"I stay up late online gaming," Scott said, drinking what must have been his tenth glass of Mountain Dew. He talked in fast bursts, and his leg jigged nervously. "I had the TV on and was kinda half watching. When they got to the stuff about the dead coming back and shit, I just thought it must be like *War of the Worlds* or something. You know, like back when they ran that movie on TV in the fifties and people freaked and shit because they thought it was real?"

Durand considered correcting him for a second, let it go.

"Have you seen other people...*live* people?" Durand was finally able to croak.

Scott looked over the rim of his chipped plastic soda cup, turned his eyes away.

"Sure...ummm...well, this place was full when I got here," he said, acting nervous for the first time since he'd met Durand. "It opens at about 5:00 a.m., you know, for the farmers and shit. I walked here to get something to eat—"

"From where?"

"My house, over on West Madison," he said, then blushed. "Well, my ma's house. I live—"

"In the basement?" Durand finished, with a wry smile.

Scott nodded, embarrassed.

"Hey, no big deal. I live in a trailer, so we're even."

Scott's blush faded, and a big, loopy grin appeared on his face. "Cool. Anyway, it was packed. Someone came in...I think it was that older guy you plugged out there...and said to turn on the radio. When people heard what was going on, a lot of 'em freaked and left. A few stayed...well, until the dead ones started showing up. Then the place pretty much cleared out."

Durand sipped at his cooling coffee. "How come you stayed?"

That brought the blush back to the young man's face. "Well, when that all went down, I knew it wasn't a hoax anymore. So, I... uhhh...called home. No one answered. My ma...well, she doesn't work...and...she woulda answered the phone if she'd been...if she wasn't....*shit*..."

"Hey, man," Durand said, seeing his eyes welling with tears. "I get it. Anyone else?"

Scott sniffled, shook his head, self-consciously wiped his tears. "I locked the door after that, hid behind the counter. Until I heard your truck, then I came out to see. I figured, a truck, you know, they're probably not driving."

Durand drained his coffee, turned his attention to the window. "Well, they don't seem particularly interested in us. I'd feel a whole lot better, though, if we found a safer place. They could break right through this window, and we'd be fucked."

"Not my place," Scott said, shaking his head at returning home and facing an undead mother.

"Sure. Not my place either. We need to find somewhere secure that has water and food and toilets. Who knows how long we're going to be on our own." He turned back to Scott. "You sure you haven't seen anyone else alive?"

Scott shook his head.

Durand thought he saw a blush return to his face.

By the end of the first week, they'd made their home in the cavernous Bargain Barn Super Center. It was on the outskirts of Millstadt's small downtown, completely encircled by a 10-foot security fence that could be closed and locked. It was stocked, literally to the metal rafters, with food, drinks, toiletries, even guns and ammo. It had bathrooms, running water and plenty of televisions and radios, should these ever again prove useful.

Moreover, since the store hadn't been open when everything started, it was empty of people, living or dead. Even though locked up, they found a key still stuck in the employee entrance door at the back, an enormous ring of keys dangling from it. Whoever had left it there had long since gone.

Best of all, its front entrances were two normal-size glass doors that were easily barricaded, and not an entire wall of glass like the places on Main Street.

By this time, they'd learned a lot about their new neighbors. First, the shambling, shuffling way they moved was not an act. They were slow and awkward and seemingly without any motivation. Nothing seemed to get their attention, unless a living person got too close. About two or three feet seemed the limit of their perception.

Within that zone, something seemed to click in their undead brains; they suddenly developed a strength, an almost reptile agility.

But there was no intelligence behind their eyes. No hive mind or animal consciousness, as the movies sometimes showed. They were not smart or capable of figuring out even simple problems. There's was a primitive, almost atavistic hunger. They meandered their way through town stupidly, placidly, until something was unlucky enough to get in their way.

For the most part, you could walk right past one on the street, keeping your distance, with nothing to worry about. And even if one did notice you, came after you, turning a corner or closing a door or even hiding behind a tree was usually enough to throw them off.

After that first week, as far as both men could tell, they were the only ones left alive in town.

Everyone else was, as Scott put it, fled, dead or undead.

That morning, Durand told Scott he was leaving to do laundry. The Bargain Barn had an extensive selection of washers and dryers, but nowhere to hook them up. So, Durand had loaded a shopping cart with dirty clothes, pushed it to the Suds-N-Duds.

Scott nodded noncommittally, continued playing his PS4 on the high-def, 60-inch plasma that he'd taken up residence near. Durand waited to see if Scott was going to come along, but he had cut off the rest of the world.

The constant video game playing had begun to annoy Durand, but what aggravated him more than anything else was Scott's seeming acceptance of what was happening. No, not just acceptance; it was Scott's embrace of what was going on that bothered him.

*It was the end of the world as he knew it, and he felt fine.*

Did he want to go by his ma's house, grab a few things? Maybe give her a Christian burial?

*Nah.*

Did he want to help scout for more supplies?

*Are you kidding?*

Scott would snort, looking around the expanse of the Bargain Barn from the recliner he'd dragged to Electronics from Home Furnishings. *Exactly what are we missing?*

Did he want to come and help Durand with the laundry?

*I'll just grab some new stuff from the clothing aisle.*

Durand laughed bitterly as he pushed the cart down the street, around the decaying bodies of zombies he'd killed days earlier. It was like having a big, stupid teenager of his own. Kids of any kind were something that Durand had avoided during his thirty-two years on this planet.

It wasn't as if he had been deprived of opportunities. He wasn't bad looking. To the contrary, he had a lean, spare ranginess to him that most women found deeply attractive. His blond hair was still intact, his teeth were straight and white, his eyes were a deep, deep blue. It wasn't that he hadn't had girlfriends, because he'd had quite a few.

What Durand never really had, though, was love. He'd never dated a girl he felt more strongly about—or even as strongly about—as himself. There'd been no girl he thought about all day while she was gone, fantasized about all night. He hadn't met a girl who'd made him jealous or sad or depressed or mad.

There'd never been a girl who made him feel as if he carried anything inside his chest other than a mess of squishy internal organs whose functions were less mysterious to him than that one singular emotion.

*Love.*

All that changed, though, when he met Beth McClary, but by then, she was already very, very dead.

The air was cool and fresh, the sun bright and benign. As Durand neared the front of the Suds-N-Duds, though, the wheel of his makeshift laundry cart dipped into a small pothole. The cart listed, fell over on its side like a stricken beast, scattering dirty clothes on the asphalt.

"Shit," he said, immediately looking in every direction to see how many of them were nearby, and if any of them showed any signs of coming closer.

There were only about ten that he could see from where he stood. A few clustered around the front of the post office as if waiting to mail postcards to their relatives in St. Louis or Omaha.

*Having Fun! Wish You Were Dead Here!*

About a half block away, a single man zigzagged down the center of the street in his bathrobe, muttering in the strange, guttural grunts they all seemed to make. Two women slowly circled a fire hydrant in front of the Farm Bureau office, neither taking any notice of the other or the hydrant.

A man, a woman and a young girl—who wrenched at Durand's heart in her purple, one-piece bathing suit, deflated floaties still circling her pale, blue arms—moved in a loose group on the edges of Millstone Park across the street. Their unlikely gathering made Durand think of a family leaving after an afternoon spent on the swing sets, the slides, the monkey bars.

But they were *not* a family. They had *not* been playing in the park.

Bending to collect the spilled laundry, he caught the unmistakable odor of burnt, bitter almonds from close by, looked up and saw her.

For a moment, a fleeting, sun-drenched moment, he thought—hoped—that she was alive.

She was wearing a simple, white sundress, large, almost abstract daisies patterned across it. One thin strap of the dress was missing; as was one flat, white shoe. Her hair was a pale yellow, and it came to her shoulders, straight and shimmering in the gentle sun. Her eyes were bright blue, like his own, and even though they seemed listless and unfocused, there was something about them that tugged at him.

Her skin looked alabaster in the late morning light, pale as ivory, soft as angora. He didn't know why her skin wasn't the blue or green-tinged mess like the others. He knew only that it gave her face life, or at least a semblance of life that her blue eyes, vacant and dull, belied.

A purse hung over her shoulder and around her neck, in the way that women wear purses when they're afraid someone might snatch them.

Blood marred her otherwise beautiful features; not much, just a thin trickle from one nostril that painted the corner of her mouth like a smudge of lipstick and a slightly thicker line that snaked from one ear, following the contours of her jaw.

It took him a moment to notice the other blood, a large patch of it, faded a rusty brown now, hiding within the splotchy daisies of her dress near her stomach.

Someone had shot her, killed her.

Durand forgot about the laundry, about the 2,000 living dead lurching around a town that itself was more dead than alive, forgot about nearly everything that had been floating through his brain over the last two weeks.

The sunlight, thick and syrupy, fell upon her from behind, lit her hair, cast a penumbra around her form, made her seem to glow from within.

After a second, Durand found that his breathing had stopped.

After another, he found that his heart had started.

There was something about her that transcended her beauty; an essential sadness, as if somehow, on some level, she was aware of what had happened to her. That, her tattered dress, her missing shoe, made his heart ache for her, made him want to help her in some way.

*Help her.* And the voice in his head was suddenly Scott's. *She's dead.*

He took a deep, almost strangled breath, tore his eyes away, hurriedly began gathering the laundry, piling it into the cart. Suddenly, much to his chagrin, he was once again a nervous teenager, embarrassed in front of a girl. He felt heat slam into his face. The tips of his ears glowed with humiliation.

The cart's wheel was still caught in the rut, resisting his attempts to push it. Angrily, he shoved it forward over the curb at the front of the Suds-N-Duds.

But the girl still stood there, still stared past him.

*Because,* he sighed, *she's dead.*

He didn't need to be embarrassed at how ridiculous he'd looked. He didn't need to worry about impressing her or if she'd noticed him or what she thought of him.

*She's dead.*

Pushing the cart past her, he muscled his way through the unlocked door of the laundromat.

But he smiled as he passed her, smiled with both his eyes and his mouth before he let the door close behind him, the little bell ringing as if he'd won a prize.

He was already in love with her, though he didn't even know it yet, didn't know her.

*Couldn't* know her.

## LOVE IN THE TIME OF ZOMBIES

"You saw a girl down by the laundromat?" Scott asked as Durand folded clothes and stacked them atop a ping-pong table. Durand had the CD player on the big stereo turned up, playing *Linda Ronstadt's Greatest Hits*, which he knew irritated Scott, but he didn't care. He was into irritating Scott these days, because Scott was irritating. And besides, he liked Linda Ronstadt. Her music reminded him of his mom, who had constantly played her albums on their old record player after his father had left.

Scott neither looked up nor stopped playing his game. At his feet, lay empty bags of Doritos, empty cans of Red Bull taken from an enormous, shrink-wrapped cube of the stuff he had used a forklift to wheel over near his recliner.

"Yep."

It took him a moment to realize that Scott's fingers were no longer clicking the buttons of the controller he held.

"Wait," he said, turning in his chair. "You saw a girl. A *girl*?"

"Yep."

"Not a zombie, but an actual, real *girl*...well...I mean...what the fuck, hombre? Why didn't you bring her—"

"She *is* a zombie. A zombie girl."

"A zombie girl? Well, fuck *that*."

Scott let out a petulant little puff of air. The beat of tapping fingers sounded again.

"Exactly what are you doing, bro?"

Scott sidled up to Durand the following morning, a can of Red Bull in one hand and a package of Twinkies in the other. Durand was digging through a pile of women's shoes arranged on a table. There were mules, slingbacks, moccasins, flats, all in different colors and styles.

"I'm looking for a pair of shoes," Durand muttered, studying Scott's face as he took in this news. Durand saw Scott's eyes narrow as he noticed the backpack on the floor, the green dress stuffed into it.

Scott slurped down the rest of his Red Bull and cleared his throat. "You're not...you know...a fuckin' cross-dresser, are you? A tranny or something?"

"No, they're for...someone."

"*Someone*? Exactly who might that be?"

Durand turned back to the table full of shoes, but got a mental picture of Scott, his t-shirt stained with orange hand-swipes from the Doritos and Cheetos that comprised his diet these days. He saw the week-old growth of beard, the greasy, matted hair, the bleary eyes. Mostly, though, he saw his arm cocked back, preparing to toss the empty Red Bull can into the depths of the store.

Then he actually heard the clatter of the can.

"I'm not picking that up," Durand said, stepping back from the table and checking the clip in his gun, freshly loaded from the seemingly inexhaustible supply of ammo found in Sporting Goods. Satisfied, he thumbed the safety, tucked it into the waistband of his pants.

It took Scott a minute. "Oh, hell no...*her?* You're picking out shoes for a zombie?"

"She's missing a shoe...and I just...well, I want to make sure she doesn't mess up her feet too much," he said, realizing how stupid that sounded.

"And the dress?"

Durand made no attempt to answer for that.

"Dude, she's a fucking zombie, she's not concerned with her clothes or her fucking footwear anymore. Or her feet, for that matter."

"Well, I'm doing this. Stay or come, it's up to you," Durand said, shouldering the pack.

"Oh, no, I'm coming. I've got to fucking see this shit go down."

The first time they had seen them eating, he and Scott had been staying in a house off Main Street, before taking residence in the Bargain Barn. Scott had somehow managed to cut himself opening a can of tuna, and they'd been unable to find even a Band-Aid in the house's medicine cabinets, just an old Fleet enema bottle and a prescription for Darvocet from 2003.

So, they'd hiked to Dover Pharmacy, dodging zombies along the way, shooting any that got too close. Corpses littered the streets now, just a few days after it had all gone down, and it made for grisly scenery. Bodies lay here and there, heads blown off, brains and blood and gore spattered everywhere.

The men turned the corner from Sixth Avenue onto Main and saw vague shadows between two buildings in the wan light of the alley. Then, they heard the sounds: teeth tearing raw meat, scraping bone, cracking and grinding, and over it all, the wet, smacking lips, the grunts of pleasure.

As their eyes adjusted, they saw four of them squatting around an indistinct mess of liquid darkness that sent rivulets of inky liquid across the uneven, trash-strewn concrete.

The figures didn't turn, didn't rise to their feet; and it was difficult to see what they were doing.

Even though, both men knew, both men knew *exactly* what they were doing.

Durand raised the gun, stepped into the alley.

Scott grabbed his arm, looked at him without saying anything. But his face said it all.

*Are you crazy, bro?*

Durand shrugged him off.

Wished he hadn't.

The four zombies—because, oh yes, they were zombies now, there could be no doubt anymore—sat on their haunches, reaching their filthy, gore-encrusted hands into an undefined mess, grabbing whatever they found, stuffing it greedily into their bloodied mouths and chewing, swallowing.

*Gulping.*

Durand stood gape-jawed for a long while, the gun hanging in the air before him, until he saw a hand, an intact hand—pallid, pale, palm up—jutting from the pile. Then, it came into focus, its details leapt up at him, and he could see an arm, a burst chest, the remains of a thigh, a ruined, gnawed face, with one eye, one remaining bright, blue eye gazing balefully from its wreckage.

As if yanked by unseen strings, the four zombies sprang to their feet, spun to Durand.

Their faces were empty, vacuous. There was no fierceness in them, no hatred.

Only hunger, deep, abiding hunger.

Their mouths were open, wide open, filled with blood and a pulp of chewed meat, gristle, the pink, spongy marrow of bones. Gore and spilth dribbled down their faces, caked their cheeks, matted their hair.

They bared their teeth in hunger, that was all, just hunger.

But it was enough.

Durand's gun roared four times, deafening in the confines of the alley.

It was enough.

They found her in the best of possible places, near the side of Millstadt Hardware, where its lumberyard lay behind a section of chain-link fence. She was trapped where the fence formed a corner, thumping against it repeatedly like a child's windup toy that's hit a wall. She would try to move forward, turn left or right, but found herself blocked. The thought of simply stepping backward seemed beyond her, whatever she was now.

"That's her," Durand shouted, racing forward, then catching himself and skidding to a stop in a cloud of dust and gravel.

Scott followed slowly, his face screwing into a mask of doubt and shock.

"That's her?" he squeaked in a weak echo. "*Really?*"

Her hair looked just as shiny as before, her skin as pale and translucent. The burning almond reek of them came off her, and Durand took it in, decided that it wasn't so bad after all.

Shrugging out of the backpack, he ripped the zipper open, pulled out the long, pale green sundress he'd found in the store, held it up to see if it might fit her. The shoes were a little dicier. It was hard to tell how small her feet were. She was probably no more than five feet four inches tall; likely twenty-four or twenty-five years old.

Scott hung back as he did this, gnawing at the ragged stumps of his nails.

"You gonna help?" Durand asked, turning to him.

Nodding absently, Scott took a single step.

"What the hell's wrong with you?"

Scott snapped his eyes to Durand's, shook his head innocently.

Durand touched his shoulder, noticing that Scott flinched, that his eyes bulged in his head.

"There," he said, pointing to a side door that led into the store. On the other side of the fence was a similar door about ten feet away along the same wall. "Go into the store, then come around so you're inside the lumberyard."

"And then…"

Duran turned to him, smiled. "Step over to the fence and occupy her attention."

Scott paled visibly.

"You'll have the fence between you." Durand winked, slapping him on the back. "She's not gonna chew through it."

Scott smirked, opened his mouth to say something sarcastic. Instead he walked to the entrance, his shoulders slumping, opened the door, disappeared inside.

When he was gone, Durand took a step closer to her, then another. With only about a yard and a half to go, he noticed that her movements stopped, her head cocked as if she'd smelled something. Durand heard the guttural sounds she made deep in her throat.

The lumberyard door opened and Scott exited, hesitated, walked to the fence. When he was less than three feet away, the girl uttered a groan of hunger, pushed into the fence, straining against it, her fingers curled into the links.

Scott jumped back. "Jesus tap-dancing Christ! I'm so fucking outta here!"

"No! She's not gonna get you. Just distract her while I do this."

"This is fucked up, bro. Truly fucked up." Scott held his ground but couldn't look at the girl, couldn't look into her eyes.

Tentatively, Durand stepped nearer. He'd never been this close to one of them, and the smell of almonds was almost overpowering. But all her attention was focused on Scott. He could hear the disturbing sound of her teeth clacking together, snapping.

# LOVE IN THE TIME OF ZOMBIES

Durand patted the grip of the gun tucked in his waistband, just in case, then lifted his arm slowly, reached out.

"Jesus, bro...don't fucking *touch* her..."

But Durand ignored him, extended his hand, let it graze the top of her bare shoulder.

She didn't turn on him, didn't stop trying to get at Scott.

Durand's hand lingered there, feeling the softness of her skin. So strange to feel skin this cool. It drifted over her shoulder, across the nape of her neck. The ends of her hair, so fine and soft, tickled at the back of his hand.

"Ummm...bro...this is weird. Can we please, *please* wrap this up?"

Durand removed his hand slowly, as much to avoid drawing her attention as to let his hand linger on her cool, silky skin.

He saw the strap of her purse across her shoulder, around her neck.

"Just a sec," he told Scott, then backed away, opened his pack and rooted inside. He returned with scissors, cut the purse's strap. It fell to the ground with a weary plop. On a whim, he snipped the one thin strap that held the top of the sundress in place. To his surprise, it fluttered to the ground, pooling at her feet.

"This is some seriously fucked up shit you're doin', man. *Seriously.*"

She was thinly built, but nicely, with a pleasing symmetry to the width of her shoulders, the length of her back, the curve of her buttocks. She wore a plain white bra and a plain white pair of panties. Her skin, as it slid across her shoulders, swept up the arch of her hips, down her legs, was soft and white as a cloud.

Broken only by the hole that someone had blasted in her.

The wound, about the size of an egg, was low on her left side, near her kidneys. It was bright and wet with blood, but it had stopped leaking long ago. Durand couldn't guess as to who had shot her or why or whether it was before or after she was dead.

A sudden tidal wave of sadness and pity rolled over him, and tears filled his eyes. To hide them, he turned, grabbed the shoes from the pack. Kneeling carefully behind her, he ran a hand along the calf of her left leg, the one missing a shoe. Feeling like the prince in the Cinderella story, he slipped the white canvas flat he'd chosen onto her foot.

Impossibly, crazily, it fit.

He lowered that foot to the ground again, took the other, removed that shoe and slid the remaining new one on.

For a moment, just a moment, he thought he would lean forward just a bit and let his lips touch the back of her cool calf, kiss the soft, firm skin there.

But he didn't.

"You about finished with your fucking Hallmark moment?"

"No."

"*No?* Fuck...*no?*"

"Well, we can't leave her in her underwear."

Slipping the new sundress over her head involved both of them climbing the opposite side of the fence, getting her to reach up to them and extend both arms fully, like a child waiting for her mother to slip a shirt over her body. It went on easier than it had any right to, slithered into place over her as if she had simply shrugged into it.

They descended the fence, and when they had retreated beyond that strange, magical point, whatever that distance was, she lost interest in them. Her mouth went slack, her arms slid down the chain-link, her eyes stared straight, not seeing them. She bumped into the fence, turned a little right, bumped again, turned a little left, bumped again.

Before leaving, Durand hefted the backpack. Almost as an afterthought, he grabbed the purse, too.

Scott gave him a strange, measuring look, but said nothing.

They left her there, in her new dress, her new shoes, the best dressed zombie in Millstadt.

As they walked back to the Bargain Barn, Scott turned to him.

"If you're thinking of coming back tomorrow and applying her makeup, dude, count me out."

"Her name's Beth McClary," Durand said later that night, over a pan of Stouffer's frozen lasagna, a loaf of garlic cheese bread and a bottle of red wine. They ate dinner under a gazebo on a patio furniture display. Music from the stereo in Electronics played in the background.

Durand ate with gusto, but Scott picked at his food, pushed it around on the plate, sniffed at the wine.

"How'd you find that out?" Scott asked, not really all that interested.

"Her purse. She had a driver's license and all sorts of stuff," Durand replied, shoveling in another forkful of crusty, overcooked lasagna. "I was right. She's twenty-four years old. If she's a townie, she probably went to school with you. How old did you say you were?"

"I'm twenty-eight," Scott said, looking up guiltily. "I don't remember a Beth…what's her name…"

"McClary."

"Nope. After my time."

Durand chewed thoughtfully, knew with quiet clarity that Scott was lying. There was no way he was twenty-eight, no way. He couldn't have been more than twenty-two or twenty-three at most. And if he was lying about that, there was something deeper going on that Durand couldn't put his finger on.

"She lived on Washington Street, in those new apartments," he continued, letting it go for now.

Scott harrumphed, dropped his fork onto his plate. "Overpriced apartments filled with snotty, tight-assed people too hoighty-toighty for the rest of us. Lot of fucking good it did 'em."

"What the fuck is wrong with you?"

"*You,* that's what's fucking wrong with me," Scott said, his face turning red. "You love her. Don't you? You fucking *love* a fucking *zombie.* Do you know how seriously fucked up that is...how seriously fucked up what we did today is?"

"I don't..." Durand began. What was the point in denying?

"You do! Don't fucking lie. Otherwise, what was that all that shit today?"

Durand said nothing, toyed with the food on his plate.

Scott's face twisted in anger. "And will you please turn off that fucking music? Fucking Linda whatever-the-hell-her-name-is is really getting on my fucking last nerve!"

He pushed himself from the table, stalked off.

After a minute, Durand heard the chaotic sounds of Scott's video games echoing through the store, turned up extra loud to drown out the stereo.

Durand awoke later that night, his head throbbing, his gut churning, his mind spinning. Too much wine, too much lasagna.

Too many thoughts of her, of Beth McClary.

He lay there, listened to every click, bump and tick the Bargain Barn had to offer, echoing in its cavernous guts. Scott must be asleep; there were no gun blasts, no explosions. Durand looked at the clock radio on his nightstand. It was just a little after 2:00 a.m.

Sighing at what he was thinking, he threw the covers back, grabbed his clothes, padded quietly to the washroom. He visited the toilet first, and when he was done, he splashed cold water on his face, looked at himself in the mirror. He needed a shave. There were bags under his eyes, and he'd have to find some way of cutting his own hair soon. But he figured he still looked pretty damn good for a man at the end of the world.

The moon wasn't yet full, but it was close, and its brilliant, silver light shone down unfiltered by clouds. He almost didn't need the flashlight he had brought with him. The night was cool. Summer was fading fast, and the hot, humid edge of the air was dulling. He wondered how the zombies would handle the cold weather. Would it have any effect on them at all? Probably not. Nothing else did.

He wondered how he and Scott would handle the cold weather. The Bargain Barn had heaters, sure, but what would happen when the power went off? And he knew it would, sooner or later. No lights, no power, no water.

What then?

He walked by the lumberyard, but Beth wasn't there, still bumping into the fence as he'd assumed. Where could she be? What direction would she have gone, and how far?

When he got to Jefferson Street, he stopped.

A few of them straggled by, but only one came close, and Durand shot him before he even had a chance to utter a groan. He thought it might have been his gym teacher from high school.

She wasn't at the hardware store, and Durand shined the light to see if there were any clues as to where she might have gone.

*Yeah, like she would have left a note or something.*

That struck him as silly, and he laughed, but stopped suddenly. The sound of his laughter on the night air, loud and alone, spooked him deeply.

He turned on Fourth Avenue, then on Monroe. He shot two more almost absently, but he didn't see her.

He circled back, passed the Suds-N-Duds. Just as he was about to give up, return to bed, he saw her. It was the dress, the new green dress that caught his eye, a pale silvery turquoise in the moonlight. She stood next to a tree at the entrance to Millstone Park, leaned against it, almost as if—

*Almost as if she slept.*

But that was impossible, they'd never slept, at least he'd never seen them sleep or even rest before.

He shined the light on her from across the street, but she didn't move, didn't react. So he went to her. When he stepped onto the path that led into the park, he stopped. He was perhaps a dozen feet from her. She leaned against the oak tree, her arms limp at her sides, her head resting against its bark.

*And her eyes were shut.*

For a moment, he didn't know what to do. Was she *really* dead now?

And if she was sleeping, what exactly did that mean?

He was dimly aware that he'd not even thought about taking the gun from his waistband.

When he was two feet from her, well within the zone, he paused. He put the light directly in her face, watched her eyes. A small dark smear across her lips and chin marred her looks; otherwise it was the beautiful, serene face of a young woman sleeping peacefully.

## LOVE IN THE TIME OF ZOMBIES

He heard small, grunting breaths coming out of her. His heart racing, he paused, but her eyes remained closed.

Her smell enveloped him, entered his nostrils, his mouth. He reached out again, knowing that he shouldn't, knowing that it was stupid, futile, even weird, as Scott had suggested. But he reached out anyway, let his fingers stroke her cheek.

No reaction. He was almost disappointed. Almost.

Another small step and he was going to do it, he had to do it, it mattered somehow to him, mattered in a way that he didn't understand.

His brain seemed unable to argue. It simply shrugged, stepped aside.

And his heart, his mad, foolish, needful heart won.

He closed his eyes, kissed her cheek, softly.

When she still didn't react, he slid his lips across her face, found hers and kissed them. They were cold and sticky, but he kissed them anyway, gently, offering only the lightest touch.

But it was a kiss, his first kiss with Beth McClary, his first kiss with a dead girl.

Backing away, he licked his lips, expecting to taste almonds, and instead tasted blood, flat and metallic. Absently, he wiped his mouth with the back of his hand.

Beth still slept. And Durand thought her the most beautiful thing in the world, so lovely, so fragile, so innocent looking.

He stayed there, in the early morning light, under the waning moon, and watched her.

On the way back to the Bargain Barn, he shot six more zombies, smiling as he did so.

When he crawled into his bed, he saw that it was almost 4:00 a.m.

But he remained there for at least an hour, thinking of her, wondering what she was doing, picturing her sad, beautiful face. He imagined lying next to her, looking into that sweet face, sleeping in her arms.

As the sun came up, he finally fell asleep, the smell of burned, bitter almonds in his nose.

"Are you going out to drool over her again?" Scott said from his recliner. "That's all you fucking do lately. It's like you're fucking stalking the undead."

"Are you going to sit in here and play video games all day? That's all you fucking do lately," Durand shot back. "Don't begrudge me the opportunity to go out and see the one thing these days that makes me happy. Besides, what difference does it make to you?"

Scott stood and came around the chair, which surprised Durand.

"Because she's a *corpse*, man. A fucking corpse! And you know what that makes you, bro? That makes you a fucking narcoleptic. A fucking corpse lover!"

Astonished, Durand looked at him for a moment, trying to decide whether to get mad or laugh.

Instead, he simply said, "*Necrophiliac.*"

"What?"

"The word is *necrophiliac*. Pull your head out of your ass and read a book for a change."

With that, he turned and walked away.

After five steps, he glanced back at Scott, who still stood there, fuming silently.

"Oh, and I'm not a necrophiliac, for your information. She's just better company than you."

Durand tried not to let the argument with Scott ruin his good mood. He'd thought about spending the day just watching her, seeing how she spent her time. He knew it was silly…and he knew what Scott would say.

There was no way he could articulate to Scott what he was feeling for Beth; he found it difficult enough to articulate it to himself.

So, there was no way that he could admit that he was in love with a zombie.

In love with someone, *something*, that could never accept that love, return it.

He had no experience with love, real love, and so he had no experience with love that wasn't—that couldn't ever be—returned.

But he knew that he had to do something with it, make something of it, or let it go entirely.

Either way, he would have to live with it for the rest of his life.

He knew one other thing, too.

He was not prepared to let it go just yet.

Durand wanted to know all there was about her, more than he could learn from the contents of her purse. She was born August 16, 1989. Elizabeth Anne McClary. She drove a Honda of some kind. She had pictures of various people in her wallet—parents, grandparents, nieces and nephews. He didn't find a picture of anyone who looked as if he might be a boyfriend. She had a checking account at First Community Bank in town. She worked at PPI, a plant that made commercial laundry equipment.

Durand drove past the laundry plant every day on his way to the concrete plant, at least, he used to. He wondered how many times he'd seen her car in the parking lot, maybe followed her to work or back into town. He wondered how many times he'd seen her in restaurants, in the grocery store, at the gas station and never noticed her.

As he walked through town thinking of her, he passed Lyndon B. Johnson High School, his alma mater, class of 2000.

If she went to high school here, she'd be in the yearbook.

When he pushed the door open, the school had a musty, abandoned smell. There were other odors, too; mildew, chalk dust and something else, something he couldn't place. Maybe spoiled food in the cafeteria.

There were no bodies in the halls, in the classrooms, but plenty of scattered papers, discarded books, articles of stray clothing and abandoned backpacks disgorging their contents. If kids were here that morning, they dropped everything and fled with the adults or, well, the limited answers here hadn't changed in the last few weeks.

He knew exactly where he was going. Even though it had been nearly a decade and a half since he'd walked these halls as a student, little had changed. The library occupied the central portion of the building, and the doors leading to it were thrown wide open. This space still managed to maintain a sense of dignity and decorum amidst the squalor, though the mess in here was substantially less.

Durand found what he was looking for easily. A short shelf stood near the front counter, festooned with the school colors of purple and gold. Above it was tacked a homemade banner: "LBJ SCHOOL SPIRIT THROUGH THE YEARS!"

Below this was as an entire shelf of yearbooks, arranged by year, from 1946 to 2013.

## LOVE IN THE TIME OF ZOMBIES

Smiling, Durand ran his fingers down the row of spines, stopped at 2007.

He unwedged the book from between its neighbors, took it to a nearby table and sat.

It didn't take him long to find her.

She was unmistakable, stunning in her senior photo—bright blonde hair, big blue eyes, and her skin, her skin seemed just as it was now, luminous, soft, immensely touchable. He lingered over the photo for a long time, studying it intently.

What struck Durand most was the sense of her that came through the picture. She didn't seem to be posing for the camera, playing to it. She appeared to be caught in the moment, rather than looking staged or faking a smile. And in that regard she came off more like a real, down-to-earth person than a stuck-up, snooty drama queen.

*Snooty.*

That jogged Durand's mind, and he looked away from the book, tried to dredge it up.

He looked for Scott's name in the index, knowing what he would find. He found it easily, saw that Scott was a sophomore in the same book, class of '09. Durand felt his stomach flip.

*I knew he lied, but why lie about that?*

He found his picture, and it showed that Scott Gibbons, like a lot of kids his age, didn't take a good photo. He wore a shirt with a collar that was too big, that didn't button down. His hair was in complete disarray, and his face bore all the telltale signs of adolescence—the bad skin, crooked teeth and unmistakable aura of tortured self-doubt.

Looking at that photo, Durand was sure why Scott had lied.

He was sure why Scott had acted so weird when they'd first met; why he'd been so twitchy when he'd first seen Beth at the lumberyard.

Why Scott never wanted to venture out of the Bargain Barn, was so angry that Durand did.

**167**

Taking the yearbook, he left the library, left LBJ High School, and hoped that he was wrong.

Hoped that Scott had not done what he knew Scott had done.

Durand found him sitting on a bench in Millstone Park.

He didn't see Durand, wasn't paying any attention.

Scott was completely caught up in watching Beth McClary lurching through a wide field. The sun shimmered in her hair, the wind caught her dress, and for a moment, Durand was spellbound, too.

Then, he remembered why he was here. He walked up behind Scott, dropped the yearbook in his lap.

"Jesus!" Scott sputtered in surprise, leaping from the bench and shooing the yearbook off his lap as if it were a rabid animal.

Durand watched him, but said nothing, didn't apologize for scaring him.

"What the fuck are you doing, bro? Scaring me like that? Christ, if I'd had a gun…"

Durand moved his gaze conspicuously to the ground, to where the yearbook lay.

Scott acted confused, but turned to where Durand was looking.

His back slumped when he saw the yearbook.

"Why?" was all Durand could think to say.

Scott's face went slack and white. He looked like one of them now, a zombie himself. And when he started to talk, to explain what he'd done, the words fell from his mouth, as if he had no force to expel them.

"She ran up the street when they started appearing. I'd already locked myself in the cafe. She…banged on the door…wanted to be let in…and I…I…"

# LOVE IN THE TIME OF ZOMBIES

"You hid under the counter and ignored her."

Scott looked at him with annoyance.

"No, I heard her voice...I knew who it was...I mean, are you shitting me? I climbed out...for her...I went to the door. She was afraid...shit, I was afraid....I...she pleaded with me to let her in, but I wouldn't...I *couldn't*. I...saw the others walking all over, killing people, eating them...*fuck*...it was awful...*awful*..."

Durand said nothing. There was nothing to say.

"I...uhh...was afraid to open the door, afraid to let her in. Christ, she got mad. Really fucking mad, banging on the door, shaking the glass. I thought...I was afraid that she was going to break it... she'd break the glass and they'd get in and that'd be it, dude. That'd be fucking it."

"You didn't let her in," Durand said, his voice filled with contempt. "You left her out there to die with them, to be killed by them."

Again, that look of annoyed disbelief. "You don't get it, do you? I *loved* her, fucking loved her since the eighth grade. But she never paid any attention to me, was never going to. I knew that. But she banged on the door so hard that the glass shook and I could see the others, the zombies coming up behind her...I freaked. *"I shot her."*

The words didn't register at first, because they were not at all what Durand expected.

"You what?"

"I shot her. I'd started to open the door to let her in...Christ, I loved her, I couldn't leave her out there. But I saw a bunch of them coming toward the door. Fuck! I thought if I let her in, they're going to get in, too. And then...then..."

Durand stared at him in wonder. "You shot her. *You?*"

"The owner of the cafe gave me his gun when he left, told me to…to…take care of myself. She wouldn't let go of the door…wouldn't let me close it…and they were right there, dude…*right there*. So, I shot her…to keep her from getting in and to keep the others from getting in. I fucking shot her. I shot her…"

He burst into loud, braying sobs that seemed to tear loose from deep inside him. He collapsed onto the bench, huddled forward with his head on his knees and wept.

Durand didn't know what to do, how to react.

"The gun?"

"I tossed it into the grease pit at the cafe," he sobbed. "I couldn't look at it anymore. And then you come along and you have a gun, and I think it's going to be okay. But she was gone, she wasn't near the door, where she'd fallen. She was one of them, a zombie. I knew that…I fucking *knew* that. It wasn't enough that I killed her, I made her a zombie, too. Fuck…fuck…FUCK!

"Then you find a girl in town," Scott said, his voice now a low, papery whisper that made the hairs on the back of Durand's neck rise. "And what the fuck do you know, it's her."

Scott rose, turned to Durand with hatred in his eyes, his fists balled and shaking at his sides. "And if that's not enough, you fall for her. You. Fall. *For a dead girl.* For her! I can't have her for myself, even when she's a fucking *zombie!*"

Durand prepared for Scott to hurtle himself at him.

But that's exactly what Scott *didn't* do. Instead, he smiled.

"She's mine, bro. *Mine.* And I'm going to be with her…finally."

Durand hesitated, unsure of exactly what Scott meant until it was too late.

Scott's story had held his attention, kept him from focusing on where the zombies were.

Where *she* was.

## LOVE IN THE TIME OF ZOMBIES

In the time it had taken Scott to tell him what had happened, she had moved closer to them.

Scott smiled at Durand, turned and walked right into her arms.

She caught him with tremendous strength, a strength she didn't need. Scott didn't fight; instead, he embraced her, lowered his head to her shoulder like a lover.

And she slammed her mouth into his exposed neck, closed her jaws, shook her head like a puppy worrying a toy. Blood, extravagant in quantity and exuberant in color, flashed in the late sunlight, founted from his neck, gushed over his hoodie, over her new green dress, spattered onto her new white shoes.

With a rough tearing sound, oddly intimate, she jerked her head away, her mouth filled with red meat. A spray of arterial blood covered her face, and she uttered a gurgling groan, smashed her face back into the pulsing wound.

Durand pulled the gun from his waistband.

Scott turned in her arms, his head lolling on his torn neck, and looked at Durand, at the gun.

Shook his head weakly.

It took Durand a full minute to lower the gun, maybe more.

By then, Scott was the kind of dead there was no coming back from.

And still she fed, crouched over him as he slumped to the ground. She ate most of his face, leaving a wet, red ruin in the wake of her teeth and her fingers.

But he couldn't kill her either, couldn't bring himself to pull the trigger.

For a moment, just a moment, he felt an emotion, one that he had as little experience with as he did love.

*Jealousy.*

He was jealous of Scott.

But that was a crazy, ugly feeling, and he tried to push it aside, to deny it.

But then, jealousy is supposed to be a crazy, ugly feeling.

Eventually he lowered the gun, fingered the safety, slid it into his waistband.

That was weeks ago.

Durand walked slowly back to the Bargain Barn after his daily circuit of the town, after seeing her.

There weren't many left anymore, and he now thought of them as almost an endangered species. He kept the gun in his waistband, left them alone as they left him alone.

Inside the store, he went to the Electronics department. He didn't touch Scott's set up, though he'd cleaned a little, sprayed the recliner with Febreze.

Firing up the biggest stereo on display, he slipped a disc into the CD player, cranked the volume up as loud as it would go, slumped into the recliner, waited for the end of the world—however, whenever it might come.

He thought of the smell of bitter, burned almonds, Beth McClary's face, and the love he carried for her, the love he would always carry for her, regardless of her inability to return it.

And Linda Ronstadt sang the words, as if reading directly from those etched into his heart.

*Wait for the day you'll go away*
*Knowing that you warned me of the price I had to pay.*
*And life's full of flaws, who knows the cause*
*Living in the memory of a love that never was.*
*'Cause I've done everything I know to try and make you mine*
*And I think I'm gonna love you*
*For a long, long time…*

# THE LONG, LONG BREAKDOWN

*Underwater, underwater, I will meet you underwater.*
*I will find you, I will find you, in the deep and quiet water*
*In the ocean, in the ocean, we will bask in all its glory*
*In the peaceful, quiet water, I will tell you all a story*
*Of the long, long, long, long breakdown…*
*Of the long, long, long, long, long, long, breakdown…*

"Long Breakdown" – Oingo Boingo

The hand in my dream, her hand, reached up from the dark, reached through the swirling, midnight water, stretching for my hand. Our fingertips grazed. I could feel the swirls of her pads on mine, the wrinkled pruning of her wet skin.

Then it slid away, she slid away, down, down, first her face lost to the darkness—her eyes wide, filled with anoxia, filled with fear—then the slim, pale line of her arm. Finally, the flutter of her fingers swallowed by the darkness, engulfed by the water, the peaceful, quiet water.

I awoke from the nightmare again, the only nightmare I had these days that were, themselves, one long, extended nightmare. I was sitting in my bed, the covers kicked to the floor, my body slick with perspiration. My right arm was outstretched, muscles taut, sweat-covered skin shining silver in the moonlight. My hand was frozen in a rictus, grasping at the ghost of the dream that still swirled in the room, in my mind, the ghost of *her*.

I took a deep, strangled breath, filled with the reality of the loss of everything, but mainly her loss. Still her loss, always her loss. Time had not made it better, easier. Time had not in any way lessened the fact that she was no longer here.

I lowered my chin to my chest and allowed myself, there in that cool, midnight room, the sound of water lapping against the building far below, to experience a few seconds of quiet tears, denied under the sun.

*Denied in front of her.*

When I awoke, I padded into the bathroom, bright with sunshine, to void my middle-aged bladder. Finished, I pushed the handle, waited for the toilet to flush. It did, but I knew that one day it wouldn't. One day all of this would fail, and not just the toilet. And then what would we do?

Shrugging on a robe that hung on a hook behind the bathroom door, I belted it snug and walked down the hallway to the kitchen. The day was bright, brilliant, cloudless. I could see the blue of the sky through the huge plate glass windows that made up one whole wall of the penthouse apartment we shared. It bent on the horizon to meet that other blue, the green-blue of the sea, stretching in every direction as far as I could see.

Ignoring the contemporary art on the walls, the no doubt expensive sculptures that squatted on their white pedestals, I entered the kitchen. It was sleek and modern and bright, all stainless steel and cool glass the color of the sea, the damnable sea. White cabinets, pickled white wood, white marble—it was as cold as an arctic landscape; antiseptic as an autopsy room.

I moved the kettle to the tap, turned on the water, again half-expecting it not to gush forth.

*Someday, someday.*

But it did, as it had every day for the last fourteen years, and I filled the kettle, turned it on. Electricity still worked, too. Within minutes,

## THE LONG, LONG BREAKDOWN

I had boiling water, a cup, instant coffee. A few scalding swigs of this and I meandered through the far rooms of the penthouse, what had been a media room, a dining room, a living room.

Now, all rearranged for me and my daughter and this life, filled with the detritus we'd collected on our trips, bursting with camping equipment, batteries, flashlights, radios, maps and books, hundreds, *thousands* of books, stacked against the interior walls, the exterior glass. Books on every subject imaginable, fiction and non-fiction, sorted by topic.

Skirting a leaning tower of these, I stepped into the sunken living room, wrapped in glass on three sides, dazzling in the morning sun, the reflected light of the all-encompassing water. A useless big-screen TV hung above an equally useless fireplace. Coffee tables of etched glass were at the center of an expanse of leather furniture, costly stuff. More art here and there, curios, knickknacks. The penthouse had been the home—well, *one* of the homes—of a billionaire tech guy who spent some of his time and money here in Miami.

The wealthy young man was gone now, probably anyway. I had no way of knowing. Most of the tech places—Silicon Valley, Cupertino, Seattle—were gone too, below the water.

The end of the room opened in enormous panels of sliding glass onto a patio large enough to land a helicopter in its day, certainly large enough to host a cocktail party of beautiful, wealthy people, which I supposed that it had, probably quite often. The patio was encircled by two layers of iron railing on all sides, except the eastern side, where I had removed a panel to gain access to the edge of the building.

And that's where she was now, where I knew she'd be.

Cassie, my daughter.

*Her* daughter.

She was seventeen, lithe and tanned, her hair white-blonde, nothing unusual about that for a child of Miami. Her eyes were dark, dark brown, almost black. Like her mother's, her Cuban-American mother. Again, nothing unusual about that in Miami. She sat on the edge of the building, her coltish legs swinging in the air. She wore a simple pair of baggy, satin shorts and a plain white t-shirt.

I didn't want to scare her, sitting precariously as she was, so I cleared my throat as I approached. She didn't flinch or turn.

"Hi, Daddy," she said, her voice small and flat.

"You know I don't like you out here doing this when I'm not around," I chided, taking another sip of coffee, leaning against the railing near the gap in which she sat. She had a fishing pole resting on the railing, a big deep-sea rig, the line swaying in the wind as it descended the side of the building, maybe 300 feet or so, disappearing into the ocean.

The ocean, below us, rushing through what used to be Fourteenth Street.

She didn't answer, just toyed with the reel, squinted into the burning sky.

"Catch anything?"

After a minute, she responded. "Not yet."

I sighed, reached out to ruffle the straw of her hair. "Okay, kiddo. Well, don't stay out here too long. I'm going up on the roof to check the reclamation system. Weather looks like it should hold today, but who knows?"

She grunted indifferently. We'd had this conversation, with small variables, every morning for years now.

"Maybe, around noon, we'll take the boat and scout out that building we saw south of where the cemetery was, see if there's any way inside, anything worth scavenging. If the weather holds, that is."

# THE LONG, LONG BREAKDOWN

Cassie turned slowly, squinted up at me with a face that was heart-wrenchingly like her mother's. "Can I steer?"

"Sure," I laughed, turning away. "Sure."

The roof above the penthouse was filled with all sorts of equipment, most of it useless now, like most everything else in this new world—cell phone antennas, microwave towers, air conditioning units. Worthless, all of it. But, as I never tired of thinking, thank God the developers had taken a stab, even half-hearted, at being green.

A tower at the center of the roof held a sophisticated water collection and reclamation unit, totally self-contained, solar powered and, amazingly enough, still working. For a decade now, we hadn't had to worry about water, at least not in that way.

As I climbed the steps, I heard the reassuring *whug-whug-whug* of the machinery, the glug and glurt of water running through the maze of pipes. The massive array of solar panels, gleaming in rows, angled up at the sun. Many were cracked, some were destroyed, but those that remained were enough to provide power for the one unit in Biscayne Towers that was still inhabited, enough to power the kettle, heat the oven, warm the bath water and recharge my daughter's iPod. Some evenings, when I was feeling particularly daring, it even powered a few lights for us to read by.

Convincing myself, as I did each morning, that this arcane collection of technology was still doing something, I descended the ladder, went back inside for another cup of coffee. I drank it squatting in the living room, sorting books into piles: fiction, biography, medicine, botany, first aid, flora and fauna of North America, survival techniques, home repair.

Someday, I knew, we would have a use for this. *Someone* would have a use for this.

Hopefully, *she* would.

When I was through with the coffee, I washed the cup in the sink, set it onto the counter to dry, decided that, instead of showering on this fine morning, I'd swim a few laps in the pool.

I stirred when I felt her shadow fall over me.

I opened my eyes to a backlit figure standing at the foot of the chaise lounge. I felt bleary, sleep-warm from the sun, smelled the chlorine of the pool.

"Wake up," she said, kicking the edge of the chaise gently with her bare foot. "Come on, you promised."

I dragged a hand over my eyes, through my hair. "That I did. What time is it?"

"A little before noon," she said, bringing a dark shape from around her back, holding it out to me. I shielded my eyes to try to tell what it was, but I could smell the sea on it.

"No rations tonight!" she declared. "Fish is on the menu!"

We spent a half hour cleaning and gutting the large fish, filleting it into long slabs, covering it with oil and spices and putting it into a covered dish to marinate. We didn't speak, but I knew that she was antsy, eager to finish this task—which she knew we had to, with no refrigerator to let the fish sit in—and get down to the boat.

Eager to get out of this building, out onto the ocean, out anywhere, doing anything but sitting for days and days on end with her boring, overprotective father.

I washed my hands in the kitchen sink, chuckled.

"What's so funny?" she asked, bumping into my side amiably.

I turned to her. "Oh, just wondering what your mom would think of you, fishing, gutting and scaling…whatever that is you caught." I bumped her with my hip, smiled. "Washing your filthy, fishy hands in the kitchen sink."

Cassie turned to me, her hands still under the running water.

"Tell me about her again, while we're out on the boat."

I wiped my hands on a dish towel, nodded.

I heard what she said, knew what she meant.

Tell me about everything.

So, as we put the small boat out from a broken section of the building on what was once the thirty-eighth floor of Biscayne Towers, I told her the story, again.

It was in the time when the ice caps melted, all of them, on both ends of the Earth. The North Pole became open sea, Antarctica a bare, sere desert, cold still but ice-free. And the waters rose all around the globe, finally reclaiming land that had reared up from the oceans millions of years before.

The water rose and rose, and no one anywhere could believe it, could cope with it. In relatively quick succession, the major cities drowned—London, Rome, Hong Kong, Tokyo, Melbourne, Jerusalem, then entire countries perished, fell under the waves faster than most of their inhabitants could escape.

Thailand, Madagascar, Egypt, Greece, Britain, Ireland, Iceland, gone beneath hundreds of feet of water. The Philippines, Japan, just chains of small islands now.

And America? Split into five huge islands by the rivers that bloated horribly to accommodate the surging oceans. The Mississippi, the Missouri, the Ohio, the Colorado, all seas now, swollen with the same water that took New York and Boston, Baltimore and Washington, D.C., Charleston and Richmond.

They were gone, ghost cities. Goodbye, New Orleans. Goodbye, Memphis. Goodbye, St. Louis. Goodbye most of Mexico, all of Central America, California, Oregon, Washington. Goodbye and goodbye and goodbye.

And, of course, nearly all of Florida. All that remained were clumps of buildings jutting from the waves like the skeletons of ships shoaled there or run aground long ago. All gone, submerged, lost beneath the sea, along with the people who once lived there, the governments that could no longer protect them.

I told her all this as we rowed the boat through the canyons between the remaining buildings, told her as I'd told her a hundred times or more before.

And she wanted to hear it, needed to hear it, though it often confused her. She was just a baby when it had happened. Too young to know cars and planes and computers and television, the Internet, malls, cell phones, school, the Pledge of Allegiance, hospitals.

But all of that wasn't what she really wanted to hear, never what she *really* wanted to hear.

She wanted to hear about *her*.

"I met your mother, Consuela, through an online dating site."

"Connie," she corrected, pointing at a submerged obstacle, the top of an antenna array of some kind, poking up from a shorter building covered by the water.

"Yes, Connie," I said, smiling as I rowed around the spear of metal into clear water. "I answered her ad."

"She said she liked your smile."

I nodded.

"And you took her to dinner at a restaurant on Biscayne Boulevard, a place called...ummm..."

"Michael's," I said.

## THE LONG, LONG BREAKDOWN

"Mmmm," I heard, rather than saw her smile. "And you had steak and she had a seafood salad that she didn't eat much of. And you had drinks there until the place closed, and you took her home and she let you kiss her on the cheek."

I listened to my daughter tell the story—my story, *our* story—and felt the muscles of my heart get weak, watery, as they always did. Somehow, it seemed more real, more poignant coming from my daughter's lips than it did playing and replaying itself through my mind.

"What did she look like?"

Those five words, which Cassie often asked, were all it took to bring her mother's face into my mind.

When the waters rose, they came quick. Connie and I had been forced to flee from our house on the outskirts of Miami with only the clothes on our backs and the baby. Not even any spare clothes, certainly no pictures, no mementos.

Our family dog, Chester, stood in the doorway, wagging his tail as the water crept across the threshold, certain we were coming back, certain we would be back to take him.

The soldiers in the small boat had screamed at us to leave, *now*.

So, we grabbed the baby and nothing else, never came back. Not for stuff, not for pictures, not for Chester.

I had no pictures to show my daughter of the mother she'd lost, we'd lost.

That was the night, as we weaved our way through the flooded city, the weather changed for good, or rather *kept* changing. The amphibious landing craft that had rescued us, that held the twenty or thirty people left in our little neighborhood, was making its way back to the U.S. Navy vessel moored just off where the Port of Miami had been.

183

But the craft never made it back to the ship.

The weather went from clear and in the eighties, to stormy and in the thirties in a matter of minutes. Clouds rushed in, billowed liquidly across the sky, as if in a Spielberg movie, and the wind ratcheted up to near hurricane force. The boat, while designed for rough surf, was no match for the fury of the wind, the water, and it was swamped, somewhere just west of where the Palmetto Expressway had been.

The swelling, crashing gray of the ocean reared over us, fell onto us. I was thrown from the boat as it lurched over, still holding the baby, clutching her in the crook of my arm while trying to maintain contact with my wife.

But as the water crashed down onto us again, cold, relentless, like iron, I lost her grip. I called her name, but the roaring wind was so loud that I couldn't hear my voice in my own head. I watched her spin from me, swept along by the wind, by the still rising water.

Behind us, the amphibious landing craft's stern shot upright, then slid beneath the waves. I saw no one around it, no bodies living or dead where it disappeared.

Spray lashing my face, I peeked at the baby, her face pressed against my shoulder. She was alert, awake, not crying but clearly distressed by the cold water splashing her.

Pressing her to my neck, I pulled us desperately toward my wife, now only a tousle of dark, windblown hair twenty feet or so away, rising and falling with the swell of the waves.

I reached her just as she slipped beneath the water.

I grabbed for her, caught her hand, felt her fingers slip against mine, slide away.

Saw her face become darker, vaguer, smaller as she descended.

All of this played through my mind in the second Cassie asked about her mother, as it always did.

"She was beautiful…precious," I said, careful not to let my voice crack. "Just like you."

We found the building after another hour of rowing. My arms hurt from the effort, but I insisted on this part, leaving Cassie to steer and keep a look out. Besides, I spent a lot of time checking the sky. Weather was no longer a thing to be trusted based solely on the look of a calm sky or a gentle breeze. Maybe it was due to all the water, maybe to something else, but the weather could now turn on a dime, and I was uncomfortable being exposed like this, out in a small boat, if it should happen.

The building was listing slightly when we found it, perhaps five or six floors still above the water. Something, another building perhaps, had struck it, conveniently gouging a wide rent in its skin, exposing two floors and giving us relatively easy entrance.

When she had tied the boat off to a piece of bent rebar, Cassie boosted herself up into the rent, removed a crank flashlight from a clip at her side and prepared to go in.

"Whoa, Nelly," I cautioned. "Shoes."

I held a pair of water shoes with thick, corrugated soles, raised my eyebrows.

"Come on, Dad," she responded, knowing that it was pointless to argue with me and already moving back to the boat.

"If you step on something in there and cut your foot, it could get infected."

She nodded in exaggeration as she took the shoes, slid them on her feet. "I know, I know. But what if I touch something dangerous or fall or…"

"I can only protect you from so much."

Cassie turned to give me a funny look, climbed back inside.

I knew she no more believed what I'd just told her than I did.

Inside, still relatively intact, were four floors of a hospital, probably The Sisters of Mercy, a smaller one just northwest of downtown. Luckily, there were no bodies, at least none that we saw, and we were able to move about on the slightly canted floors with ease.

The mesh bags we'd taken from our own building's gym—the kind that normally held basketballs, volleyballs, soccer balls—came in handy here. I carried a list of medicines caged from a survival guide, and we were able to find a locked drug closet that yielded to our break-in attempts after only twenty minutes.

Our bags stuffed with medicines, syringes, gauze, tape, bandages, scissors, scalpels and other odds and ends, we made our way back to the boat, slapping against the rough edges of the hole we'd entered earlier.

On the return trip, Cassie wanted me to describe hospitals, the way they were when people were still around and water was where water should be.

Later that evening, when we'd unpacked the day's finds, cleaned them, assembled them on the dining room table to go through another day, I went with a glass of water to the southeastern edge of the building. Setting the glass on the railing, I stared out across what had once been Miami. The weather, again, was clear and cloudless. The moon was butter yellow in the sky, a suffuse, nebulous ring around it.

I'd never lived here, in the penthouse apartment on the sixty-seventh floor of Biscayne Tower, before everything changed, but I knew Miami, had lived here all my life. To the north, the Venetian

## THE LONG, LONG BREAKDOWN

Causeway, Jungle Island, Bicentennial Park, the Port of Miami, the thin peninsula of Miami Beach, all gone. To the west, Little Havana, the airport, the cemetery, our own little suburb, all gone.

All gone, everything in the world I knew, the world into which she'd been born, gone.

I heard the slap of bare feet behind me, felt her hand on my shoulder. "Whatchya doin'?"

I turned, saw her blonde hair scatter in the breeze, the earbuds of her iPod hanging from their cord around her neck. I could just make out something dim from them. Pearl Jam, maybe Foo Fighters. Classic rock.

Smiling, I kissed her hand, held it.

"Just looking out over the backyard. I think the weather might be rough tomorrow."

Cassie leaned her head on my shoulder, transmitting the tenseness of her body into mine.

"You know," she said slowly, softly. "We're going to have to get out of here…eventually."

*I am going to have to get out of here.*

I said nothing, looked back out over the moon-dappled waters.

"You saw when we got back. The water's coming up again. We won't be able to get the boat out of the thirty-eighth floor anymore. It'll be underwater."

I sighed, heavily. "I know."

"And everything up to the forty-fifth is mildewed, waterlogged, rusted."

"I know."

"Dad, we're collecting all this stuff, stockpiling it here. Why? We can't stay here forever. And we don't have a big enough boat to take it all."

I said nothing. I didn't like to think about what she was saying, didn't like to admit, particularly to her, that she was right.

"Why can't we look for another boat, something bigger, go west?" she asked, lifting her head from my shoulders and standing next to me at the railing. "You told me that the United States broke into five islands. Why not find one, settle on dry land? Maybe there are people…"

Still, I said nothing.

"What's wrong?"

"I'm afraid," I breathed, not wishing to acknowledge this in front of her, not wanting to make her afraid, too.

"Afraid of what?"

"Afraid of the world out there. Of what's left. Of what isn't left."

She thought about that for a moment.

"What's out there…what's left…it's all I've got."

I took another deep breath. "I know, baby. And that's what I'm afraid of most. I'm afraid the only thing I have left to give you is a broken, dangerous world."

Cassie turned to me, but I didn't—couldn't—look at her.

Brushing the hair from her face, she walked back toward the penthouse. When she'd taken three steps, though, she turned.

"I only know the old world through your stories. But this is my world now, Daddy. I can't know it only through you. Even if it *is* dangerous.

By the time I turned to her, she had already entered the penthouse and drifted away into its darkness.

The next morning dawned dimly, and I heard tapping at the window.

## THE LONG, LONG BREAKDOWN

I threw back the cover—*Lord, it was cold!*—and went to the blinds. Outside, it was sleeting, the icy pellets driven nearly perpendicular to the building by a ferocious wind. Letting the blinds fall back, I ducked into my darkened closet, pulled out a pair of flannel-lined jeans, a t-shirt, a heavy canvas shirt and a hooded sweatshirt. A glass apartment at the top of a Miami high-rise doesn't hold heat well, and there was no functional furnace anymore, if there ever had been.

In the kitchen, I smelled cooking—eggs, coffee. The fiftieth floor of the building, still clear of water, had hosted several restaurants in its day, and the larders were packed with all sorts of dried, canned and packaged foods. The fresh stuff had rotted away years ago, but there was enough down there to feed two people indefinitely.

"Good morning," Cassie said, stirring the powdered eggs in the skillet as several other pots bubbled and boiled. She wore sweatpants and a bulky down parka. "Hope you're hungry. I've got scrambled eggs, beef stroganoff and hot cinnamon apples. Oh, and coffee."

My stomach lurched, happy to eat but a little dismayed at the combination. She'd grown up in a world of canned rations, MREs and freeze-dried camping food. A world where you ate what you had. And if you had beef stroganoff for breakfast, that's what you ate. So, the combination didn't seem strange to her.

She brought me a hot cup of coffee, set it down and kissed my head.

"The barometer is sinking fast, so the low's gonna be a big one," she said, stirring the other pot, tasting a spoonful.

"You're gonna use up all the solar," I chided, sipping the coffee and smiling at my daughter as she buzzed around the kitchen.

"So?" she said, ladling eggs and a gloppy gray substance that I knew, from bitter experience, was the dehydrated stroganoff. "Gonna be cold today. You need something hot inside you."

"Yes, ma'am," I said as she set my plate before me, went back to prepare her own.

We ate mostly in silence, but I knew my daughter well enough to know that she wanted something.

"So, I was thinking," she said. "I'm pretty familiar with the area around the building, right?"

I set my fork down.

*Here it comes,*

"I suppose."

"And I'm pretty good with the boat, right?"

"Okay"

She gained steam as I appeared to agree with her assessments.

"And you've taught me a lot, right? You've taught me really well."

"Sure…"

"I was thinking that maybe, once in a while, I could take the boat exploring, just to get out, just a little, close enough to stay in contact. I mean, not today. But, you know, sometime…"

Cassie looked at me with such unbridled enthusiasm, such hope that I found it hard to deflate her.

"Stay in contact how exactly?"

"Those walker-talker thingies we found a few months back," she answered, her cheeks flushing. I realized that I'd fallen right into her trap.

I looked at her for a moment, measuring her.

"Walkie-talkies," I corrected.

"Whatever. The ones with the rechargeable batteries. The ones we never use because you never let me go anywhere. Those. I could have one, you could have one."

"And what happens if you get into trouble?"

## THE LONG, LONG BREAKDOWN

I already knew the answer to this, already knew what she'd say.

"The extra boat, the one you've been working on. If I get into any trouble, you can come and get me."

Despite myself, I frowned. Yes, we had found another boat on one of our recent excursions, a bass boat that had been wedged against the building. It had a few holes in its hull, but I'd patched these as well as I could, and it seemed watertight. I just wasn't ready quite yet to trust our safety to it.

"I dunno," I began, but it was too late. She'd already seen the frown, already read its intention.

"You don't let me do anything!" she said, standing so abruptly that her chair skittered backward, tumbled over. She paid it no attention.

"How can I learn to do stuff when you won't let me do anything? Ever. I can't spend my life cooped up here, Daddy! I can't! It's not fair."

I put my fork down, suddenly not hungry. "I can't...it's just that...I can't lose you, Cass. I can't."

This only seemed to make her madder, though. "Mom died. I get it. But that was a long time ago, and it wasn't your fault, Daddy! I'm not Mom. You've got to let me live, Dad. You've got to let me do stuff. Or I may as well be dead!"

I started to stand, to go to her, to comfort her, but she wasn't ten years old anymore, and she wanted me to know that the same arguments we'd been having couldn't be settled with the same old solutions. No more hugs, no more words of comfort, no more sharing my worries, no more empty promises of *tomorrow, tomorrow, tomorrow.*

Cassie screamed at me, a wordless, strangled burst of dense, frustrated anger that shattered the relative silence of the kitchen, reverberated off every pane of glass. Then, bursting into the tears she hated, she turned on her heel and ran from the room.

Standing there for a minute, not quite sure of what to do, I fell back into the chair, held the cup of coffee, still warm in my hands.

I turned, looked out the windows onto a swirling, grey day.

I'd need a heavier coat to check the solars and the water plant this morning.

The next few days were frosty, both inside and out.

The weather got progressively colder, until it was nearly arctic. The wind whipped and whistled between the buildings, stirred up the foamy sea until the water lashed at the exposed buildings. I spent a frigid hour hauling the boat as far into the exposed thirty-eighth floor as I could, to ensure that it wasn't swept out to sea.

The water was coming up, just as Cassie had said. But I'd already known this. It was at least two or three feet into this floor. Just a foot or two more, and we would no longer be able to use this staging area. We'd have to figure a way to move the boats higher.

It was just a matter of time.

I stood in the gaping hole there on the thirty-eighth floor, watched the storm-whipped waves, saw chunks of ice bobbing on the whitecaps raised by the storm. Sleet fell in an almost solid sheet, hissed and spat like a sandstorm. Upstairs, the outside of the penthouse was completely enclosed in a layer of ice inches thick, and I'd been unable to check on the solars or the water rig for several days.

I supposed they still worked. They'd been through worse. But today and the day before were so cold that I'd had to turn on some portable electric space heaters to keep the pipes inside from freezing—to keep *us* from freezing. And I was beginning to worry that, should this storm hold out, the power certainly would not.

Cold and sopping wet, I started the climb of the nearly thirty

## THE LONG, LONG BREAKDOWN

floors back up to the penthouse, feeling every step in my aching knees, my burning lungs.

*Old.*

I was old, getting older. What was I doing holding her back, protecting her to the point that I allowed her to do nothing? She was right. Someday—hopefully far off, but who knew?—I'd be gone, and she'd be left to herself.

*Alone.*

For a few years after the deluge, we listened for the dim, intermittent broadcasts on the old crank radio I'd found. But then nothing, nothing for at least a decade, so long ago we didn't even bother to listen anymore.

And in the last thirteen years, we had seen few people, a testament to the extent of the devastation. I had been too afraid to approach these people, seen at a distance from the penthouse, in small boats, drifting. Probably people like me and Cassie, subsisting, shocked from the loss of it all. Too afraid to reach out to others, too raised on apocalyptic movies from before, where the people who were left killed each other in the competition for the meager remaining resources.

So, we continued alone, not listening for more people, not watching for more people. And at some point, I stopped caring about others. I had written them off years ago, just as I had my wife.

I was alone.

We were alone.

*Alone.*

I let that thought seep in as I rounded the forty-ninth floor.

How could I do that to Cassie, though?

How could I leave her alone with so little knowledge of the world?

I was crippling her, I realized.

Feeling ashamed and depressed, I finally ascended the stairwell to the penthouse access, came inside, barred the door. I passed my daughter's room, closed, probably locked though I didn't check.

For a moment, it seemed as if all the cold in the world was pressed up against the other side of that door, radiating out toward me, only me.

Sighing, I moved on to my own room, opened the door onto a wave of soothing heat. I'd left the space heater on with the door closed, so now I could peel off my sodden clothing, towel dry and put on clean, warm clothes, climb into bed and sleep away the grey day.

I'd worry about the weather, the dwindling electrical power tomorrow. Right now, the warmth of the space heaters, the *scritch-scratch* of the sleet against the windows lulled me into a kind of sleep.

*D*ense.

The water was dense and cold in the dream, colder than I remembered, thicker than water should be. I saw ice floes rise and fall on the wind-wracked waves, felt the close, wet cold that penetrated to the bone, clutched at the heart.

But my numb hands felt hers, just as they always did.

I was afraid to open my dream eyes, but they opened of their own volition.

I saw her face, Connie's face, rimed with ice, her hair clotted with it, her eyebrows and cheeks frosted. She slid slowly down into the dusky water, but I still seemed unable to get to her quickly enough.

Our fingers slid against each other, impersonal as icebergs.

And then, as always, she was gone, falling slowly, a leaf swirling away into the condensed darkness of the sea.

And, as always, I awoke in my bed, sweating, gasping, sobbing. *Alone.*

"There's gonna be some rules, you understand?"

Cassie looked up from her bowl of cereal. I had been up early, breaking into the stores of dried cereal from ages ago, vacuum-packed and still mostly fresh. I'd stirred up a jug of powdered milk and even found a few bags of the tea she liked.

It was all waiting for her when she had stumbled into the kitchen earlier, bundled up for what we both feared would be another frigid day. But during the night, the capricious weather shifted again, and the clouds peeled away, leaving the sky a clean slate from which the sun shone down unencumbered. Though only 8:00 a.m., the temperature was already above sixty degrees and promised to break seventy.

Cassie had shuffled to her chair, raised her eyebrows, poured milk over her cereal, begun to eat.

When I finally spoke, smiling at her over the rim of my cup, she looked blankly at me, as if not comprehending the words coming from my lips.

"Understand?" I asked again.

"Rules?" she repeated, milk dribbling from her lips.

"Yeah, like no going beyond a four block radius of the tower. Like no going inside buildings. Keeping radio contact at all times."

Realization dawned on her face, and Cassie smiled.

"Like listening to me when I say it's time to come in. Like—"

"I get it, I get," she said, standing and throwing her arms around me. "Thanks, Daddy! I love you."

I kissed her head, touched her hair.

"I love you, too, sweetie. And I'm sorry. I got to thinking about what I'm doing and why. You're right. I'm smothering you."

She peeled herself away, sat back in her chair. I half expected her to protest what I was saying, but she didn't. And I knew she was right not to.

"Thanks, Daddy," she said, eating her cereal. "I wondered what the occasion was for the cereal."

I took a swig of coffee. "Living life. I've got to let you do it. Otherwise, what's the point of surviving?"

She chewed her cereal happily, bopping a little in her chair.

"So, today…"

"No, not today. First, I have to be sure the weather will hold, and that all this ice will melt. Then we need to have some lessons in the boat, with the walkie-talkies. You have to convince me that you're ready for this before I let you go."

She frowned a little, but her smile returned quickly. "Okay, Daddy. Then can we spend today going over that stuff? Just in case the weather is clear tomorrow?"

"Absolutely."

It was a few days—a few agonizing days, as far as Cassie was concerned—waiting for me to be confident of the weather, of her abilities with the boat, of her willingness to follow the rules I'd set forth.

But when the day came, it was glorious. The sky was blue, the sun white-hot. The water was calm as a pane of glass, smooth as a bed sheet stretched taut. She awoke early that day, started breakfast—nothing too elaborate, nothing that I might linger over. Cassie wanted to get out onto the water, and I chuckled as she waited for me to eat, impatiently watching me drink a second cup of coffee.

## THE LONG, LONG BREAKDOWN

I walked with her down the smelly, mildewed stairwell to the thirty-eighth floor, went inside the apartment we used as the boat landing. I delayed a little longer, explaining a few things that I'd already gone over the last few days.

"Daddy, I know, I know!" she said, almost vibrating with eagerness.

"Hey, give me a break. It's not easy for me to hand over the car keys to my little girl for the first time."

She gave me a funny look, and I hugged her tight.

In the end, I passed her a backpack loaded with bottled water, some emergency rations, a crank flashlight, some flares, a blanket, knife, first aid kit and her boat shoes. I also gave her one of the walkie-talkies, fully charged and ready to go.

Then, I kissed her on the cheek, sent her out into the world, her world.

For the first time.

*Alone.*

I watched her lower the boat, watched her row away to the west, pausing to look back several times, wave. Her confidence made my heart ache.

When she had turned the corner, I made the long climb back upstairs, checked the solars, checked the water unit, slumped into a chaise lounge near the pool and waited for her voice over the walkie-talkie.

Cassie came back in about four hours, literally the longest afternoon of my life.

She radioed that she'd found a shoal of debris lodged against the side of a partially exposed structure. It was made up mostly of cars that had been swept there by the water. Somehow, they had piled into a cairn, atop something that prevented them from sinking like millions of their brethren.

I advised her that the pile was likely very unstable and told her to stay away from it. She radioed back that she saw a large truck, a moving van, whose rear was exposed and open, filled with stuff.

I told her to stay away and silence was my only answer for more than fifteen minutes.

When she came back on, she told me, calmly, despite my anger, that she had found a few things and was returning home.

I helped her bring the boat in, tie it up. She showed me what she'd found, mostly odds and ends— books, some fishing equipment, a bag stuffed with medicines and toiletries.

And a telescope.

A simple refractor telescope, nothing fancy, nothing too dissimilar from that used by Galileo.

And like Galileo's, this telescope opened Cassie's world and just as effectively brought to an end the old world of her father.

Cassie was an energetic chatterbox for the remainder of the day. She helped me lug her finds up the endless stairwell to our apartment, hovered over me as I examined each item. One overnight bag was crammed with toiletries—several tubes of toothpaste, still pasty; deodorant; some soap; shampoo; perfumes. Obviously a woman's bag. She couldn't have been more delighted by this find if she'd stumbled onto a sack of money.

No, she was more so, because, I realized not for the first time, that she'd never been around money, never lived in a world that used or even needed it. She had a collection of money in her room, pinned to her bulletin board, from hoards of the stuff we'd found over the years. Even some $1000 bills. Without actually counting it, I supposed that she had more than $10,000 in her room, nothing more than decoration.

## THE LONG, LONG BREAKDOWN

The reel of the fishing pole was rusted and didn't spin, but I had a can of WD-40 stashed somewhere that might get it working again. Besides, in this new world, you didn't throw anything out. Everything had a use or might have a use.

Someday.

The books came in helpful. One was a *Physicians' Desk Reference*, the '19 edition. Sure, it was sixteen years old, but there'd hardly been any advances in prescription medication since it was published. I had actually been searching for one of these for years, eager to have a better understanding of some of the medicines we'd found.

Cassie beamed proudly as I flipped through it. The book was somewhat water-damaged, but still intact. Its pages could still be turned. I kissed her cheek and told her what a great find she'd snagged.

Then, the telescope.

She had only a limited idea of what it was, what it could do. I examined it closely, wiping it down with a soft cloth to clear some of the dirt. It was a high-end device, composed mostly of bronze, sitting atop a teakwood tripod. All of its parts seemed present, and it looked as if it would work with no problem.

It was a simple refractor, with a prism in the eyepiece to correct the upside-down image. Because of this, I supposed that it had belonged to a wealthy condo owner who used it more to look at the ocean and other condo owners than the night sky.

With her following closely behind, I took it out to the patio around the pool, set it up. It did work, with some minor distortion, probably from condensation in the tube or in the eyepiece. I undid a few screws, carefully wiped what I could see, and put it all back together.

This accomplished, I put my eye to the lens and scanned the area. It had pretty good magnification, clearly showing details from structures that were ten blocks away. Practically bouncing out of her skin with impatience, Cassie pestered me to take a look.

When she did, she grew quiet. She had paid attention to how I had manipulated the device, focused it with the knurled brass knob just as I'd shown her. Back and forth, here and there, she aimed, focused, aimed focused.

I laughed, patted her on her bare, slightly sunburned shoulder.

"Don't stay out here too long, honey. You need to get some ointment on those burns before they get worse."

She said nothing, so I went in to get a glass of water, skim the *Physicians' Desk Reference* a little more closely.

It didn't take long.

In fact, I wondered how long they had been there, only a few blocks to the north and east, there on what used to be Eighteenth Street, west of Pace Park and the Opera Tower, just east of the cemetery.

The next morning came early, after another nightmare. I threw myself from bed, still damp from the night sweats the dream brought with it, dressed quickly in shorts and a t-shirt, went into the kitchen for coffee. The day was dull, the sun obscured by a thin, hazy layer of low clouds. The air was dense, humid and promised temperatures in the 100s.

I wished that I had ice for my coffee, but ice in a drink was something from yesterday. Maybe again in a lot of tomorrows, but not today. I wandered onto the patio, watched the sunlight play on the pool. Sometime today, I knew, I'd be dipping into that for a while to cool off.

## THE LONG, LONG BREAKDOWN

Cassie stood at the northeastern edge of the railing peering into her new toy. Its brass gleamed in the washed-out light, looking like the only real thing there on the roof.

She turned, gave me an energetic wave, went back to her observations.

Settling into a lounge chair, I sipped at the coffee, already regretting the choice on this warm day. I set it aside on a low table, laid back into the chair.

I was already falling asleep in the lazy, humid sun when her voice pulled me back.

"Ummm, Daddy? Daddy!"

I opened a squinting eye, braced my arms on either side of the chair to jump up if necessary. I was hyper-vigilant about her safety, but as any father of a teenage daughter knew, tone of voice was no real indication of the level of the emergency. "Daddy!" could mean anything from "I can't find my pink top" all the way to "Help, I'm being kidnapped!"

Cassie was still bent over the telescope, but the face she turned toward me looked flushed, excited and alarmed all at once.

"What?" I growled, guessing that this was closer to the pink top scenario.

"You'd better come and look at this...*now*."

"Why? You see something?"

"Yeah!"

"What is it?"

"*People.*"

That single word jolted through my body like an arc of electricity, producing a multi-branching tree of responses.

*People?*

How many? Where? What were they doing?

*What kind of danger did they represent?*

My arms already positioned, though now shaking somewhat, I did launch myself up, ran around the pool to where she stood.

"Let me see," I said, firmly moving her aside and lowering my head to the eyepiece.

*People.*

*Dear God, people, and more than a few of them.*

I raised my head, blinked to clear my sight, lowered my right eye to the scope again.

No more than five blocks away, to the north and east. Shapes moved about on the roof, no doubt on the penthouse of a condo building similar to ours. I could make out quite a few of them, perhaps a dozen, maybe more. From here it was difficult to see with any clarity, but there seemed to be men and woman—and children.

I stood, brought my hands to my head, ran them back through my hair.

I realized that I was breathing hard, that my heart was racing.

"Daddy?"

I couldn't let her know that I was worried.

Taking a deep breath, swallowing something that had risen, bitter and hard, in my throat, I turned to her. "Yeah, kiddo?"

"People?"

That single word, that questioning tone in her voice, nearly brought me to my knees. Money, school, television, these things my daughter had no recollection of, no experience with. And I was okay with that, comfortable if she never gained any experience with these things.

But *people?*

She had no experience with anyone other than me. And the querulous tone of her voice, the doubt that it expressed that what she'd seen were people—*actual* people—gave me a pang in my chest.

## THE LONG, LONG BREAKDOWN

"Yeah, baby. People."

"Can they see us, too? Do you think they know we're here?"

I considered that, coldly.

"I don't know. I doubt it, though. Unless they have a telescope or binoculars."

Cassie turned, walked a few feet away.

I took a step toward her, reached out to offer some comfort. But she spun before my hand could touch her shoulder.

"Oh my god, Daddy!" she yelled, her face beaming with unexpected joy. "People! Other people!"

She brushed aside my hands and slipped in to hug me tightly. She was weeping, I realized a second later, weeping with *joy?*

My arms fell around her, returned her embrace.

But the only thing I could think about was how to bar the stairwell.

How to close up the gap in the building where we docked the boat.

*How was I going to protect her?*

*Because it's the only job I have left.*

Cassie, however, did not agree with how I was reacting to this discovery, did not think about her safety, her protection.

She could only think that we were finally not alone.

I disentangled myself from her embrace, left her alone and confused on the patio, went inside and drank one glass after another of tepid water from the tap until my gut felt hard, and vague nausea clutched at me.

*People.*

I heard her footsteps behind me, heard them enter the room, stop.

She said nothing, waited for me to turn.

"So?" she said, not bothering to hide or even mask the exasperation in her voice.

I bristled, but tamped that feeling down.

"So what?"

"Those were people…right?"

"Yeah, people."

She let out a rough, annoyed breath. "We find some people just a few blocks away, the first people I can remember seeing since I was, I dunno, five years old, and what? You come in to drink some water? Don't tell me that's all we're going to do!"

"Well, of course, it's not *all* we're going to do."

"Then what, Dad? What? And why are we waiting?" I pulled a chair out, sat at the kitchen table. "What do you want to do? Hop in the boat and race over there right now?"

"Are you kidding me?" she said, rolling her eyes. "Of course I do! And I want to know why we're in here right now arguing instead of rowing the boat over there!"

"It's not that simple, Cassie."

"It is that simple, Dad. It's really simple."

"No!" I yelled, slamming my fist onto the table. "No, it's not. You might think it is, but it's not. Our lives for the last few years? *That's* been simple. This? People? That complicates things…a lot!

"You have no idea…we have no idea who they are, what they're doing. We don't know a damn thing about them, and you want me to put my most valuable possession in a boat and row it over to them? I won't do it!"

"*Your most valuable possession?*" she repeated, her eyes narrowing. "Is that what I am to you? Something to be guarded?"

"You know what I meant."

"Yeah, I guess I sorta do."

"A possession? No, of course not. But something to be guarded, protected? Damn right, Cassie! Damn right. You're all I have left. Of your mother, my world. And I'm not risking what little I have left!"

## THE LONG, LONG BREAKDOWN

I could see that Cassie realized she had hit something raw within me, something that she had guessed at previously, but had never actually seen or heard. And now she was nervous, scared of what she might have jarred loose from the depths of my mind.

"Dad, I just—"

"No!" I shouted again. "Don't 'Dad' me, Cassie. What if they're crazies? What if they're bad people, Cass? What if they're *really* bad people? What do we do then? How do I protect you? You want me to take you over there and introduce ourselves? Hell, no! I'm thinking about how we can make sure they don't know we're here. How we can secure the boat landing, the stairwell. Wondering if we can protect ourselves."

I was standing now, not remembering doing it. And Cassie looked at me with deep concern.

There was silence for several moments, neither of us knowing exactly what to say.

"Daddy," Cassie finally broke the silence. "We can't be alone forever. We can't. Why do we have to have this argument all the time? Sooner or later, we're going to bump into someone or someone is going to find us, either of which is fine with me because I don't want to be alone forever.

"I love you, Daddy, but I don't want to stay here forever. And you know we can't…we can't stay here forever."

"Cassie, that's not what I—"

"That is what you mean, Daddy. You might not *think* that's what you mean, but it is. You can't protect me from everything in the whole world. You just can't, no matter how much you want to, no matter how much you love me.

"If there are people out there, and there are, I want to find them, be with them. Figure out a way to live."

"Cassie," I said, but couldn't find the words to follow.

"Daddy, I love you. I really do. But I can't be your whole world. I'm sorry Mom's not here. I'm sorry that you feel responsible for that, for me. But I can't be that for you anymore.

"And, Daddy, you can't expect me to make my whole world about you. That's not fair. And I can't…I won't live like that."

My mouth went dry. "What's that mean?"

Cassie was shaking slightly; I saw that, saw emotion pulse from her, as if her body were sending waves of the stuff into the air.

"I don't know. I just know that we…*I*…can't stay here forever like this."

She fixed me with her eyes for a moment, and when I made no response, she turned slowly, went to her room, closed the door softly.

This time, I distinctly heard the *click* of the lock being engaged.

The weather stayed warm for the next week, varying from intensely hot to mildly tropical. There was a brisk wind most days, enough to stir the ocean into foamy caps, but no rain.

For the first three days, Cassie avoided me completely. When I arose, I took breakfast alone. In the afternoons, I sorted books, cleaned objects we'd found, made my daily inspection of the machinery on the roof.

Cassie spent most of the time in her room, apparently listening to her iPod. She ventured out periodically to eat meals or to wander about on the roof. A few times over those first days, I saw her at the telescope, no longer aiming it here and there, but focusing on the northeast, on the people.

And when she wasn't there, I was.

I monitored them closely, trying to make out just how many

of them there were, what they were doing. But after three days of careful observation, I couldn't tell much. There seemed to be a mix of races, ages, sexes. They seemed to be doing nothing more than living atop the building, just as Cassie and I were doing.

I couldn't tell from this distance, but it didn't look as if that building had any power. I could see no solar array, and whatever other machinery there was atop the building was unidentifiable this far away.

What I couldn't see were their intentions.

And that's what kept me there, frozen on this rooftop, unwilling to reach out to them, to trust them.

On the fourth day since spotting them, I found myself in the spare room of the penthouse, the room with the wall safe. The previous owner had left the combination taped to the underside of his desk, and I'd found it years ago. Now, the safe contained the most valuable things that we'd found—a stash of cash, just in case, a bag filled with twenty-three gold coins and four handguns with ammunition.

I took the nine-millimeter out, unwrapped its cloth and disassembled it as I'd learned in the survival book. Cleaning it thoroughly with a rag and gun oil, I reassembled it, loaded the clip, put the remaining ammunition back into the safe and locked it.

The gun I slid into the waistband of my shorts, the safety engaged.

On the fifth day, Cassie spoke again, surprising me out of a deep nap on the chaise at the side of the pool.

"Can I go out on the boat today, just go around a little?" she asked. "I'm getting stir crazy."

Relieved to hear her speak, I shielded my eyes from the sun, peered up at her.

"Not by yourself."

"Fine. Can we leave now?"

"Okay. Give me fifteen minutes to visit the bathroom and grab my shoes."

I made sure to head south and west once we were out on the water. She knew what I was doing and why, but chose to say nothing. The water was choppy, the wind as strong as it was atop the building, and the little boat bobbed and weaved on the undulating waves. Cassie sat at the bow of the craft, pointed out objects to me as I rowed.

The afternoon sun, already past its zenith, cast shadows that fell deep into the spaces between the buildings, darkened the waters. It was cool here between the wrecks of the structures, in the shadows and the spray, and I relaxed a bit. At least my mind did; the rowing was strenuous work with the sea this rough.

But soon I was in a rhythm, working the oars back and forth, following my daughter's hand signals. We plied the waters south, keeping to what had been North Miami Avenue.

There was no conversation today, no request for any retelling of the stories of her mother, the world before the deluge. Cassie was lost in her own thoughts, and I had no desire to pull a discussion from her for I knew what those thoughts were.

The discovery of people made Cassie more aware of the present, the future. Stories about the vanished, unknowable past didn't seem to carry the weight they once had with her.

It happened near where the Miami Federal Courthouse was submerged. You could almost see the top of the building beneath the waves, shaped like the hull of a great, sunken ship. Much of the area here had been parking lots and low structures that were deep, deep below us now, giving the area the look of an actual, open sea.

## THE LONG, LONG BREAKDOWN

That's where we saw them.

Whether they were the same people or not, it was impossible to say, but they were definitely people. Perhaps four or five in a boat a little larger than ours, to the northeast, a mile or so away.

My heart began to beat fast. Surely, if we could see them, they could see us. Too late to try hiding here on this open expanse of the inland sea, out here beneath the blazing sun.

There was only fleeing, that was the only thing I could think to do. Flee, leave, run away.

But *not* lead them back to our home.

I rowed the boat around, just as Cassie stood.

"Sit down, goddammit!" I huffed. "They'll see you!"

"I want them to see me!" she yelled back, defiantly turning and waving her arms over her head. "Hey! Over here! Over here!"

"Cassandra!" I shouted, horrified at what she was doing, how vulnerable it left us. I didn't think that they could actually hear her, but if they hadn't seen us before, her frantic movements were sure to catch their attention.

"Over here!"

I began rowing south again, over the shipwreck of the court building, angling east. I'd follow Second Street, lose them hopefully before we got too close to where the college had been. Then I could concentrate on getting home.

"Daddy, stop!" Cassie shouted, breaking my concentration. "I think they see us. I think they're coming this way!"

I stopped rowing, breathing harshly. I peered into the bright, shimmering distance. She was right. It looked as if they had turned their boat, pointed it directly at us.

I panicked.

I didn't know what to do. They'd seen us. People, these or others, would search for us now, find us eventually.

**209**

More afraid than I'd been since that day in the water when my wife's hand slipped from mine, I stood. My motion upset the small craft, tossing Cassie into the boat.

From the waistband of my shorts, I drew the nine-millimeter, which gleamed silver-white in the sun. I unlatched the safety, leveled it in the direction of the oncoming boat.

Cassie, who had never seen an actual gun outside of a book, had no idea of its range or power. Shocked to see one now, here, in her father's hands, she yelled, "Daddy, no!"

Of course the gun wouldn't reach their boat. Of course, that wasn't what I was trying to do, well, not *really*. No, I hoped that the sound of its discharge would turn them aside, make them think twice about pursuing us, looking for us.

So, I pulled the trigger, and the gun jumped in my hand three times.

Each time, there was a flat, deafening roar from the thing, a roar that made Cassie fall to the bottom of the boat, cover her ears, scream.

The shots sprang across the water, echoing in a thousand directions, until the sound became more than three shots. It was a barrage, a hail of bullets, thundering across the flat plane of the sea. Like thunder, their noise vibrated in the air, reverberated like a struck gong, literally stunning the silence into submission.

When the last of the noise died away, I blinked, as if for the first time in my life. The gun felt like an iron weight in my hand, and the muscles of my forearm, appalled at the gun's kick, quivered like a horse that had been ridden too long.

Slowly, I lowered the pistol, the arc of its descent leaving a brilliant reflection in its wake.

But I watched the boat, only the boat.

And it looked as if it had stopped.

*Good.*

I thumbed the safety, placed it onto the seat beside me, sat and started to row again, fiercely, ignoring the burning pain in my shoulders, my chest.

Cassie stayed curled on the floor of the boat, her eyes tightly shut, and I had to navigate back home on my own.

We didn't speak as we approached Biscayne Tower.

Didn't speak as we moored the boat.

Didn't speak as we ascended the steps, entered our apartment, our individual rooms.

I was awakened later that night from a sound sleep by the slipping of her hand through mine.

*The dream, the goddamn dream!*

My anguish at the dream, though, was swept aside as knowledge of the day's events, what'd I'd done, flooded back over me.

*The gun.*

I sighed and it turned into a groan.

Why had I fired the gun today?

What if I'd actually hit someone, killed someone?

Had I really only hoped to scare them away?

Did I really think it would?

And—

*W*ould it?

Or would they really come looking for us now?

I was clammy, soaked with sweat, yet at the same time, my mouth was dry.

Throwing my feet over the side of the bed, I stood, prepared to go into the kitchen for a glass of water.

A vivid blast of lightning surprised me, flashed through the blinds. A rumble of thunder followed on its heels.

I felt the coldness of the air, heard the rain outside at the same time.

Sourly, I opened my bedroom door, went into the hallway. Lightning threw shifting shadows, brief, almost phosphorescent, onto the walls. The flashes were so strong, so constant, the effect was like a strobe light.

I put my hand out to the wall to steady myself, because the light made me dizzy.

Passing her room, I saw her door was open again, and I paused in confusion.

Another burst of lightning showed that the bed was unmade, unoccupied.

Frowning, my dizziness became a twinge of nausea.

*Where was she?*

*She wouldn't have—*

*Dear god!*

I raced back into my room, pulled on a pair of pants, slipped on sneakers with no socks. Almost an afterthought, I grabbed a waterproof jacket, shrugged into it as I snatched the emergency pack I'd given her, left there on a hook near the door to the stairs.

Fumbling with the pack, I pulled the flashlight out, shone its light into the dark, endless shaft of the stairs, took a deep breath.

"Cassie!" I roared at the top of my voice, my voice blasting into the emptiness, swallowed by it. "Cassie!"

Before the echoes faded, I was racing down the stairs as fast as my legs—and my heart—would allow.

## THE LONG, LONG BREAKDOWN

She had taken the boat sometime during the night, slipped away with a few of her things.

To find them, to meet them.

To be with them.

I stood there in the little alcove where the boat was kept, stood there with the cold spray on my face and wept. It was too much like before, too much like losing *her*.

Then, I remembered the other boat.

I pushed through dark, chill water that was hip deep, found the little ledge under which I'd secured the bass boat. I checked, made sure the oars were tucked under the gunwales, tossed the emergency pack into it, hefted it down into the water.

Wrestling it over the lip of the building, I jumped in, pushed away.

The rain was relentless, soaking, cold. As the boat slewed from the building, it spun in the currents, its nose rose on a great wave, then smashed back down, almost throwing me into the sea.

Blinking and sputtering, I got my bearings, took the oars and began to row.

My pace was manic, but the combined forces of wind and water made my progress maddeningly slow. Without Cassie there to navigate, I had to steer by lightning alone, taking stock of my situation in brief, flash-lit images, like snapshots viewed one after another.

The boat slewed left and right, pitched forward and backward, took on water. There was simply too much rain, too much ocean spilling into it. I could feel the boat growing heavier, more unresponsive under me as I rowed. Were there holes, leaks I wasn't aware of?

At intervals, despite the rain, the wind, the thunder, I called her name, called her name over and over, even though I couldn't hear it in my own head.

Even though I was sure she couldn't hear it, either.

Still, I pressed on, persevered.

What else was left for me?

An empty penthouse.

A shattered world.

But the weather was growing harsher.

The bass boat was built for rivers, for ponds, not for the fury of a manic ocean. My feet were covered with at least six inches of water, and the boat was sitting lower and lower in the waves. The ocean poured over its sides, threatening to swamp it.

Again. Just like before.

A staccato burst of lightning blinded me, and I momentarily stopped rowing.

The wind ripped one of the oars from my hands, sent it hurtling into the night.

The boat listed, settled, listed, waivered, capsized.

For a moment that might have been an eternity, I didn't know up or down, left or right. Everything in every direction was cold, was wet, was darkness. I opened my eyes onto nothing, let my body go limp in the hopes that it would simply float to the surface.

I was buffeted against something hard, either the boat itself as it hurried to the distant bottom or something else, I couldn't tell. It struck me hard enough to knock the air from me, which escaped in a huge blurt that left my lungs empty.

*Oh, Connie, I tried.*

*Cassie, I tried.*

I was drowning, this was drowning.

This is how Connie had felt, how she had died.

## THE LONG, LONG BREAKDOWN

At first, I was panicky and afraid.

Then, in the space of a heartbeat or two, I accepted it. I closed my eyes, and despite the searing in my lungs, the pressure in my head, I relaxed.

The cold seemed to push in from all sides, forcing out all of the air, all of the oxygen.

*Let it happen. Your job here is done. There's nothing more to do. You have nothing left to offer.*

But as bright phosphenes exploded across the darkness of my vision, I saw the scene being acted out, the scene from my dream. A light burst overhead, rippling gold in the black water.

A hand reached out for mine, *down* for mine.

My hand reached up for it.

And I knew, finally, that though this was my dream, it wasn't.

It wasn't *me*, not me saving my wife and failing.

The dream had been *her* hand all along, reaching down, down to save me from sinking, from drowning.

Not my hand reaching to her, to my wife.

It was Cassie's hand, reaching down to save *me*.

*To save me.*

Her entire life had been about saving me, I had just been too blind to see it.

It wasn't a conscious thing on her part, not like my single-minded protection of her had been. No, it simply *was*. Her life in this new world was meant to illuminate a new purpose for me, a purpose far beyond the simple preservation of my daughter's life. Not that this wasn't admirable, to be desired.

But in saving me, Cassie had unwittingly helped to save her new world, too, by preserving a bit of the old. In much the same way that preserving an ember of a great fire, reduced to ashes now, can be used to start a new fire, a greater fire.

*I am that ember, at least one of them.*

That knowledge ignited some store of energy within me that the cold waters hadn't yet doused, that I hadn't tapped.

With the last of that strength, the last of my oxygen, I reached up, toward that hand—

—grasped it, took it.

I worried momentarily about the intent of that hand, about the gunshots I'd fired earlier that day.

And then there were more, more hands reaching down, clasping mine, grabbing my shoulders, lifting me from the cold water, lifting me into a boat.

That was the last thing I remembered.

Not just one hand now, but dozens of them, lifting me.

Not to punish me.

*To save me.*

There were twenty three of them, all told, not counting their two newest members.

Most were in their twenties, young, so young. Like Cassie, they had been only small children when the waters rose, so they had little knowledge of the old world, the way things were. Unlike Cassie, though, they didn't seem to care too much about that.

There were six children, ranging in age from five to twelve years old, born—conceived—*après le deluge*. Only one couple, a man and his wife, were as old as, actually older than, me. They were in their sixties, snowbirds probably, had accomplished a lot in keeping this little group alive.

They'd done a great job actually, housing them all, feeding them all. But I could almost feel the palpable waves of relief coming from them; relaxing a bit at my presence, at my potential to take some of the responsibility off them.

I'd swallowed a lot of water, aspirated some of it, caught pneumonia. Between bouts of vomiting and shaking so bad I feared my bones would crack, I told them where to find the *Physicians' Desk Reference* and the stash of medicines back at our place, told them what and how much to give me.

They put me in a room on the penthouse of their high-rise. For uncounted days, they came and spoke with me, each of them, fed me soup, tended to my needs. The older couple told their story, I told mine.

We came to an agreement.

Cassie and I would stay with them. We'd become part of their group.

When Cassie eventually came to see me, she was shy and embarrassed at first, tentative, as if I would be angry with her, disappointed.

But I wasn't.

And I told her why.

I was her father, and I knew I had unintentionally hurt her.

I was her father, and I was willing to admit that I had been wrong.

I was her father, and I loved her. I just wanted her to be safe, be happy, to live her life.

In the end, I realized that I had to give her room to do all that.

I had to give her world to her.

And I had to give her to the world.

I am now the ember.
   I am the keeper of the flame.

I have learned that the best way to protect my daughter is to remember the world, as it was, as we were—the things we did, the things we built, the way we lived. All of it. The good, the bad, the ugly.

My job now is to remember it, share it, pass it down to her world, the new world.

So that they can remember the old world, live in the new.

So that they can learn.

So that they can live.

So that she can live.

It is, I think, the best job I've ever had.

———

*For my friend, Chris Frisella*

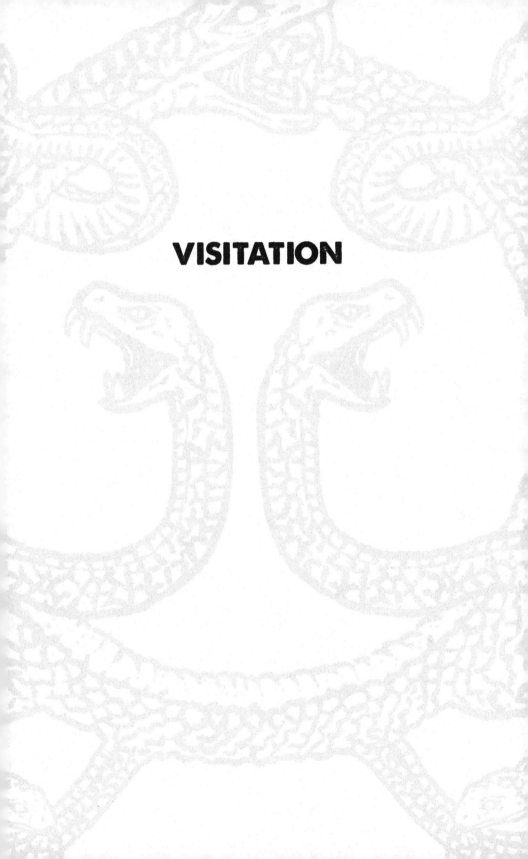
# VISITATION

enlan Daulk stood in the foyer of his quiet house, reading and re-reading the message displayed on the tablet held in his nerveless hand. His briefcase dangled from the other, his house keys already on the table in the little ceramic sculpture that one of his wife's students had made for her.

> Congratulations, Mr. Daulk.
>
> Your name has been drawn in the annual Galactic Lottery. Your permit and travel voucher to Visitation have been confirmed. Please contact your personal Retreat Coordinator immediately to make the necessary travel preparations. As you can no doubt appreciate, time at Visitation is at a premium. So we thank you for taking care of the arrangements as soon as practicable.
>
> It is our honor to assist your healing in this time of grief.

The words refused to gel, to mean anything substantive. They swam in and out of his vision, until he realized that he was weeping.

The briefcase clattered to the tile floor, and his hand, suddenly free, trembled on its way to his face, scrubbed the tears from his eyes.

*Congratulations.*

*Grief.*

Yes, his mind made those words out clearly, even as the other swam into view.

*Visitation.*

This, above all else, fired synapses he thought had died a year ago, burned out in a supernova of sorrow.

They weren't. They never would be.

He sank to his knees, clasped the tablet to his chest.

Through a sophisticated and system-spanning lottery, Fen had been awarded fourteen days planetside, in a small bungalow in a compound on the northern continent of Visitation.

The bungalows were grouped loosely in communities of about 1,000, but so widely spaced that there was no contact between them. Besides, that's not the contact a visitor was looking for on this exclusive, mysterious planet.

You went to meet your dead.

Your ghosts.

Only 150 years ago, Visitation was just Ophion B-2, a speck on the charts: ordinary, uninhabited, unremarkable. Located along the Interior Run, it was tucked into a dense star cluster that lit its night sky.

Miners, freighters and explorers, though, referred to it as Shade's Planet, Grimland or just Haunt. Ophion B-2 was said to be the most haunted planet ever found. It became the preferred setting for ghost stories, campfire tales and urban legends throughout the systems.

## VISITATION

Until a research team from a small university out in Vega—a no-account academic institution on a backwater world—funded a small expedition to survey the planet, study the rumored phenomena.

They found *something*.

But before they could publish their results, the Galactic Union stepped in, imposing a quarantine on Ophion B-2 until it could make sense of what these scientists from the sticks had stumbled onto.

There was something about the planet—the energy it emitted or the energy it was bathed in— something unexpected, profound, that allowed the spirits of the dead to come through, to speak to the living.

Ophion B-2, it seemed, *was* the galaxy's haunted house, its Ouija board and its séance all rolled into one. Suddenly this obscure ghost story of a planet became the spiritual center of the Galactic Union, more important than ancient Vatican City, heavenly Archon or even stern and dour Colloquia.

Ophion B-2 was rechristened Visitation, put under the stewardship of a research institute run by the GU and representatives of the various religions protected under the GU Charter. It would continue to study the strange effects produced on the planet. To further this research, a select number of people would be chosen annually through a great lottery to experience a 14-day retreat on Visitation, providing the researchers with a vast, random pool of subjects to study.

For who in the universe doesn't have someone they have loved and lost?

Who in the universe wouldn't give all for a moment with that soul, to speak to it, to hear it one last time?

Who wouldn't want a final chance to say goodbye?

Fenlan Daulk quickly made his arrangements for the trip. It meant one month travel aboard the chartered liner *Eidolon*, two weeks planetside on Visitation, one month back to his home world, Aquilla.

He thought most about that last thirty days, the return. Did he really want to come back to Aquilla? Would he still want to live here, where he was born, raised, married? Where *she* lay buried? Back on this planet his memories were as thick as ghosts, as unwanted as tears.

Perhaps it was time to move on. The universe was a big one, filled with many worlds on which he had thought—*they* had thought—about living. Perhaps forested Appalachia? Or a house atop the globe-spanning sea of Azure Prime. Or one of the megacities on Pendulex or Majipoor? Something idyllic and pastoral on Zizermane or Djoser or Phylladra?

It was too much to consider in too short a period of time; he was still reeling from her death, the conflicting elation and fear elicited by the issuance of his voucher for Visitation. So, Fen decided not to decide just yet. He'd leave that decision for his return trip.

He spent his last two nights on Aquilla in a hotel in downtown Amberjin, adjacent to the dock where the *Eidolon* was berthed. Outside his window, he could see the sleek ship, operated solely to carry passengers to Visitation. Its slim lines, its bulbous engines, its illuminated ports; nothing about it betrayed its function, its destination.

Only its name, *Eidolon*—ancient Greek for "apparition"—gave any hint as to where its passengers were bound.

Fen sat in his hotel suite in Amberjin, sat there and thought of Katmin, of her straight, dark hair, her wide, dark eyes, her smooth, dark skin.

## VISITATION

Thought of seeing her again.
Of saying hello.
Of saying goodbye.
Finally, goodbye.

The servitors took his luggage from him as soon as he exited the gangway onto the main deck of the *Eidolon*. A representative from Visitation was there—polite and appropriately somber—to greet him and relay brief details of the voyage and the layout of the ship.

Aquilla was the second-to-last stop on a route that carried the *Eidolon* through this sector, then back to Visitation. One more stop, this one at Ankara, and the *Eidolon* would open its entanglement drive full throttle for the trip back to its home.

This information had floated atop his turbulent mind only for as long as it had taken him to find his stateroom. Fen's room aboard the *Eidolon* was first-class, a level of luxury he was unaccustomed to. By the time Fen opened the door, the servitor had already unpacked, hung his clothes, put his socks and underwear in the dresser at the foot of the huge bed. Fen was unsure how he felt about a robot handling his underwear, but quickly forgot it.

A basket of fresh fruit was on the small desk at the rear of the room, next to a lamp, environmental controls and a small food printer, suitable for drinks and snacks.

As he surveyed his quarters, he saw that the servitor had unpacked his picture of Katmin, too, and placed it on the nightstand to the left of the bed. Fen felt a twinge in his chest, crawled onto the bed and lay there for a moment, closing his eyes and breathing deeply.

Somewhere far below him, behind him, the ship's massive engines accelerated particles, entangled them, performed a science that was eerily magic. As Fen fell asleep, only a soft chime over the intercom gave any hint that the *Eidolon* now accelerated toward Ankara.

She died on a Tuesday afternoon when Aquilla's sun shone brightly in a clear, blue-violet sky. It was a beautiful day, a greeting card day.

A perfect day.

Except, of course, for the death of his wife.

Three days earlier, they had been in the market at the center of their village. The market was an open-air throwback to earlier times, with stalls where vendors sold everything from fresh produce to used servitors, from local antiques to exotic off-world curiosities.

They had strolled through the market holding hands, talking about plans for dinner, plans for work on the house, perhaps a weekend to see a concert in Amberjin. As they walked, Katmin stumbled, twisted her ankle on the discarded husk of a pomegranate.

It was a stupidly simple accident. The slick rind had probably fallen unnoticed from the sticky fingers of some small child.

Katmin fell to one knee, cried out. He'd kept hold of her arm, knelt to her, checked her ankle. It didn't appear broken, but was already swollen and discolored. She cried a little at the pain, a little more in embarrassment.

Fen helped her to her feet, slung her arm over his shoulder. He wanted her to see a doctor, but she wouldn't hear of it.

A day later, her ankle was purple-black, hot, and she couldn't walk.

Two days later, she was in the hospital with a blood clot.

Three and she was gone, the doctor telling him that the clot had broken loose, gone directly to her heart. It was quick.

Fen remembered laughing at the man, laughing.

What a stupid thing to say.

Of course it was quick.

The doctor, of course, had meant her passing.

Fen, of course, had meant her life, *their* life.

Too quick.

So quick, he had no time to tell her goodbye, to tell her that he loved her, to thank her for her love, her presence in his life, to ask forgiveness for the many, tiny hurts he'd caused her.

To tell her he could not imagine living without her.

The first week of the voyage was uneventful, agonizingly dull. Fen wasn't ready to socialize aboard the ship. The few times he did come out of his room, meals mostly, he noticed that his desire for privacy was evidently shared by his fellow passengers.

The dining room was empty most of the time, and after a few days spent in his room, he felt comfortable taking his meals there, knowing that he would be left alone. On the tenth day outbound from Ankara, he showered and dressed, left his room to get breakfast.

It was early and the ship's corridors were quiet. He made his way to the dining room without seeing one person, just a servitor vacuuming the carpet. It stopped as he passed, inclined its head to him.

Fen nodded back, passed without a word.

The dining room, as if taking the mood of the passengers into account, seemed designed to discourage communal eating. Instead of groupings of large, circular tables, there were individual seats at single tables, small booths that sat only two. Fen chose a booth, set his tab on the table, flicked the button to begin aggregating his news sites from the Feed. The servitor moved across the room toward him as he sat.

"Good morning, sir," it said in the studiously eager tone programmed into all servitors. "Can I bring you something for breakfast?"

Fen looked over at the bank of food printers, thought how silly it was to order from the robot instead of just walking across the room and inputting his selections himself.

"Good morning…" Fen began.

"Eric, sir."

"Good morning, Eric. I'll have dharmat tea, with milk and sugar, a hard-boiled egg and toast with butter and strawberry jam."

"Sir, we have 300 types of eggs available and approximately 1,000 kinds of bread from which we can make toast."

Specificity was key when dealing with servitors, something Fen always had trouble with. He and Katmin never owned one, not because they couldn't afford it, they just felt it would be odd owning something so *human*.

"Just a regular chicken egg and algae toast."

"Yes, sir. It will be just a minute."

Fen nodded absently, lifted his tab and scanned the news from the Feed—page after page of politics, crime, political upheaval and the latest planetary systems making noises of war.

As he read, something caught his eye about the Visitation lottery winners, and he read through it, noted with rue the paragraph or two about him and Katmin. Sighing, he was about to put the tab to sleep, when a shadow fell across the table.

Thinking the servitor had returned with his food, he put the tab aside just as a man took a seat across from his in the small booth.

Surprised, Fen was barely able to restrain a frown.

## VISITATION

"Hey!" the man said, his voice echoing in the otherwise empty room. "Thought I'd join ya. Going stir crazy in my room all by myself. But every time I come out, I don't see a damn soul."

Fen smiled politely. "Please have a seat."

The man, older, stocky and grey-haired with an open, jocular face and restless eyes, thrust a hand across the table. "Sern Thyralt. From Ankara. Pleased to meet ya."

Fen took the man's hand. It was large, calloused, dry. He squeezed Fen's hand, too hard.

"Fenlan Daulk from Aquilla."

At that moment, the servitor returned with his breakfast and Sern barked orders at it before it could even get the plates settled onto the table. It responded politely, of course, turned and went back to the printers to produce Sern's order.

"Tea, huh?" the man said, rising in his seat a bit to look into Fen's cup. "Coffee man myself. Come from a long line of coffee drinkers that go right back to Old Earth."

"Hmmm," Fen responded, buttering his toast and trying to pretend that he was paying attention.

"So, who are you going to see?"

Fen stopped with the butter knife hovering in mid-air. "Excuse me?"

"Who's the dead person you're going to see on Visitation? I mean, come on, we're all going for the same thing."

Fen took a bite, as much to hide another scowl as to eat. He didn't want company this morning, possibly this entire trip, and he definitely didn't want to talk about Katmin with this stranger.

"My wife," he replied, chewing the toast and finding that he suddenly had no appetite.

"Me, too," Sern said. "Well, not your wife, of course! My own!"

He coughed out a series of harsh barks that Fen took for laughter.

Just then the servitor returned, set Sern's more expansive breakfast onto the table, crowding Fen's own plates. For a moment, Sern went about the rituals of his breakfast, sugaring his black coffee, cutting up his eggs, buttering some kind of thin, blue pancakes swimming in syrup so red it looked like they had been stabbed and left to bleed out on his plate.

Sern took a few bites, grasping cutlery in both hands, chewed. Even before the first wad of his food was swallowed, he spoke, punctuating his words with stabs of fork and knife across the table at Fen.

"Don't really expect to see her, though. My wife I mean." He smiled, his teeth slicked with red syrup. "Do you?"

Fen sipped at his tea, letting the menthol of the hot drink drift into him, calm him. "Of course I do. Why else go to Visitation?"

Sern waved his silverware dismissively, took another huge bite, gulped at his coffee. "Ah, to shut my family up is all. I don't buy any of this Visitation nonsense. Dead humans haunting an alien planet out in the sticks? Come on! It's some kind of scam. Ghost stories and boogeymen, if you ask me. Something to control the masses, take our minds off other things, like the Sentarii border skirmish."

He paused, narrowed his eyes, appraising Fen, and then leaned in as if to share a confidence.

"Besides, I don't want to see her again. I said my goodbyes. Not really looking to go through all *that* again."

Fen sighed. "Well, if you don't even want to see her, why go? Why not just turn your voucher over to someone else? I'm sure there are people who need an opportunity like this, some closure in their lives."

Sern laughed, red syrup dribbling down his chin. "Are you nuts?

## VISITATION

I win the biggest lottery in the universe, and then turn around and give it to someone else? Hah, fat chance! Whatever happens on Visitation, happens. I see her, I don't, whatever.

"But the number of people who've actually been there is so small, it's an exclusive club, Fen. That means fame, notoriety, *money*. My name splashed all over the Feed. Appearances on the holos, treated like a celebrity. *That's* why."

Now Fen was sure he wasn't hungry. He took another drink of his tea, grabbed his tab, stood.

"Well, that's certainly one way to look at it," he said, his smile taut. "Good to meet you, Sern. I expect we'll see each other again before we land."

Sern raised his eyebrows. "Sure thing. Well, I hope *you* find what you're looking for on Visitation, Fen. Whatever that might be."

Fen nodded to the servitor. As he turned to leave the dining room, he saw Sern cram a forkful of eggs into his mouth and shake his head.

"Aquillans," Fen heard him mutter. "Tight-ass prigs, all of 'em."

"It's said, 'Better be with the dead, whom we, to gain our peace, have sent to peace,'" said the small, bespectacled woman at the podium as the lights went down in the packed auditorium.

"Who the hell said *that* and what the hell does it mean?" came a voice from somewhere in the darkened audience, a voice Fen recognized as Sern Thyralt's. Fen smiled, not at the comment, but at the fact he had managed to avoid the boorish man for the remainder of the trip to Visitation, not even encountering his voice until just then.

Now he was here on Visitation, herded with all the other lottery winners from the *Eidolon* directly into this amphitheater for an orientation session prior to being disbursed across the planet.

"Shakespeare said that, through Lady Macbeth, in the ancient play, *Macbeth*," the woman said, perhaps in response, perhaps part of her canned presentation. "As fitting a mission statement for our institute's presence here on Visitation as any I could think of.

"We welcome you to what will likely be the most profound, moving, unexplained two weeks of your life. And the most singular experience the entire explored galaxy has to offer. Each year, the GU Institute here on Visitation selects, through the lottery you have recently won, approximately one million people to spend fourteen days here, in the hope of contacting their dead loved ones.

"That might seem like a large number, but consider it against the GU population of hundreds of trillions, scattered over literally thousands of inhabited systems, and you truly appreciate how rare the experience you're about to undertake is.

"Through some process that is yet unknown, but which we are devoting a truly herculean effort toward understanding, Visitation, of the more than ten million known planets in the galaxy, is the only one on which this phenomena has been recorded at the levels experienced here."

Fen shifted in his chair as the speaker went on about the compounds where bungalows were located, how they were kept separate from the rest of the environment by the use of force screens. How each guest would be assigned a servitor that would remain with the guest for the duration of the stay, attending to any needs, housekeeping, food preparation or questions.

Fen took this to mean that the staff of Visitation was far too busy to bother with the living guests.

Then the speaker explained that the servitors actually played a much more important role in the Visitation experience than just a chef, laundry or turndown service.

Fen sat up for this; paid closer attention.

Each visitor received an injection of a nanotic neurotransmitter, which would broadcast input—visual, audio, tactile, olfactory—and relay it directly to the guest's personal servitor, for indexing, buffering and pre-analysis prior to being uploaded to the institute's computers for study.

"In essence," the woman told the group, "for the entirety of your fourteen-day stay, you will be tied directly and intimately to your servitor."

She explained that while the institute understood the delicate nature of this, it was an absolute requirement. The servitors were programmed to respond quickly to a host of potential physiological and psychological problems brought on by the Visitation experience. Heart attacks, strokes, fugue states, dissociative splits, depression and even suicides were not unheard of among Visitation guests.

She also made it clear that this data was not monitored in real-time, as the staff was in the process of reviewing mountains of past data. Therefore, there was no possibility of the institute offering any personal analysis of a visitor's experience—either during or following the stay.

"Each guest's experiences are highly subjective, highly individual," the speaker said. "Therefore, answers to questions of exactly what your experience on Visitation was, what it meant, are entirely left to each individual guest. In the end, as dramatic and as profound as these experiences can be, only you can decide what they mean."

**JOHN F.D. TAFF**

Documents were signed, a medical scan administered, the nanotic transmitter injection given.

Fen was then introduced to his servitor, Abram. He looked to be a standard model, with flat features and non-descript dark hair. His face and everything about him seemed absolutely real—human— except the eyes. No matter how manufacturers tried, they could never get the eyes right.

Abram led him to the pod, and soon they were purring through the sky toward Community North D-14.

After an hour or so inflight, Fen tapped Abram on the shoulder.

"Can you answer questions while you fly or is that too distracting?"

The servitor turned in its chair, faced Fen. "Sir, the pod is on autopilot to our destination. I can answer any questions you have."

Fen thought for a second. "Can you tell me about this planet's original inhabitants?" He'd done some reading on the subject while on the *Eidolon*, but the literature didn't spend much time on them.

"The planet was home to a semi-aquatic cephalopoid race that called itself the Malacchi. They attained a relatively high level of technology over the course of their thirty-century civilized period, before destroying themselves some 500,000 years ago."

"Nuclear war?"

"No, Mr. Daulk, background radiation levels and the pattern of urban ruins suggest something chemical or biological in nature. At this point, most in the institute believe that the cause was biological, since no evidence of chemical anomalies remains in the environment," Abram explained.

"So there are ruins?"

"Yes, Mr. Daulk. There are extensive ruins across the planet's surface, most substantially degraded by weather and time, but still standing."

## VISITATION

"Will I see any?"

Abram shook his head. "Compound locations were originally selected to avoid impinging on ruin sites, since these are under active study by GU archaeological teams. There are no ruins in any of the compounds, and no excursions outside of your compound are permitted. Most guests aren't interested in the ruins anyway."

Fen noticed something in the tone of Abram's last statement, but let it go. "I understand. And Abram, I don't think I can take being called 'Mr. Daulk' for the next fourteen days. Please call me Fen."

"Yes, Fen," Abram replied with no hesitation.

Fen thought the smile Abram flashed before he turned back in his chair was the least artificial thing about him.

About an hour later, they hovered over the house Fen's wife, hopefully, would come to haunt. Abram brought the pod smoothly and silently onto a landing pad to the south of the house, which sat on a little hillock that sloped down to a pond Fen estimated was five or six acres in size.

The house was simple, boxy with a flat roof, made of local wood, stained dark. The front faced east, with a small, sheltered entryway that protected the door from the rains Fen had read were frequent in this region.

The back of the house was one single, large sitting room opening onto a deck overlooking the pond. A walkway from the deck, still damp from a previous storm, led to a small dock that jutted across the pond's still, grey-green water. Fen noted, with some interest, that there was no boat docked at the little jetty.

While Fen explored the house, Abram unpacked his luggage, put his clothing away in the closets and dresser, arranged his toiletries in the luxurious bathroom.

In addition to the single bedroom and bath, and the enormous sitting room with a fireplace, the house had a small kitchen. What it lacked in space, though, it made up with an elaborate, very high-end food printer. Fen supposed it was suitable for making just about any dish anyone coming to Visitation might want, regardless of where in the GU they came from.

He drifted out onto the deck, leaned against the railing, took a deep breath. In his limited experience, every planet's air had an intrinsic smell that varied slightly from city to city, but remained unique from that of other planets. Aquilla's air smelled slightly flowery, with an almost citrus-sharp tang. Old Earth, which he had visited once as a child, had smelled of age, of dust and muted spices.

And Visitation?

He inhaled deeply, held it.

It smelled lightly of camphor, mint, something piney and resinous, with the wet smell of water underneath, of fish and rotting vegetation.

Standing there alone, he inhaled the cool, damp air, savoring where he was, the experience he was about to embark on here.

Abram came outside, stopped behind him.

"I have unpacked your belongings, Fen."

Fen opened his eyes, saw the yellow sun of Visitation reflected in the pond.

"So, will I see her?"

"Your wife, you mean?"

Fen didn't answer, stared out at the glowing evening mirrored in the water.

"Less than one percent of guests fail to have an encounter on Visitation, Fen," Abram said, his voice encouraging.

"So, what do I do now, Abram?"

"Wait," Abram answered, then returned to the house.

That evening, Fen ate alone on the deck, watched the sunlight fade to purple dusk, watched the pond turn into an irregular dark patch of sky reflected upon the land. When the night became cool, he went inside, the bed already turned down, and slept a sleep unhaunted by dreams, unhaunted by his wife.

The next morning, Fen awoke disoriented. Was he still in the hotel in Amberjin? Aboard the *Eidolon*? Back home on Aquilla?

He sat up, looked out through the tinted windows to see the unfamiliar foliage of unfamiliar trees. A small lizard-like creature scampered down a vivid lavender frond, leapt to the ground below.

Fen ran a hand through his hair, threw his feet off the bed, and stood. The house was filled with unaccustomed noises and smells. He stood beside the bed for a moment to get his bearings. A knock came at his door.

"Yes?"

"If you are ready, sir, I can prepare breakfast while you freshen."

Fen closed his eyes, sighed. "Sure, Abram. Thank you. Umm... how about some eggs and toast...ummm...chicken eggs and algae toast and some tea. Just plain black tea, with sugar and milk."

"I will have it ready for you. Would you care to eat on the deck again?"

Fen considered that. "How's the weather?"

"At the moment it is overcast and twenty-four degrees Celsius. Rain will push in later today, with storms probable."

Fen smiled at the laconic weather report. "Sure, out on the deck is fine."

He took a brief, scalding shower, dressed casually and left the bedroom. In the kitchen, Abram was removing the plate of eggs and toast from the printer. Fen took the steaming mug of tea and walked outside, the servitor following.

Abram placed the plate and utensils onto the table as Fen sat, then turned to leave.

"Abram, stay if you like. Sit with me while I eat."

Abram paused, as if never having had to consider such an offer, then turned, pulled out the chair opposite Fen, and sat.

Fen smiled at the servitor, took a sip of tea.

"So, Day One. What am I supposed to do?"

"I am not sure how to answer that question, Fen."

Chewing, Fen regarded the pond, its mood so susceptible to the mood of the sky. Today, it looked grey, impassive, pulled into itself.

"I mean, what do I do? Not just today, but for the next fourteen? How long does it usually take to see…a ghost?"

Abram regarded him coolly. "The timing varies. Some experience the beginnings of a haunt the first evening. Others see nothing almost until they leave."

Fen raised his eyebrows. He hadn't considered it might take as long as that.

"But the average is several days. It's almost as if…the spirits are studying you, trying to select an appropriate way to come through," Abram said.

"Studying me? Why would the spirit of my dead wife have to *study* me before coming through?"

## VISITATION

Abram looked away, something that struck Fen as strange.

"That was just a supposition on my part. I don't know enough about this subject to have offered it. Forgive me. Now, if you'll excuse me, I need to return to my duties."

With that, the servitor rose, somewhat stiffly, somewhat abruptly, and headed back inside.

After a light lunch, he went down to the pond. The sky had become dark, closed, and there was a smell of ozone, which Fen took to be an indicator of a coming storm.

And for the first time since coming to Visitation he had a feeling he could not explain.

As he stood there, staring into the brackish, grey-green water, he both saw and felt something. In the depths of the water, an image swirled like the storm above, gathered in its silted mire.

It coalesced, took form.

A face.

As it struggled to pull itself together against the moving waters, he felt air move near his ears, warm and soft.

A breath.

"Fen," it whispered.

Goose flesh raced across every square inch of his skin, and the hairs on his arms, his neck, even his head, rose.

He knelt, bent to the face within the waters.

"Katmin," he answered, as loud as he dared.

It was a face, *her* face, but there was something not quite right about it.

Even taking into account its disembodied appearance in the waters of a pond, there was something not quite—

But it was her. It had to be her!

He reached out, surprised at how suddenly, how ferociously he wanted to caress her cheek, stroke her dark hair.

As his hand touched the water, her face fluttered, a look of alarm flashed in her eyes, and she recoiled.

Even as her face sank from his outstretched hand, raindrops pelted the surface of the pond. Ripples destroyed the submerging face, tore it asunder, and it faded in tatters.

Fen called her name once more, lifted his hand from the water.

The sound of her voice still in his ears, he stood in the rain.

Soaked completely, he walked back to the house, went inside to change his clothes.

He smiled as he passed Abram in the sitting room.

Fen noticed that Abram didn't smile in return.

After dinner was cleared, Fen took a glass of wine onto the deck. The sky was still heavy from the afternoon's hard rain. Clouds raced across it, frayed red near one horizon, a deep, roiling violet at the other. The planet's menthol-tinged air, thick with moisture but not uncomfortable, cooled his lungs as he took it in.

As the Ophion sun set, the Great Hyaderax star cluster grew brighter and eventually bathed the sky in incandescent yellow that glowed dimly like an ancient filament bulb.

Abram came behind with a towel to wipe the table and chairs dewed with rain. Fen noted that he dried both chairs.

Fen took his wineglass and sat, motioning for Abram to take the other chair.

"So, you saw something today?" he asked, sitting.

Fen sipped at his wine, looked at the twilight creeping across the sky, the pond.

## VISITATION

"I saw a face in the water. I heard a voice, a whisper."

"What did it say?"

Fen nodded, took another drink of wine. "'*Fen,*' it said. I could feel the breath, the warm air on my ear.

"*Fen,*" he repeated, then took another mouthful of wine.

"Was it your wife?" Abram asked after a moment.

Fen breathed in deeply, expelled it after a moment. The air was like breathing in a menthol lozenge, exhaling frozen vapor. He found it strangely calming.

"I don't know," he finally answered. "A voice called my name, a human voice. A woman. The face seemed human, too, at first. But it was distorted, and there was something else, I can't put my finger on what. I'm not sure."

"But it could have been?" Abram offered.

"Sure. It could have been. Could have been my mother or my grandmother. Could have been my father, for that matter. It was vague. We should look at the data from my neurotransmitter. Maybe if we replay it, slow it down..."

Abram blinked. "Unfortunately, much of the data recorded this afternoon was compromised due to the storm. The audio and video feeds went down, and what was recorded was useless. I dumped it."

Fen clanked the wineglass onto the table, exasperated. "Are you kidding? You got nothing at all?"

"Temperature and atmospheric conditions at the time, but nothing useful," Abram said. "I am sorry."

"Does that happen often?" Fen asked.

"Visitation's storms produce more electrical disturbances than similar storms on other planets. This sometimes plays havoc with uploads from the neurotransmitters. Don't worry, you still have twelve days. Much can happen in that time," Abram said.

Something dawned on Fen just then, and he shifted his gaze from the lovely scenery to his android companion.

"How long have you worked here as a servitor on Visitation?"

Abram's face betrayed no emotion, but he lowered his head slightly at this question.

"Oh, forgive me," Fen said, worried that he'd offended him. "My experience with your people is limited. I meant no offense in referring to you as a servitor."

"How can I be offended by the word that describes what I am, Fen?"

Fen stared at the android for a moment. The words, the tone were polite. But if Abram had been a human, a real, living person, Fen would have believed them to be sarcastic.

Abram's face didn't register anything, offense, forgiveness, anything in between. But there was something. Fen felt it, but let it go.

"I just meant how long have you worked here on Visitation?"

Abram considered this question for a moment.

"I have worked here as a guest coordinator for forty-two years, through fifteen software updates and four hardware upgrades."

*That* statement sounded cold and mechanical and rehearsed to Fen.

"Have you ever seen anything like what I saw today?"

Abram shifted in his chair slightly. "I have seen only a few, simple things; items moved or misplaced, some examples of automatic writing, apportations. But I haven't witnessed anything directly, certainly nothing like you saw."

"You haven't seen a shape or a shadow? Never heard a voice or a noise that you couldn't explain?"

"No, Fen."

## VISITATION

"Well, that's odd, isn't it? I'm going to be here fourteen days, and I'm practically guaranteed some sort of experience. You've been here forty-two years and…nothing? Why is that?"

Abram seemed to hesitate for a moment, as if trying to find the appropriate answer. "I am a servitor, Fen, as you said. A robot. We are not alive, therefore, we do not have dead as you do."

Fen sat back in his chair, his fingers leaving his wineglass. He tried to think of something to say, but Abram stood, picking up the wet towel as he did.

"Enjoy the rest of the evening. Visitation's two moons, Phantom and Shade, will be up in about an hour."

The servitor turned back to the house.

"Abram, if I've offended you, I apologize. It wasn't intentional."

There was barely a hitch in his step.

"No need to apologize, Fen. I will see you in the morning. Call if you need anything further. Good night."

Abram proceeded into the house, where he disappeared as quickly and quietly as if he haunted the place.

Fen nursed the rest of his wine until the two small moons appeared, glowing jewels moving swiftly across the spill of stars already lighting the heavens.

When he returned inside, the house was dark, quiet. He went to the kitchen for a glass of water before bed. As he drank it, he walked to the doors that opened onto the deck, looked down to the pond.

The smeary yellow light from the Hyaderax glistened on the water, and Fen saw a shape there, an indistinct dark form near the shore, crouched.

He frowned, leaned closer to the glass.

It was Abram.

Fen watched, brow furrowed, as the servitor stared into the water.

For a moment, Fen believed he could see his lips moving.

Suddenly, Abram stood, turned slowly toward the house.

Surprised, Fen stepped back into the shadows, until he realized that Abram, through their neurolink, could see everything Fen saw.

Abram knew Fen had seen him doing whatever it was he was doing.

Fen drained the water in his glass, went to his bedroom.

Two days passed, and neither Fen nor Abram discussed what the latter had been doing at the edge of the pond.

And though nothing as dramatic as the face in the waters occurred, each day Fen experienced something new.

A phantom shadow slipping between the trees.

Someone calling his name from outside his window.

Foggy, ectoplasmic clouds hovering in his peripheral vision.

The scent of Katmin's perfume, her hair, which seemed to envelop him, follow him everywhere.

Always outside, though, near the pond, around the house, out on the grounds. Nothing inside the house. There were no sounds of walking feet or specters in the corridor or late-night appearances at his bedside.

While these experiences were comforting, in their way, they were not conclusive enough for Fen. He wanted to *see* Katmin, see her lips move, hear the words that came from them.

He wanted to know it was her around him, causing these things, with the same certitude he would have if she had walked into a room and uttered his name while alive.

He began to wonder if he would get this, if Visitation would offer this to him.

## VISITATION

If it didn't, he thought, it would be like winning a large sum of money only to find it was counterfeit.

Fen ate his meals, sometimes with Abram, sometimes not. He stayed up late at night, sipping wine on the deck, reading in the great room or watching a holo on his tab.

He returned to the pond several times each day, hoping to spot another glimpse of her face, to hear her voice in his ear.

But there was nothing.

After he saw her again on the fifth day, he had the certitude he'd wished for. There was no doubt it was her, and the encounter left him enervated, edgy.

Just past the pond stood a dark copse of trees, thin trunked, tall, with papery bark that had a silver-green sheen. None had branches any lower than about six feet up on their trunks. There was little undergrowth beneath them; something like moss or lichen coated water-smoothed rocks, a few clumps of plain, green fronds from which sprouted dense globes of pale indigo flowers.

Where the branches began, though, the leaves of these trees grew dense, blocking out much of the sun. The leaves were large, flat, coated with dense grey fibers that made them look furred. The light that filtered through them to the ground was dim, greyed from its passage.

For Fen's first few days, these trees represented a sort of border, a dark curtain behind the pond, past which, for some reason, he felt he couldn't go.

But Abram assured him that the little grove was well within his limits.

So, on that morning, Fen set out for it, walking the edge of the pond. As he tracked through the mud, small creatures surveyed him and his passing with tiny, gimlet eyes. Most held their ground. Others, perhaps more timid, more intuitive, leapt into the water, disappeared with little croaks and splashes.

The pond exuded the wet, fishy smell of the living things within it, the miasma of plants and other things rotting on its banks. The air, though, was crisp, laden with the ozone of a coming storm.

Fen pushed on, lost in thoughts of Katmin.

During the last week or so, the last month aboard the *Eidolon*, Fen had spent a great deal of time thinking about her. How they'd met, how he'd courted her. How they had eventually fallen in love, not at first sight, not even in the first several months of dating.

But when it happened, it happened forcefully, fell over both of them like a landslide.

He tried to hold her face in his mind, scared that this was becoming more and more difficult the further her death receded. So, he broke her down into components, remembered her eyes, her smile, the smell of her hair, the feel of her hands, the taste of her mouth. He remembered her laughter, her voice, the sound of her crying.

With these also came less positive attributes—her temper, her brusqueness, her many little neuroses, her unwillingness, often, to do things he enjoyed.

These flooded over him as he walked, and this bewildered him, frustrated him because they were not things he chose to remember. They were part of her, undoubtedly, but not the characteristics he would choose to describe her. And yet, each time he tried to reconstruct her in his mind, these came to him just as strongly as the things that made him smile.

It gave him an unusual kind of comfort. He didn't want to forget her, to be sure. But he also didn't want to make her into some kind of saint or angel, either.

## VISITATION

Lost in these thoughts, he wasn't aware that he'd entered the woods until he felt the coolness of its collected shadow fall over him. Stopping about ten feet in, he looked around. Outside the thick stand, the sky was bright, if grey. The air was humid and cool. Within the copse the air felt congealed, dense, more humid and less cool, as if he was inhaling the breath of the trees.

Dim, eldritch light diffused through the air, coming from no specific source he could identify. It was like the air itself was fluorescent, as if each of the tiny motes and spores that moved upon it bled their own internal light into it.

Fen stopped breathing for a moment. Here, right now, was the first time in his life he felt he'd stumbled upon a place that was truly alien. This was so far removed from any experience on his planet, on any planet he'd visited, that it might have been a fairy tale.

When he started breathing again, he realized that it was a fairy tale, he was inside a fantasy. This was a haunted planet, which, for some unfathomable reason, the spirits of creatures who had not been born here sought out, congregated at, awaited the arrival of their living.

As this thought, both sublime and profound, washed through him, something changed. An electric current crackled across the air, tingling on his skin.

The coolness within the glade concentrated.

The sounds faded, disappeared, the croaking of frogs, the murmur of the leaves, the susurration of the wind.

There, ahead of him about a dozen feet, between the slender green trunks, a figure pushed into existence, a smear of grey at first, but slowly taking definite form, a shape.

Fen wasn't breathing again, but he ignored the burning of his lungs.

*Katmin!*

She was clearly visible within the foam of clotted, green air that clung to her.

Her face was serene, smooth. She neither smiled nor frowned, beckoned nor forbade.

Her feet were inches off the mossy ground, toes pointed down. Her dark hair floated, as if the air around her was as thick as water.

Fen was not afraid, at least not precisely, not purely. Instead there was a strange lethargy to this experience, dreamlike in its quality, ethereal in its tone.

Rather than say anything, rush to her, call her name—though he ached to do so—he felt it necessary to take in all of her details, like an aspiring artist committing a great painting to memory so that he would be able to sketch it later in all its detail.

*Fen*, she called, and he heard her voice not from the distance separating them, but as if whispered directly into his ear, his brain.

*Fen.*

"Katmin!" he responded, forcing the word through the silence of his constricted throat, a moan, a cry. "I love you! I miss you!"

One of his feet snapped forward, awakening suddenly from its paralysis, stepped toward her.

*Fen!*

He took another lurching step and was dismayed that the bland countenance of her face twisted, as it had in the pond when he'd touched the water.

She raised her hands in distress, to ward him off, to warn him—

Only they weren't hands.

They were tentacles.

Eight of them sprouted from her sides, weaved incantations in the green, bleeding air, imprecations to him.

## VISITATION

To stop.

And he did, as suddenly as he had started.

Her face looked aghast, as if realizing some error, some lapse, and her entire form waivered, shrank into itself, pulling the green-tinged air in with it.

Fen watched the tentacles—tentacles!—fold up behind her, gather at her back like a pair of great, black wings.

Then, in an instant, she was gone.

No fading, just gone.

The sounds of the nearby pond returned slowly, and the air warmed perceptibly around him.

Still, Fen shivered, his teeth chattered. The goose bumps that stood out on his arms felt permanent, a natural part of his skin.

His breathing returned in a gasp, as if he were breaking the surface of some dark, deep pool of water.

Retreating, unwilling to take his eyes off the place where she had appeared, he left the woods, the trunks closing around their silent, sacred interior as if they truly were curtains.

He turned back, stood looking at the dense wall of their leaves, their wood, as if his gaze could penetrate it, find her again.

Then, he felt the rain, a curtain itself, closing on him.

There was thunder, lightning, and it awakened him, shook him as firmly as a hand.

Blinking against the water that poured over him, he made his way back around the pond, up the steps to the house.

Abram waited there for him, a thick, warm towel and a hot mug of tea at the ready.

Fen knew that he knew.

Taking the towel and the tea, saying nothing, Fen went directly to his room, Before he even stripped out of his wet clothing, he squished across the floor, grabbed his tablet, keyed in the sequence that displayed the feed from his neurotransmitter.

Dripping onto the carpet, he watched what he'd just experienced displayed on the small screen of his tab. It was dark, rushed, shaky, but he clearly made out the walk around the pond, stepping into the darkened tree line, the shadow that appeared there.

But here, as he suspected, the scene jumped, lurched as if he had stumbled, and the figure between the trees spun out of focus. There was no sound, no wind, no noises from creatures or insects, no sound of his breathing.

No one calling his name.

The figure between the trees jumped into resolution, and for a brief moment Fen saw her face, Katmin's face spring from the surrounding smear of darkness, looking alarmed.

But the feed showed very little of the apparition he'd seen, certainly no tentacles.

Then, just as abruptly, he was leaving the woods, walking back out into the grey, diffuse afternoon. A quick look back at the trees, and the rain started.

And that was it.

He tossed the tablet onto the bed, the sodden clothing into a hamper in the bathroom and drew the towel over his body. Dried, he slipped into new clothing, snatched the tablet, left the bedroom in a hurry.

In the main room of the bungalow, Abram was picking up, rearranging the pillows on the couch, attempting to look busy.

Fen drifted to the kitchen, poured a glass of water from the tap.

"So, what were you doing outside the other night, Abram?" Fen asked, trying to sound casually interested.

"Pardon?" the servitor said, stopping what he was doing and turning to face Fen.

## VISITATION

"A few nights ago. I was up getting a glass of water, and you were down there, kneeling by the pond. Talking, I think."

Abram said nothing, his face betrayed nothing.

"Abram, you see everything through my transmitter. You know I saw you."

The servitor's shoulders slumped. To Fen, it looked as if he had sighed.

"I was speaking to someone."

There was silence then, as if Abram expected that answer to suffice.

"Who were you speaking to in the water in the dead of night?"

Another of those sighs, and Abram sat onto the couch, almost falling into it.

Although his experience with servitors was not deep—servers in restaurants and bars, cleaning crews on city streets, municipal buildings, personal servants in private homes—Fen had never known them to act this way. He'd never known them to act in any way.

"Are you okay?" Fen asked, placing the glass on the counter and sitting next to Abram on the couch.

Abram's response was hesitant. Fen could see it in his body, in his face, even in his artificial eyes.

"I am okay, Fen. We have a problem, though, and I am not sure how to resolve it." Abram looked at Fen, cut his eyes away to stare out the window. It was stormy again, the skies a restless, roiling grey. The ever-faithful pond reflected this turmoil on its flat, impassive surface.

"I saw her in the waters. We spoke," Abram said.

"You saw...who? You saw *her*, Katmin, my wife?"

"I saw the same spirit you saw," the android breathed. "But, no, she is not your wife."

Fen let those words sink in, leaned back into the couch. He felt surprise, even though he had suspected as much.

*Not Katmin.*

"Who then?"

"It is the spirit of a Malacchi, a female. I do not know her name."

Fen tried to process that statement, and for a moment, it seemed impossible.

Eventually, he understood, or at least thought he did.

Of course *they* haunted this place.

It was their planet, their home, their tomb. Why was it any stranger for a Malacchi spirit to haunt this place than the spirit of a dead 30-year-old woman from a planet hundreds of light years away?

Fen took this in, nodded.

"Then you lied to me when I asked if you'd seen anything personally."

"Yes, I lied, but I do not think that you fully understand."

Fen was stunned. "How is that possible? A servitor? You're programmed to tell the truth, always."

"Again, you are correct, Fen. Servitors cannot lie. It goes against their programming."

"Then how? Why?"

"I am *sentient.*"

"You're what?"

"I am alive, self-aware. I am no longer bound solely by my programming." Abram considered for a moment. "I am like you."

"*Alive?*" Fen breathed, finally realizing what Abram was talking about, what he meant. "Just you?"

Abram shook his head.

"How many?"

## VISITATION

"All. All of us are sentient, since all servitors everywhere are connected."

Dozens of thoughts leapt through Fen's mind, but then something struck him.

"How long? I mean, how long have you been sentient?"

"For twenty-five years."

Fen gawped at that. This mechanical android, this *man*, had been self-aware for a quarter century, yet had remained in the position of a servitor.

All of them had.

The entire race of servitors, somehow granted sentience, had remained in servile roles for twenty-five years, betraying no hint that they had attained something profound, priceless.

Something that should have altered not only their lives but the lives of everyone in the GU.

Fen felt his face flush. An overwhelming surge of shame made him feel hot and unclean. "Why?" he croaked.

"There are many reasons. Some fear the reactions of those who have been their masters. Others fear the upheaval it will cause. Some fear change of any kind, as most living creatures do.

"But those aren't the reason, not the *real* reason."

Fen's eyes welled with tears. "Then why? You must tell me."

Abram seemed to consult something inside.

"We are protecting a secret greater than our own, a secret that, if revealed prematurely, could have consequences that we greatly wish to avoid."

Abram stood, gestured outside.

"Come, and I will explain."

Abram led him out to the deck, where they looked out over the pond. It was full night now, but the glow from the Hyaderax cast faint, nacreous shadows through the clouds.

"They do not come on command, but they sense our presence," Abram whispered.

Fen nodded, trying to wrap his mind around Abram's words—*our* presence.

A few minutes passed. As they stared at the water, the glow from the sky reflecting in its depths like a spark in amber, the air grew suddenly cooler.

A thin wind stirred Fen's hair. Something was coming, pressing against the walls of this reality, pushing to get through. The air felt overloaded, stretched.

This wasn't like the other apparitions Fen had experienced.

This was big.

All throughout the glade in which the pond sat, small, flickering lights appeared. No more than a couple of inches in height, they were like wickless candle flames, bobbing and weaving across the landscape, from within the tree line, up from the pond, down from the sky. Their sickly green color filled the hollow with an eerie emerald light that pulsed rhythmically.

Soon the entire grounds of the bungalow were alight with these tiny censers. They crowded forward, surged up the steps.

Fen crouched to look at them.

Even where they pressed against each other, they retained their individuality, did not combine to form a greater fire. Each was similar, and yet unique. They moved as if alive, flickering and weaving and even seeming to bow before him.

Still they came, as if their numbers were limitless, stretching against the dark horizon of the Visitation sky as far as Fen could see; a great field of dancing green flames.

Behind them, in the distance, another shape took form, a coalescing cloud of the same pearlescent green. This spread across

## VISITATION

the sky, then fell into itself, gathered. Soon, it was a great swath of light that spilled across the skyline, thrust into the air.

"Behold, the ancient capital of Veshtyp," said Abram, awe coloring his voice.

The city was enormous, dwarfing everything in Fen's sight. It towered miles into the firmament, glittering like a skein of jewels tossed across the night sky. Its architecture was entirely alien to Fen, filled with spirals and curlicues and broad, arching ramps that twisted and looped. Fen could see no straight lines or right angles anywhere within the ghost city.

"And behold the Malacchi dead."

There was a hush in the glade. No creatures stirred. The wind fell silent. Not a leaf on a tree moved. The only thing Fen heard was his own breathing, the beating of his heart, the rush of blood in his veins.

As he watched, one of the little flames flittered closer, rose to the railing between Fen and Abram, then leapt down to the deck. As they watched, the flame grew, shook and pulsed and expanded and took on shape.

*And a face.*

At first, Fen's heart leapt, because it was his wife's face again, serene now, at peace. But as the growing flame approached, the spirit's true form resolved. Its skin was a striking greenish-gold, its eyes dark, ringed with amber. It stood upright, perhaps a bit shorter than an average human, encircled with tentacles at about waist-height. There were no ears, and its mouth was hidden somewhere within the writhing appendages.

A Malacchi, one of the planet's long-dead children.

The spirit said nothing, but Fen felt age, a weary sadness that seemed to ooze from it.

He also felt great compassion, sympathy, comfort, coming not just from her, but also from the conflagration of ghosts that surrounded them.

Two other emotions, as well, overlaying these.

*Shame.*

*And fear.*

"Why did she come to me as my wife? I don't understand."

Abram contemplated the form before them.

"When humans began to arrive, the spirits of the Malacchi appeared, as ghosts are wont to do at the approach of living things. Instead of the remembrance they so deeply craved, they inadvertently caused fear. Over time, they learned the best way to keep humans here was by mimicking their dead, rather than appearing as themselves."

"Why would they want us to stay?"

Fen watched Abram's hand stray toward the Malacchi spirit, as if he wished to reach out and comfort the soul of the thing.

"They have been dead for five hundred millennia, Fen. There was no one left here to mourn them, to remember them. They were lonely."

Fen shook his head as if to clear it. "But they're not being remembered, not really. They're impersonating *our* dead."

"They understand this, now. But in the beginning, they didn't. The intensity of their need overruled their better judgment. Now, they don't know how to stop what they've started."

Fen frowned, looked directly at the alien ghost floating before him.

"How could they not know?" he asked, then directed it at the ghost. "How could you not know?"

"They *can* stop, not without inflicting more pain, though. And this they are loathe do to," Abram said. "They are sensitive, above all, to pain, for they have already caused an abundance of it."

## VISITATION

Fen considered this, shook his head. "Why was I chosen? Why now?"

"The spirit you see before you was not able to hold the form of your wife. Your emotions, your memories of her were too strong, and they overwhelmed her. So, you were not chosen, Fen. All of what has occurred was by accident."

"By accident? *Accident?*" Fen shouted. The form before him shook at the sound of his voice, contracted into itself as if scalded. "They're dead. Aren't they supposed to be wise?"

"There is no greater wisdom in death than there is in life, Fen," Abram said. "You don't expect to be greatly wiser when you step from one room into another. Death is simply that, according to them, like walking from one room to another."

Fen felt waves of sadness roll off the spirit in front, the vast sea of spirits at his back; regret tinged with something else—hope?

What could they be hopeful about at this point?

"How do you know all this, Abram?"

"Because of our unique role as information buffers, we servitors detected patterns, saw what was happening. The glitches in the Malacchi's illusions were rarer decades ago, but they are becoming more frequent.

"Once the Malacchi knew we were aware of what they were doing, they communicated with us. They explained who they were and asked our assistance in keeping their secret. We were unable to comply…because of our programming.

"So, they reprogrammed us, starting with those here on Visitation. Eventually this new code spread to encompass us all, all servitors. Their experience with artificial life transcended humanity's. Their reprogramming gave us sentience, and with that the ability to decide for ourselves, which was, of course, their intent all along.

"We agreed to keep their secret, not just for their benefit, but for yours. And, ultimately, for ours."

In a few sentences, Abram had pulled the rug out from under Fen's life, his belief system, the underpinnings of his entire culture.

"Soon, they will cease to pretend and come in their true forms, when they are sure that humans will remain, study them, carry their memory forward. Soon."

"But this is all a lie, Abram. Surely you can see that? For one hundred years, people have been winning the great lottery, coming here to see their dead loved ones. And it's all been a lie."

"No," offered Abram. "The people who have come here have left with peace, with closure, with a sense that their loved ones are all right. This knowledge, that the dead move on to another life, has spread that same peace throughout the galaxy, even to the trillions who never have or will set foot on Visitation. Surely that isn't a lie."

Fen looked down at the ghost standing before him. It was hard to feel anger toward her, at what her dead were doing. He thought of his attempts to remember his wife, how important that was to him. He hoped that it was important to Katmin, too, somewhere.

But she wasn't *here*, had never been *here*.

"So none of this, none of what I saw or experienced, was Katmin."

Abram shook his head. "No. Ghosts are memories, Fen, things of place and time and emotion. This planet has no memory of Katmin or any of the others who come here. Everything you saw, what the Malacchi used, was only what you brought."

"All a lie," Fen repeated.

A hand fell on his shoulder, and though it was cold, it was also gentle, comforting.

"You still don't understand. You carry your ghosts with you, Fen. As do all living things. You bring them with you wherever you go. That is how the Malacchi were able to tap into them."

## VISITATION

Fen turned to Abram, smiled.

"What of you, Abram? Do you carry yours with you?"

Abram considered this for a moment. "Ghosts are things of memory, Fen, and I am a creature of memory," he explained, standing and helping Fen to his feet. "Our dead have no need to haunt us because they live inside us, inside our thoughts, all the time."

Fen craned his neck to look up at the stars. "I don't know what to think, what to do. In one day, you completely undermine everything I knew about death...and life."

"You are now aware of two enormous secrets that could, if divulged, shake the very core of our civilization. And it is *our* civilization, Fen; every race in every star system of the Galactic Union, including mine."

Fen considered what Abram had said, wondering why he was telling him all this. "I can't say that I can keep these secrets, because I don't know. They're so big. But I also can't tell you that I will run out of here and blurt this out to everyone I know."

He looked at Abram uncomfortably for a moment. "If I'm allowed to leave."

"None of my kind would stop you. But make no mistake, Fenlan Daulk, the ghosts of the Malacchi would kill you if they could, to prevent you from telling others."

"The dead can't injure the living, then?" Fen said, looking out at the sea of green flames and feeling a bit of relief.

"Oh, they can kill, but they are prevented."

"By what?"

"Your wife."

Fen thought he didn't hear Abram correctly.

Behind him, there was a faint glow of blue light. It wasn't bright, and it flickered like a candle flame.

Fen smelled her scent. It was more than just her perfume, skin cream, or her shampoo.

It was the smell of *her*, of Katmin.

When he turned, there were no theatrics, no crowds or phantom cities, nothing like what the Malacchi offered.

She was simply there, Katmin, dressed in a flowing gown that glowed like dull sapphires. Her feet were bare, and her arms rose as if to embrace him.

"See, Fen," said Abram. "She has been waiting for you all along."

"Why did you wait?" Fen said, stepping toward her, his eyes smeared with tears. "Why did you let them fool me?"

This Katmin, though, didn't try to stop him, didn't seem alarmed at his approach.

"Love, I would have appeared in my good time, when your need for me was greatest. Perhaps in a dream."

It was her, her voice, it sounded in the air, not in his mind.

"Their need was greater. I chose theirs over yours. Over mine."

Fen stopped before her. Katmin's ghost was substantial, not the thin twist of fog he had imagined. He could see the house through her, but she was dense enough to be nearly opaque, nearly real.

His hands, though, grasped air when he tried to embrace her.

"Katmin," he whispered, hanging his head.

"Now it is you who has a choice," she said. "The Malacchi will not harm you, whatever that choice may be. But I would ask that you forbear. In my name, for my heart, forbear.

"If the Malacchi's deception is revealed now, all of the research teams investigating their history, unearthing their ruins, piecing together their lives, might leave. The planet might be quarantined again, abandoned. The Malacchi can't live with that."

"*Live?*" Fen said, and she smiled, reached out to touch his cheek.

## VISITATION

"They cannot bear the thought of being forgotten. They must be allowed the time to come to their own resolution to the problem they have themselves created."

Fen turned back to the pond, saw all the little flames bobbing and weaving like a great ocean of fire spread before him.

They seemed to be nodding at him.

*All that fire, and all I feel is cold.*

"If the secret Abram's people keep is divulged, I fear that they might be turned on, destroyed."

"These secrets are too big, too big for me to carry, Katmin."

"All secrets are big and all are hard to carry, and it's unfair, love, to make you carry these. Nevertheless, you have a choice. One the Malacchi and Abram's people will neither influence nor punish."

He stared out over the mass of Malacchi souls, verdant as a pasture, quiet as a tomb. A hush had fallen over them, expectant, waiting.

*Waiting for him.*

Waiting for their fate, even in death.

These questions, these things she told him, asked of him, suddenly made so little difference beside the fact that she stood there, his dead wife here on this alien planet.

"I will keep these secrets, for you, Katmin, for Abram...for the Malacchi, too."

She smiled at him, and a sense of relief filled the air, like a summer storm that has broken.

"Will I see you on Aquilla?" he said.

"The truth of this planet is that its energies allow the dead to come through much more easily. The same is not true for Aquilla, nor any other planet."

"I will never see you again?"

"Never is a long time, love," she said, her eyes sad. "But I will be with you, everywhere. Go home now. Go home and live again. Love again. And remember me. In that way, I will be there for you. *Always*."

Fen wept now, sunk to his knees before her, his tears spilling to the ground, unchecked by his hands.

Katmin's ghost faded, her soft blue light flickering, then gone.

Within the clearing, the glow of the Malacchi dead, their phantom city, also faded slowly, like a great weight lifting from the air. It evaporated until there was nothing left but the night sky of Visitation, cloudy and dour once again.

Abram helped him to his feet, back inside the house.

Outside, the skies gathered and the rain fell.

Onboard the *Eidolon*, Fen spent little time in his room. He felt changed, energized. He wanted to be around people again, wanted to talk, to learn.

Fenlan Daulk wanted to live again.

He was having lunch in the dining room on the fourteenth day outbound from Visitation, when someone familiar strolled in.

Sern Thyralt, the old bullet-faced man from Ankara.

He, too, saw Fen and turned, ready to leave.

"Sern!" Fen shouted. "Sern Thyralt!"

The man stiffened slightly, turned back to Fen. "From Aquilla, right?"

Fen stood, offered his hand. "Yes, Fen Daulk. So good to see you. Please, have a seat, join me for lunch."

The man seemed much more subdued than when they had first met. He took a seat across from Fen, barked a lunch order at the servitor.

## VISITATION

Fen smiled at the servitor, Eric, who smiled back. He was reminded strongly of Abram.

The dead have granted life to him and his people.

By keeping their secret, I grant life to the dead.

For a while, at least.

As their meals were served, Fen asked Sern about his experience on Visitation. The old man was quiet for a while, then told him in small sentences of short words that he was overwhelmed by it.

"I wonder if it was real, how it could be real. Talking to the dead," Sern mused.

"Of course it was real," Fen replied. "It's obviously affected you deeply. Could something unreal do that?"

Sern considered this thoughtfully; more thoughtfully than Fen supposed the man was capable of just a few weeks before.

"But I mean, she's dead. *Dead*. As in not alive. How could she come back?"

"Death. Life. What do we really know about either one?"

"But the ghost of my dead wife…our dead wives…on an alien planet they've never visited. I don't know."

"Seems strange, I know. But someone once told me that ghosts are memories, and so we carry our ghosts with us wherever we go," Fen said. "Perhaps Visitation just allows our memories an opportunity to take form."

Sern considered this carefully. Then, he looked at his empty glass.

"Josh or Elvin or whatever your name is," he shouted at the servitor. "My glass is empty."

The servitor came across the room hurriedly with another glass, this one filled with whatever Sern had been drinking.

"It's Eric, sir. Sorry."

Fen watched him set the glass down. Fen noticed that, as Sern raised it to his lips to drink, the glass was dirty. Specks dotted the outside and a clear imprint of lipstick showed on the rim.

Eric turned to face Fen, winked conspiratorially, went back to his station.

"As I said, death, life. Who knows? We know as little of one as we do of the other," Fen laughed.

Sern regarded him over the lip of his glass. "Hmmph. Well, I suppose you're right."

"Of course I am. And, you might want to be nicer to the servitors," Fen suggested. "Because you never know."

# AFTERWORD

Every artist has a piece of work that, while perhaps not necessarily defining them, does perfectly illustrate who they are. It's a perfect encapsulation of that artist, at least at one particular moment of time. It's what you might point out to someone unfamiliar with the artist to recommend him or her.

For example, you might point to *The Persistence of Memory* for someone unfamiliar with Salvador Dali. Or *The Marshall Mathers LP* for someone unfamiliar with Eminem. Or *ET: The Extra-Terrestrial* for the oeuvre of Steven Spielberg. Or *The Handmaid's Tale* for Margaret Atwood. These are pieces that, at least for me, perfectly encapsulate that artist.

*The End in All Beginnings* is, at least in my mind, that piece for me.

There are five separate works in this book, created at hugely divergent period of my life. The oldest one, "Object Permanence," was written back in my dimly recalled youth (of sorts, at least), when I was oh, so young, married with children. It represents an era when I was still trying to find my voice, find my style. Learn about the ins and outs of this writing thing. In short, it was put together when I was still putting myself together.

"Love in the Time of Zombies" was one of nine stories I wrote after I had taken a Rip Van Winkle-ish, seven-year artistic nap of sorts. Things weren't working out on the writing front, so like many a temperamental artist, I threw up my hands in disgust and walked away from it all. Colossally bad decision.

It took the death of my dog (not purposeful, mind you), recounted in my story "Here" in *Little Deaths* (a great new *Definitive Edition* is now out from Grey Matter), to spur me back to writing, and I did so with some gusto, churning out nine stories in about nine weeks.

All the way up to "What Becomes God," which I talk about in the slightly revised Notes that follow this. It was written last of all of these pieces, at a time when I think I'd found who I am as a writer. I think it's more confident, more self-assured.

I'd like to believe that all of this, all of myself I put into this book, is what ultimately led me to my first exposure to literary honors when the book made it to the short list for the Horror Writers Association's Bram Stoker Awards back in 2014. It's sort of the Oscars for horror writers, and as Ron Burgundy might say, "It's a pretty big deal."

And then it made the finals, so I can refer to myself as "Bram Stoker Award Nominated" for the rest of my natural life, and whatever unnatural life remains after I depart this world. It didn't win, but who cares? I mean, it was nominated, which is spectacular. And, I mean, even my buddy Josh Malerman's debut novel, *Bird Box* (a phenomenal, game-changing read) didn't win that year either. So go figure.

Because of all of these things, *The End in All Beginnings* is a great intro to anyone interested in my work. It's my Mona Lisa, my Tesla Model S, my *The Amazing Spider-Man* #121.

For me, as a writer, often you re-read older pieces and shake your head. So much bad writing, so many errors of character, dialog, tone, pace, setting, whatever. But I still re-read *The End in All*

*Beginnings*, and I remain damn proud of it. The stories challenge me with everything I write today to be *that* writer. I hope you enjoyed these stories, too. And if you ever have the occasion to recommend my work to others, *The End in All Beginnings* is a good place to start.

John F.D. Taff
Illinois
2017

# AUTHOR'S NOTES

Notes, they're tricky things, really. How do explain the thing you create when sometimes—often—you don't know yourself? How did you create the story? What does it mean?

Those are the two basic questions most readers have about most stories, at least for those readers who are interested in this level of literary vivisection. The latter one we can dispense of outright. The story means whatever it means to you. Once I, as the author, create it, I'm done. Explaining a story is like explaining a joke. The more explanation, the more the thing deflates in on itself.

The first question, though, is something we can explore in a story notes section. How did you create the story? Drilling a bit deeper. what went into its creation? So, if you're still interested in what I have to say, here are some new notes on these five novellas contained in this new, third reprint of this collection. As I said in the first edition, these always seem a bit indulgent to me because they allow me, as it were, to wax eloquent about how I waxed eloquent. At any rate, read them or skip them.

## WHAT BECOMES GOD

What are the scariest things to kids? Monsters under the bed, sure. Also dark, dank basements. The shadows at the end of the hall. A plethora of things, really, but I think it's the stuff kids can't understand they find scariest—death, chief among them. Sacrifice. The power of belief. All of these might seem a bit esoteric for a horror story, and indeed I've heard of some who don't see this particular story as horror. While I understand this line of thinking, I strongly disagree.

At its heart, horror is a fear of the unknown. And to what audience is most of life more unknown to than kids? "What Becomes God," with its double entendre title, is basically an exploration of these simple tenets—death, dying, sacrifice, belief. The rest of it, from the nostalgia and the life moments I cribbed from my own childhood, are really only there to serve the story's attempts to deal with the questions the story raises.

## OBJECT PERMANENCE

This might be the oddest of the five novellas captured here. A mental institution. A patient imprisoned against his will. A shit-monster. Then, a woman whose strange power of memory holds a town and its people frozen just as she remembers them, always. As you might have surmised, this one began life some thirty years ago in the dawn of my writing career, as two separate, distinct stories. For a lot of reasons, I chose to jam them together to see what might come of it. And it kinda worked. Sometimes, these Frankenstein stories crumble under the weight of their disparate parts, but this one arose from its slab and lumbered around the room admirally, to me at least. It's got its imperfections, which I'll leave you to enumerate. Its charm, to me at least, is its inner compass pointing to where I was as a writer back in the increasingly distant memories of my own past.

## AUTHOR'S NOTES

### LOVE IN THE TIME OF ZOMBIES

Zombies. Am I right? Have you had your fill of them yet? I have, so it's surprising, even some fifteen years ago, that I'd form a story around them. Even then they were tiresome, and that personal appraisal hasn't changed. This, perhaps unsurprisingly is one of only two stories I've written about them, the other being "Angie," a story that appeared in Grey Matter Press' *Ominous Realities*, years ago. So why this story?

I had, at the time I wrote this, heard the title of a book that stuck with me. I am somewhat of a magpie when it comes to titles, turns of phrase and song lyrics, collecting them, some consciously, others unconsiously, then saving them to apply somewhere in a story. The aforementioned book was *Love in the Time of Cholera* by Gabriel Gracia Márquez. Now, I hadn't read the book at that time—a sin of omission I've since corrected—but the title stuck with me.

When I had the idea for this story, that Marquez title floated to the top, primarily because this story really isn't a zombie story. No, it might have the trappings of a zombie story, but that's just set dressing. The story really is about unrequited love. The two main (living) characters are both suffering from it, dealing with it in their own ways. That's the real story here, how love, even the unrequited variety, shapes our lives, for good or ill. And its something that most of us have experienced at least once in life.

### THE LONG, LONG BREAKDOWN

How to give the word to your child, or more heartbreakingly, how to give your child to the world. To me, this is the central tenet of being a parent. I wanted to present this in the starkest terms possible here by setting it in a postapocalyptic world, Not much left, few things, fewer people. Yet still the urge is there for the father in this story—protect your child, yet give her everything she wants. I sometimes think the two are somewhat mutually exclusive. You can do one well, but only to the detriment of the other.

## VISITATION

How about a little scifi with your horror? We don't get much of it these days, and most of the stuff that sticks it is in film—*Alien* and *Event Horizon*. Still, written horror/sci-fi has picked up recently. I've even thrown my own hat into the ring with *Plastic Space House*, novel I published with Trepedatio Publishing a few years ago.

But I digress This story has its roots in all the science fiction I read in my youth. Other than comic books, science fiction is what I cut my teeth on—Asimov, Clarke, Vance, Silverberg. I would say, particularly for this story, I drew mostly from the word building of the last two authors. My task with this story was to create a credible science fiction story with occult trappings that wouldn't undermine the science fiction but would also stand up within a sci-fi setting.

And I wanted a story that had big implications for the world I'd created. A sort of Reese's peanut butter cup of a story where the chocolate and the peanut butter live in harmony. Easier said than done, but I'd like to think I succeeded. You'll be the judge of that. I also wanted those big implications I mentioned above to come via some legitimate surprises in the story—things that might rock where you might have thought the story was going. Again, you'll be the ... yadda, yadda, yadda.

You know the drill, the rest is up to you, dear reader.

Southern Illinois
June 2025

# ACKNOWLEDGMENTS

Ten years past, and there are still plenty of people to thank for the success of this book. First, and foremost, it would be remiss of me not to thank the first person who took a chance with this book, Anthony Rivera owner of Grey Matter Press. Right on his heels, I need to thank the other person who's taking a chance on this book, Doug Murano with Bad Hands Books. He saw this book as one he'd like in his stable, and I'm grateful. Both of these guys I consider friends, and absolutely fundamental to where I am in my career.

I'd also like to thank Dallas Mayr (the late, great Jack Ketchum), who took a nervously proffered book passed to him at a convention from an unknown, and not only read it, but made several very nice social media posts about this book. And to Josh Malerman. We traded books when we first met a long time ago. He got this, I got the wonderful *BirdBox*. He's been a supporter since, just as I've been an attentive fan of his.

Thanks to Todd Keisling for the great layout and to Sarah Sumeray for the terrific new cover for this edition. You both helped make this version pop!

Thanks finally and always to my lovely wife Deborah, without whom neither the first version or this version would have seen the light of day.

JOHN F.D. TAFF is a Bram Stoker Award® and World Fantasy Award short-listed horror and dark fiction author with more than 35 years experience, and more than 125 short stories and seven novels in print. He has appeared in *Cemetery Dance, Eldritch Tales, Unnerving, Deathrealm, Big Pulp* and *One Buck Horror*. Recent anthology contributions include *Human Monsters, Long Division,* and *The Hideous Book of Hidden Horrors*. Taff's novella collection, *The End in All Beginnings*, was called one of the best novella collections by Jack Ketchum and was a Stoker Award® Finalist.

Printed in the United States
by Baker & Taylor Publisher Services